THE ACTOR AND HIS SECRET

BEN ALDERSON
LAURA R. SAMOTIN

Copyright © 2024 by Ben Alderson & Laura R. Samotin

All rights reserved.

No part of this book may be reproduced in any form or by any electronic or mechanical means, including information storage and retrieval systems, without written permission from the author, except for the use of brief quotations in a book review.

Cover Art by Kloe Bennett @Kloe.bennett

To every person who day-dreamed about bumping into their favourite movie star, and both falling head-over-heels in love with each other. This is for us. The de-lu-lu of it all. - Ben

If you've read enough that you know every trick in the book - this one's for you, because book people are the best people, and you deserve your own HEA (and genius publicist). - Laura

CONTENT WARNINGS

- Alcoholism
- Cheating on a romantic partner
- Extortion and blackmail by a parental figure
- Threats to disseminate illegally obtained nude photographs of the main characters
- Threat of a closeted character being unwillingly outed
- Off-page mention of breaking and entering, robbery
- Mentions of spousal abuse; spousal abuse resulting in accidental death
- Mentions of past physical and emotional abuse of a child by a parent
- PTSD, anxiety, and depression; on-page depiction of panic attacks
- Blood
- Physical fights/violence
- Vomiting

PART 1

THE BEFORE

1

OLI

I'M SHAKING JUST a little bit as I step off the tube. The train ride from Reading to Paddington was most of an hour, which I spent reviewing my interview answers over and over in my head. By the time I was out of the train station and on the tube, I'd given up on rehearsing in favour of just trying to even out my breathing.

And now as the crisp fall air hits my face, I'm doing my best not to be visibly nervous. To embody the calm, cool, collected publicist that I know I can be. Years of doing freelance marketing work had given me something vaguely approaching an impressive portfolio, mostly working for local businesses and people wanting to build a following on social media for their brands, and now I'm ready for prime time.

I bounce on the balls of my feet to dispel the nervous energy coursing through my veins as I check my phone, making sure the directions I'd memorised the night prior were accurate. The small indie publisher who'd somehow found the breakaway success of the last year - the steamy, action-packed *An Age of Dragons* - has a small office on the floor of a corporate tower in central London. I'm sure that they're going to outgrow it sooner rather than later, given that the book has been at the top of every bestseller list for over fifty weeks running, now. And with a movie in production, it's going to blow up even further.

Which is why they need an in-house publicist to start handling all the incoming media requests and start actively shaping the story instead of just responding. As I always tell my clients, marketing and PR are about being proactive, not reactive. I help to get the narrative out that *we* want to see, as opposed to what reviewers and customers want to believe.

And I know that I can do a bang-up job on *An Age of Dragons*. I've read it three times, and I have a crystal-clear vision of how I'm going to tie together the grassroots fan base already churning out fan art and other content with the mainstream media attention the book has already gotten. All of it will be able to support and coordinate with the PR effort around the movie's release in a little under a year. I have a PowerPoint presentation on my iPad to back it all up, complete with data and mock-ups for the ads I'll create.

It's not just that I'm excited to level up in my career and finally land somewhere that's hopefully permanent, with benefits and everything. A real job title, a way to be taken more seriously in the cutthroat world of publicity. It's the chance to be *here*, in London, instead of over an hour away from the posh neighbourhood where my long-term boyfriend Geoffrey lives.

No one thought we'd end up together, least of all me. Geoffrey works in finance and has the demeanour to match - suave, sophisticated, always wearing a perfectly tailored suit and a watch that costs more than I make in a month. We'd had a rocky childhood growing up together, me with an artist and a teacher for parents and a wardrobe full of secondhand clothes, Geoffrey the son of one of the richest families in town. He'd picked on me for years - for being less well-off, for being tiny, for having freckles and glasses and curly blond hair that was always falling into my eyes.

I'm still tiny, but at least now Geoffrey claims my lean frame and short stature are appealing because he can toss me around in the bedroom. And I've gotten better haircuts and trendier glasses - looking good is, after all, fairly important to convincing people that you can make *them* look good - and shaped up my wardrobe. Now I squeeze into designer jeans and button downs, even if I tend to throw a baggy cardigan on top most of the time, given that I'm always cold.

I've done so much to try to fit in with Geoffrey and his banker friends, all of whom are dating or married to people who could be supermodels and also have doctorates. This is the biggest step - getting a job in London so that I can move here, taking that step of moving in with Geoffrey. We haven't done it yet because he wants me to be able to pay a fair share of his sky-high rent, and because he's almost never home. It makes more sense for me to stay in Reading with my parents whilst I save up, given that I can work from anywhere.

Except, if I get this job with Sky High Publishing, I'm going to be making more money - a *lot* more money - and I'm going to need to be in London every day. It will be a no-brainer move for us to live together, and maybe I'll even impress his friends with the red-carpet events I'll be attending as the man in charge of making the author of *An Age of Dragons,* and the whole team behind her, look good.

I take a deep, steadying breath as I weave through the crowds on the street in front of the office tower, making my way into the sparkling marble lobby and presenting my ID to the security guard on duty.

'I'm here for an interview,' I announce, chewing my lip as he scans my ID into the computer system. 'With Megan, of Sky High Publishing.'

'Go on.' He hands me back my ID and waves me through the barrier. I make sure to discard the gum I've been chewing nervously all the way from home into the trash can by the lifts before getting on.

The doors open and reveal a small yet sleek office, full of young bookish-looking people bustling around. The sequel for *An Age of Dragons* comes out in four weeks, and I can feel the frantic energy coming off the staff, a couple of them standing in the lobby cradling coffees and having an urgent conversation about possible delivery delays to Waterstones. They must all be under incredible pressure, with the astronomical number of copies that the book is expected to sell.

I stand a bit awkwardly, clutching the straps of my backpack, because there's no receptionist to introduce myself to. But luckily a harried looking woman with a pencil tucked into her bun and paper hole punch scraps all over her black turtleneck makes a beeline for me.

'Oliver Cane?' she asks.

'Yes,' I reply, extending my hand for her to shake, hoping it's not covered in sweat. 'Although you can call me Oli.'

'Great to meet you,' she says, her grip firm. 'Megan Smith, managing editor here at Sky High. We're so glad you came in. We can *really* use the help.'

Stay calm, I tell myself, trying not to start blathering on about how much *I* need *them*. 'It's an exciting opportunity,' I say instead, my voice level and professional. 'I've been a huge fan of *An Age of Dragons* from the beginning, and I'm quite eager for the chance to help take Sky High's profile to the next level.'

'God knows we're in deep,' she says, guiding me to a hall and then into an office. There are books cluttering the desk, what looks like every special edition of *An Age of Dragons* that anyone in the world has ever produced. My fingers twitch with the urge to examine them - I'm nothing if not a book whore. 'With the movie in pre-production, and the media company's PR team hounding us daily for quotes and assets and interview answers and the like, we're underwater. You would think that we'd have gotten on the bandwagon and hired an in-house publicist long before this, but our owner wanted to be cautious with finances. Publishing runs on a shoestring margin, you know, and we were always half-expecting the book's fame to just…go poof one day and disappear. We have around a year until the film is out, which equates to a year of managing this fucking inferno around us… pardon the French.'

I give her what I hope is a comforting smile as I put my bag down besides the chair she motions to and sit. 'I understand that. For you to have found such success is honestly incredible, but I imagine it also brings with it an incredible amount of pressure.'

Megan sighs and tucks back a strand of the blonde hair

currently trying its best to escape from her bun. 'I never thought when I pulled that manuscript out of the slush pile that we'd be here today, but when life gives you lemons, you go into your tenth print run.'

'Well,' I reply, 'I'd be happy to take a load off, especially with coordinating with the production company.'

'That would be a dream,' Megan says, her blue eyes wide. 'With the casting news that's about to come out, we're going to be beating off reporters left and right.'

'Oh?' I quirk an eyebrow. There'd been some contract dispute or another with the lead actor who'd been cast to play Armin Wolfe - the hunky dragon-rider who somehow managed to vanquish armies, save his friends and gorgeous lover, and fight to reclaim the throne all whilst never wearing a shirt - and there's been no news of who is replacing him yet. And obviously the whole movie hinges on casting the exact right man to embody the black-haired, violet-eyed, totally ripped hero. If they get it wrong, the fans will undoubtedly riot, and that will be the end of that.

'You'll see.' Megan winks at me. 'Check the entertainment news tonight. But for now, let's talk about how you can help.'

'Of course,' I say, nerves giving rise to excitement. I know my stuff, and I know I'm the right person for the job. 'As Armin says in chapter fifty-one, the only way to win a battle is to go in with firm determination and an iron-clad plan. So, I've got a *PowerPoint*.'

Megan's mouth drops open, and I launch into my marketing and publicity plan. I know within five minutes that I've got her hooked, and I pray to all the gods in *An Age of Dragons* that I keep her that way.

I walk out of the office an hour later with a job offer, a contract on the way, and a start date of next week.

This is going to be my big break, I know it. I smile all the way to Geoffrey's apartment and let myself in, slumping into the huge leather sofa and kicking off my trainers. The sun is setting over the London skyline, framed through the huge floor-to-ceiling windows.

It's going to be hours before Geoffrey gets home, which gives me plenty of time to build out my schedule for the next week. I pull out my laptop and open my email to check for the contract, but what catches my eye instead is a breaking news update from one of my favourite media roundups.

Greek God Nikos Ridge to Play Armin Wolfe, Star in An Age of Dragons.

My breath catches in my throat looking at the picture of the actor underneath, a smouldering gaze above razor-sharp cheekbones and a strong jaw dusted with stubble. He's shirtless in the picture, and my mouth waters as I count the ridges of his abs. Fuck me - he's got an eight-pack. I don't even know how that's physically possible. He looks like he just stepped off a pedestal, a Greek statue come to life.

I reel in my lust and calm down the warmth in my groin, ordering it to cooperate, because this is *perfect*. Just perfect. *This* is our Armin, So much better than the golden retriever, Captain America-looking generic hunk that they'd originally cast. This man looks like he could rip someone apart with his teeth. I want him to bite me until I scream -

Okay, Oli. Calm down.

I take a deep breath and get to work figuring out how to convince every *Age of Dragons* fangirl how to support our new leading man. It's not even going to be *hard*.

I crack my knuckles, pop three pieces of gum in my mouth, and start to type.

2

NIKOS

Even in my lucid state, I know I should've drunk more. The dreams may not have been vivid, not as they usually are, but they're still playing out. Torturing me. They unspool in black and white, poisoning my mind, refusing me the rest I long for.

In my dream, I'm a child again. It's always the same when I'm sleeping. It isn't so much a knowing, but a feeling. Utter terror as I watch it happen, almost in slow motion. Broken glass and blood. Screaming until my throat bleeds. Screaming until my lungs puncture from the splinters of my fear.

Screaming from -

'Nikos Ridge, I swear on all things holy and sacred, if you're high or drunk, I'll personally smack it the shit out of your system.'

Reluctantly, I open my eyes to the sudden glare of harsh light. Daylight sweeps across my room as the curtains are thrown open. I wince against the glare, my eyes aching. It takes a moment to settle, for the claws of that nightmare to ease, for me to see an endless blue view, ruined by the tops of a city skyline.

New York. Safe. Home.

My head aches and my throat burns. I need water, badly.

As suddenly as the light appears, a shadow blocks it out. It's enough of a reprieve to open my eyes and stare dead into the - extremely pissed off - glare of my manager, Selina Tate.

But she isn't glaring at *me*. Her eyes are pinned to the empty bottle of vodka tipped over on the floor, just shy of where my hand is dangling.

'Get up.' Her two words are like the icy crash of sobering water.

'Morning to you too,' I croak, feigning a smile, although my skull feels like it's splitting in two.

'It's afternoon.'

Selina is dressed in her usual pantsuit combo, brown hair slicked back into a tidy bun, lips painted cherry red. She's Italian in origin, with the striking features to match. While no older than me, Selina still has the uncanny ability to scold me like a parent.

It was why she's my manager. I like her, but it doesn't mean I have to tell her that.

'I must've missed my alarm,' I drone, stretching long arms over my head. Fuck, I stink. From the crinkle of her nose, even from a distance, Selina notices too.

'Are you going to get up, or am I going to drag you out?' The air is driven from my lungs as something heavy is dropped onto my stomach. I clutch my chest, wheezing as the sudden urge to vomit passes over me.

'I regret giving you a key,' I moan, picking up the pile of bound pages Selina has just dumped on me.

'To an apartment which is days from being claimed by the bank if you don't pay up on your arrears? Really, Nikos. It's a fucking Wednesday and you smell like the floor of some dingy nightclub downtown.'

'Are you flirting with me?'

I don't need to watch to know she just rolled her eyes. Selina always follows an eye roll with the kiss of her tongue over her teeth. It's an Italian thing.

'I've come to throw you a bone.' Her heeled boot - red bottomed, most likely, she's got expensive taste - kicks the velveteen sofa I've fallen asleep on. 'Are you going to be a good boy and take it?'

'Go away.' I hoist the bound pages and drop them to the floor, right next to the puddle of vodka. 'I'm vegan.' Well, if consuming nothing but alcohol counts as vegan.

'Fuck you.' Selina kicked again, knocking over the empty bottle of spirits I had downed last night. 'Up. Now.'

I pinch my eyes closed. If I can just tell the universe that Selina is going to leave, maybe the manifestation will work. 'I don't pay you to give me orders.'

She leans over me, painted nails digging into the material of the sofa. Not that it matters – with the stains, sweat, and unknown bodily fluids matting the once soft velvet, there's no hope for it anyway.

As there's no hope for me.

'May I be the one to remind you, you *don't* pay me.'

'Then leave already.'

Selina chuckles, a deadly, dangerous sound. 'Oh, no, you're not getting rid of me that easily.'

I don't open my eyes until the click of her heels disappears in the direction of my kitchen. Problem with these luxurious apartments is the architects think an open plan, modern design is more desirable. I suppose it would be if that didn't mean I could smell the rotting take-out food left on the counter from my place on the sofa.

My ears itch with the sound of running water. It's brief, shuts off, and then Selina is back in the living room. There's barely a warning before a cup of water is dumped on my head.

'Okay, okay!' I bark, gasping at the icy bite of water as it soaks through my dirty white tee.

Selina has a terrifyingly pleased grin on her face, her arms crossed and sharp shoe thumping a rhythm on the hardwood. The empty glass is tinkering against the tap of her nail.

'Enjoying yourself?' I ask, sitting up as the room sways violently. My living room really is a mess. It wouldn't be impossible to believe a tornado entered, unannounced and uninvited, but it's simply the way I've been living.

Beyond the wall of windows at Selina's back I have the perfect view of Central Park. Even from the height of my home, I can still hear the calls of runners, coffee vendors selling pastries from carts, and the bustle of foot traffic as New Yorkers continue with their day.

Is it really afternoon?

I rub the sleep from my eyes, still not bothering to look at the papers Selina had dumped on me. They now sit in a puddle of vodka and water, two opposing liquids - which is rather a good metaphor for the war currently waging inside of me.

It's a script, with the tell-tale typography of a catchy title plastered on the front page.

An Age of Dragons.

So it's not bank letters or an eviction notice - the same I've been dodging for almost a year.

'No thirty-year-old lives in such a state,' Selina says, grimacing as she looks between the table covered in old pizza boxes and warped cans of beer. 'If your Yiayia saw you now, she'd murder you.'

Yiayia, my weakness. My grandmother who I'd left behind in Thessaloniki, Greece. No, not left. Ran away from. I didn't go back to visit her a single time before she died.

'Why are you here?' I'm not in the mindset for talking. Not with the drums pounding in my head and the snakes writhing in my stomach.

'You got the gig.'

I look down to the script again, squinting as if that would help my mind make sense of where I'd seen the title. 'Sorry, I don't think my thirty-year-old brain is awake enough to make sense of this.'

Selina smiles down at me, flashing every single perfectly placed tooth. 'If I could say it in Greek, I would. You got the fucking job, Nikos.'

'But it's been six months…'

'Six months and a stroke of luck.' The sofa shifts as Selina sits beside me. She plucks the glass bottle from the floor and holds it, studying the peeling label with a grimace. 'No more of this. Time to get in the shower and put on the mask of Nikos Ridge, America's beloved Greek god. The box office is welcoming you back.'

It's easier to focus on her than the reeling emotions storming within me. I can't believe it, won't believe it.

But it's there, in black ink on white paper. 'How?'

'Talent, but that would only be half a lie.' Her wink tells me she's joking, but I catch the faint whiff of truth beneath her tones. 'Turns out the actor they hired dropped out due to a conflicting schedule. Enough time has been wasted, and pre-production is almost up. Filming starts by the beginning of next week. No other actor was willing to take it on, not with the wildly compressed schedule they'd be facing coming in at this point. Casting didn't want to spend time auditioning for another so…'

'So, they picked me.'

Weak. Pathetic. You're worthless.

I pinch my eyes closed, pressing the heels of my hands into them. I don't say it aloud, but I whisper to the dark, telling my father's voice to shut up.

He doesn't, of course. He never does.

There would've been a time for celebrating such news but gone were those days. The world once felt like such a small place, but that was the perspective I had looking down from great heights. Now it's large, endless, and ready to devour me. I'm sitting in the middle of it, in an apartment I can't afford, pockets dry and opportunities always out of reach.

Until now.

Selina starts to cry. I hear it in the sniffling, in the way she wrings her fingers around the bottle of spirits as though she wants to strangle the life right out of it.

'This is your last chance, Nikos.'

I know it before Selina says it.

'I know,' I reply.

She grips my knee and squeezes. 'You can't fuck this up. Not for you, not for me.'

I haven't worked in three years. Once I withdrew into

myself, once what was going on grew too much to bear and I just started to hide, the opportunities dried up. Who would want a movie-star who'd rather be locked inside his apartment than promoting the film? Who has panic attacks so bad he has to lock himself away until they pass? Hollywood hasn't called, the press has left me alone. For the most of it, I've stayed in this apartment, festering like mould, sinking my future with every shot of vodka I drink.

This is your last chance.

I inhale deeply, feeling no different than fragile glass in careless hands. Selina picks the script up, and this time, places it carefully in my numb, shaking hands.

An Age of Dragons - I remember it now. The script was for some new book-to-movie adaption with a moderate budget. I trace my finger over my name, seeing it in black and white, dried ink, and still it doesn't feel real.

'I don't... I don't deserve this.'

It's not me who speaks, not entirely. It was the little broken boy who had once been buried beneath the success, the fame. The little broken boy who clawed his way out of the cage I made. The little broken boy who ruined everything for me by trying to escape.

'Yes, you do,' Selina says, laying a gentle hand on my shoulder. 'There is no one more deserving I could see this happen to.'

The pause which follows draws out for a millennium. I dare to shatter it.

'Is that Selina talking, or the fifteen percent fee you get if I accept?'

Her grip falters. 'It's me, your friend before the manager. Now, your plane leaves from JFK tomorrow morning. You'll be out of state for eight months on set. A month for rehearsals, followed by seven months of filming - '

'I can't...'

'Eight months. That's all I am asking of you.'

I shake my head, burying it in my hands. 'I can't do it, Selina.'

'I wish it was a choice you had. But if you don't get the work, you don't have the money to pay for this apartment. Your lifestyle. Fuck, Nikos, if nothing else matters then perhaps knowing you'll have no more money for the drink and the drugs will. Eight months, that's it. Then you don't ever have to do it again. You'll be free.'

Helpless tears fill my eyes as the secrets fill my head. I wish I could tell her, but even she doesn't know. I look up at her, hating the pity in her brown stare. 'I'll never be free, Selina.'

She'll never know just how true those words are.

'This is big,' Selina says, catching her emotions and hiding them behind the closed door of manageress. 'The team is thrilled. You may not have been the first choice of romantic lead, but this is exactly what your career needs. A fresh start. A new chance to remind the world who Nikos Ridge is, and what he is capable of.'

My knee bounces, my heart fluttering as though a flock of birds just took flight. I look to the empty bottle in Selina's hands and regret finishing it last night. I could've done with a swig now. Better to wash the anxiety away then let it drown me.

'Eight months?' I repeat, trying to convince myself.

'It'll fly by. And it's filming in the UK. You've always wanted to go, haven't you? Anyway, the agency came up with a deal, to ensure you got this role - '

'There's no refusing this, is there?'

Selina shakes her head. I can almost hear it, the scratch of a pen as it signed me away in a deal with a devil. I'm all too familiar with the sound.

'The production company have paid off your outstanding debts.' Selina speaks as though she is reading off a prompter. Emotionless, as a way to protect herself and me. 'A second payment will be made to you once filming is complete. The final instalment will come to you once the run of press for the film is over. Eight months of work. Another two for media. Then it's over. No more films. No more work. If you decide to give it up, you can, no ties attached. But until then, you *must* do this.'

You must *do this.* It's as though I'm sitting in another place during another time. Urging someone else to do something, which all went wrong.

Selina brushes the creases from her trousers, giving her hands something to do.

I look up at her, feeling as though I'm watching the world through a lens isn't wasn't my own. 'Please, don't make me do this.'

I shake violently, my chewed nails grasping my bare thighs until the skin breaks and bleeds. If Selina notices, she shows no signs.

'My hands are tied,' she replies, looking around the messy state of the room. In seconds, her sadness is gone, replaced by the steel mask of the manager I'd become all too familiar with. There was once a time we were best friends, navigating the entertainment world together. Now, we're strangers with the thorn of money wedged between us.

'It's five percent.'

I narrow my eyes at her. 'What do you mean?'

Selina picks at her nails, looking anywhere but me. 'You accused me of doing this for the fifteen percent, but that isn't true. I'm taking five. The extra ten is going to you.'

That shocks me back to silence. I open my mouth, close it again, and repeat that like a gulping fish for air. It's just extra for *him* to prey on, more stones tied around my ankles as I sink.

'Have a shower,' Selina snaps, preventing me from saying anything. 'Get a haircut. And tidy yourself up. A driver will be sent for you tomorrow. Make sure your breath doesn't smell.' *Doesn't smell of alcohol.*

There's no need for her to finish.

'This is it,' I hiss, the pages crinkling beneath my fingers. 'I do this last film. Then I'm done.' Because I know what this is going to mean. Doing this movie all but ensures that the demons of my past are going to come for me once more.

'I know.' Selina glances up at me, sorrow pinching at the corners of her eyes. 'I've already ensured it was included as part of the deal, Nikos. This is your great come back and farewell, all rolled into one, a publicity campaign to end all publicity campaigns. After this, you're free.'

You're free. There it is again. And yet, I know that will never be the case. Demons have long wrapped their claws around my neck, and there's no freeing myself.

'I'll be checking in on you tomorrow. I expect to see you looking... looking more like Nikos Ridge the heart-throb, and not like this sorry excuse for the man I once respected.' Selina doesn't mean to hurt me with her words, but she does. Although she's right.

I've let everyone down. I always let everyone I love down. I always hurt them in the worst ways.

Selina waits a moment for a response, but I don't give her one. I sag forward, spine aching as her footsteps fade through my apartment, followed by the thud of a door slamming.

You're free.

Words I never believed I'd hear. Words I never knew I would crave so dearly.

I place the script beside me. Just looking at it makes my stomach twist with sickness, which has nothing to do with my hangover.

'One more,' I say to myself, 'this is what you've been hoping for. One more, then it's all over.'

It's a concept I've been willing into existence since the…incident. Over and over I visualised this very moment. But now I'm facing it and I feel nothing but dread.

Because doing this means I suddenly won't be able to hide from the world I ran from. Although I never wished to simply *hide*.

I wanted to completely disappear.

You're free.

Behind the pillow, where Selina had sat, another bottle waits for me. This one is half full.

You're free.

I pull the cork free with my teeth, eyes trapped to the tops of trees and buildings beyond my window.

You're free.

I lift the bottle to my mouth and tip it back, pouring the liquid down my throat. It burns.

You're free.

This time another voice registers in the far reaches of my skull. The voice that haunts me every single day since I tried to get free.

You'll never be free. Not from me, son.

PART 2

THE CURRENT DAY

3
OLI

NEARLY EIGHT YEARS into dating Geoff and I never expect to find him buried five and a half inches deep in a stranger.

I drop my phone onto the hardwood floor with a clatter loud enough to startle the both of them. They're *in our bed*.

Geoffrey is fucking some twenty-year-old twink *on my sheets*, the ones I picked out from Frette because Geoff was whining that the perfectly good ones I'd bought online were '*too scratchy*'. The boy's head is on *my* special anti-allergy pillow. His feet are practically touching it too, where he's folded in half.

'Um,' I say eloquently as Geoff turns his head, still balls-deep in an arse that is definitely not mine. 'What the *fuck?*'

'Oh.' Geoff's brown eyes fly open. His hips give another thrust. He *doesn't even stop thrusting.* 'Oli? Why are you home?'

I didn't call because I wanted to surprise Geoff, who'd

been complaining for weeks about my work schedule. Never mind that now that he's a managing director at his investment bank he's hardly ever home. He claims all the time that *I'm* the one who works too much, but I think it's really that he's angry that I'm not always immediately available to him in the moments he's actually here and not at work.

So when I got off work early today, I didn't go out for drinks with the rest of the team. Everyone wanted to blow off steam after another intense week - with the premier happening next weekend, pressure is at an all-time high. The buzz we've been getting has been *incredible*, but I'm not counting my chickens.

Although right now I'm not counting anything at all. I'm watching my long-term boyfriend fuck another man.

I know we've been having problems. I've been pushing for us to see a couple's counsellor. I've been chalking it up to being so busy, to having fallen into a rhythm of domesticity after a year of living together, sex dropping off to almost nothing because we sit and watch each other floss our teeth every night. Never for a minute did I think that it was because he was getting it somewhere else.

'I wanted to surprise you with a meal.' I even went to the shops and got a bottle of nice wine, ingredients to cook some fancy pasta recipe that I'd found online. Geoff pulls out, and my entire body goes numb watching his dick withdraw. He's not even wearing a condom.

Selfish fucking disgusting piece of shit *cunt*.

'I can explain.' He gets up, flicking his fingers at the boy on our bed like he's a dog that he's ordering to sit. The intruder gets up, blushing furiously, and starts to get dressed. I can't help but stare at him, because he looks just like a younger, fitter me who has genetically blessed skin and infinite time to spend at the gym. 'Oli, you've just been so obsessed with this stupid book, I was lonely. A man has *needs*, love.'

'Don't fucking call me that,' I hiss. The pieces are all clicking into place at once. The way that Geoff had reacted with disappointment instead of excitement that night a year ago when I'd announced my new job. He'd covered it up quickly, but I never forgot it. 'How long has this been going on?'

The lookalike-me finishes dressing, pulls on his shoes, and scampers out the door, his feet pattering on the stairs.

'You're always so jealous,' Geoff rolls his eyes and pushes a hand through his generically dirty-blond hair. He's still wearing his Rolex. It's fucking galling. 'It's not that big of a deal.'

'Oh,' I snap, stepping forward to jab a finger into his sweat-coated pec. 'Turning this around on me, are you? It's *my* fault that you're home from work early so that you can bareback fuck me from five years ago *in our bed?*'

'I make all my sexual partners show me their test results,' Geoff mumbles, not looking at me.

'You're saying there's *more of them?*' I scream. '*That makes it not one fucking bit better!*'

Geoff finally has the grace to look just a bit embarrassed. 'Plenty of people are in open relationships. Monogamy isn't for everyone.'

I step back like I've been slapped. I can't believe he's trying to rationalise this away. It's probably been going on the whole time we've been together. It's probably why he didn't want me to move to London, so he could fuck me on the weekends and fuck other people the rest of the week.

'Open relationships rely on *consent*, you prick. I cannot believe you.' My anger is starting to give way to tears, and I absolutely don't want to cry in front of Geoff. Not right now. 'Get out of my sight. Go get a hotel. I'm sure you can find someone else to warm your bed.'

Geoffrey looks stunned, like he can't believe I'm telling him to get out, his mouth dropping open. If he hadn't gotten so much Botox, there might have even been a furrow in between his eyebrows.

I wish I had a dragon on hand to roast him alive. Instead, I turn on my heel, storm out of the bedroom, go down the stairs, grab the bottle of wine I'd left on the kitchen counter, and lock myself in the office. I realise too late that I forgot a corkscrew, so I distract myself from the angry tears running down my cheeks by using a pen to dig out the cork. It's hard. I stab myself three times, but the pain is a welcome distraction.

There's clattering coming from outside the door, and I can't really breathe until I hear the front door to our townhouse open and shut. Geoff left his iPad here, and I'm tempted to open it to see if it has Grindr on it and just how many matches he's made in the last year while we've been living together. But I start chugging the wine - no *way* am I going to waste a fifty-pound bottle, not when I'm probably about to break up with my rich boyfriend - and open Instagram on my desktop instead.

I'm crying and well on my way to being drunk, but even still I take solace in looking at the metrics on our latest ad campaign, the one I hit *go* on before I walked out of the office two hours ago. We're doing well. Really well.

I'll be going to my first-ever red-carpet event alone next Friday, but I feel like someone on RuPaul's Drag Race once said that success was the best revenge. I'm going to give Geoff an enormous metaphorical middle finger by making this movie a smashing success, sending the book back to number one on all the lists, and earning every quid of my performance-based bonus. The one large enough that I could definitely move out into my own flat, now that that's something I'm going to need to do.

There's an indecent amount of snot coming out of my nose, which I wipe on the sleeve of my jumper because I'm a disgusting gremlin of sadness and rage right now. I click on Nikos Ridge's Instagram account. His social media manager does a great job interspersing normal pictures - the star going about his day, making a smoothie or working out at the gym - with sizzling nearly-naked shots clearly done by professional photographers. I try to file away some tips from the latest caption, on a post from an hour ago which has already garnered eighteen-thousand likes, and yet my brain fails me.

How is it that I'm on top of the world professionally, about to have my greatest ever success, and yet my personal life has just gone to shit in an instant?

My head hits the keyboard with a *thunk*, my shoulders shaking. I cry into the arm of my jumper until my head is pounding and my body is wrung out. The wine is gone by then, and I'm well on my way to being shitfaced. I haul myself over to the couch, bury myself in a blanket that I wish could hide me from the world permanently, and pass the fuck out.

4

NIKOS

I CAN'T BREATHE WEARING this four-thousand-pound Armani suit. Even though the cut fits looser then when I had it tailored - thanks to the loss of muscle that fell off me when filming finished, given the stress of everything and the lack of three-hour daily weightlifting sessions - I still feel as though I'm drowning in black silk, cotton, and polished leather shoes.

My room is so quiet I can hear the fans screaming from outside the window. The five-star hotel I've called home during press week is just opposite Trafalgar Square, giving a perfect view of the crowds waiting outside the film premiere. I wonder if I should dare look outside, or if the tiny lunch I had would rush up my throat and ruin Selina's outfit of choice if I do.

Who needs to waste money on a stylist when your manager is Italian?

I step up to the window, hiding like a stalker behind the long curtains. I pull them back enough to see the sea of people outside. People waiting for me. There comes the urge to vomit again, which I quell with a long drink from the vodka in my hand. I told Selina it was water. She didn't believe me, but she didn't take it off me either. I've eased up on my drinking significantly since filming started, pulling myself out of the depths of what was probably a full-blown addiction, but I still need a drink when I'm nervous. I can't steady myself without it, and if I'm not steady, the panic attacks are going to come for me.

'I can't do this,' I say to the reflection in the window. It's slightly tinted, enough that anyone looking up would see the outline of a figure, not the details. But that means I get a long, hard look at myself.

Tired brown eyes. My hair had been dyed pitch-black for the film and the director loved my long 'I don't care about my appearance' hair length so much that he made me keep it. Since then, we've cut it back, still keeping enough length that I can effortlessly brush it away from my forehead.

I hardly look like the character I'd just embodied for almost a year. Between the hair style, normal brown eyes with no purple contacts, muscle loss, and untanned skin, I don't even know who I am in the reflection.

Effortless. That's the one word that's been put next to my name in all the recent reviews remarking on my performance. It's a word that I should carry with pride, and yet it makes me sick.

A thunderous clap of screams echoes from outside. I imagine the premiere is about to start, so I look out again. But the reaction is because a small portion of the crowd are looking up at my window, pointing, faces excited.

They're looking at me.

I step back, breathless. The glass almost slips from my

hands. I have the urge to turn my back on it all, head into the bathroom, lock the door, and stay in it for as long as I can keep Selina away.

But alas, tonight I can't. Tonight, I'm Nikos Ridge, the lead in the world's biggest predicted film release of the year - hell, of the past twenty years. That's a lot of pressure to carry on my shoulders. It's a pressure that I can barely withstand.

'Two more days,' I promise myself, finishing the vodka, pouring another and finishing that until my throat hisses with the burn and the panic fades just a bit. 'Two more days.'

Contractually, I'm almost finished. All in all, it's been a rewarding year with the filming, re-shoots and the publicity campaign. Work has kept me busy, diverting my attention away from reality to this made-up world of flashing lights, cameras, and adoring fans. But beneath it all is the truth of why I did it in the first place.

Him. Dad. Father. The Devil.

I'd wired the last of the money to him a week ago and haven't heard from him since. I'm paid in full, every penny that he's demanded. I am, as Selina promised, free. Free to return home, live my life, and never need to work again - as long as the residual checks keep coming in.

And yet I don't feel free. I feel selfish, pathetic, and unworthy. All the words my father would put next to my name, far different than the trade reviews. Because I have this life, and yet I continue to be ungrateful.

I'd give it all up to remove the scars of my past.

A light knock taps at the door. I lower the empty glass, glad for the Dutch courage the vodka has offered me.

Selina opens the door slightly, enough to poke her head in. 'Ready?' she asks.

I fake a smile, straighten my back and adorn the mask of the man everyone expects me to be. 'Born ready.'

Selina steps into the room, a swarm of people behind her, all watching me expectantly. Like them, Selina has a glint of emotion in her eyes. It wets her painted lashes, threatening to ruin her makeup.

'You look...' she begins, pausing to find the right word. 'Ravishing.'

I pull at my bowtie, hoping to ease the sudden constriction around my throat. 'You don't look too bad yourself, Selina.'

She closes the space between us and stops just shy of where I stand. To distract herself from her emotion, she fusses over me, flattening the lapels of my suit jacket, brushing hair from my shoulders and dragging a single strand of my bangs down over my eye.

'Now you look like you're worth the swooning crowd that's waiting outside for you.'

Another chorus of screams hits the windows. I can't help but wince, which Selina notices - she never misses a single thing. 'Smile. Shoulders back. Prove to yourself that you deserve to stand in this spotlight.'

I lower my voice, which is hard when it's so deep that even a whisper can carry. 'What if I don't deserve the spotlight?'

More cries of excitement, my name slowly building in a demanding chorus out on the red carpet. 'Let them prove to you that you do.'

And with that, Selina threads her fingers in with mine and guides me out of the room.

THE RED CARPET passes in a blur of blinding lights and flashing cameras.

It's acting, I tell myself. Playing the part of a man who wants to be here, a man who enjoys the attention. Maybe the reviewers are right, and I do it effortlessly. After hundreds of photos are taken of me standing beneath a 3D model of my dragon - Eratrix - from the film, I'm shepherded down a line of press. Fluffy-headed mics are pressed so close to my face that by the time I finish, all I can smell is their plasticky scent. My mouth is so dry, my head aching so much that I can't imagine how I'm going to make it through the film and the throng of after-parties set up by my co-stars.

I see Michelle, the second lead of the film, skimming down the red carpet - which is actually gold to match the film's aesthetic. She looks beautiful, long auburn hair falling down her spine like a river, the silver dress she wears something hand-picked from Aubrey Hepburn's closet.

We hug, for the cameras and the crowd. Our small talk is exaggerated so the people watching think we are the best of friends, when the truth is she *fucking* hates me. It wasn't always the case, but then she made advances on me during filming which I politely declined, over and over and over. She doesn't know it, but she's not for me. Our chemistry on screen is unmatched, but that doesn't translate to real life. At least, not for me.

Michelle isn't my type. I don't really have a type. I've never given myself room to explore it. I've fucked around, yes. But with the life I choose to lead, the constraints placed on me, it's better doing it alone.

Fewer people get hurt.

'Sign some posters, take some selfies. I say you've got about ten minutes before we need to head inside.' Selina has to shout over the hustle and bustle. The soundtrack for the film is blaring out of speakers, turning all of this side of London into a rave.

She offers me a quick drink of water, which I've never been gladder for. Alcohol would've been better, but that will come when the credits start rolling.

'Wish me luck,' I say, stepping towards the line of people waving copies of *An Age of Dragons*, collectable figurines of my character and other merchandise like t-shirts, mugs, and the many topless photos of my character scowling on the back of his dragon.

Maybe Selina was right. Because for the first time, I'm swept away by the love. I'm surrounded by it. I think it's love, anyway. Maybe a form of it. Certainly something that could replace the type of love I crave, even if it won't last.

That thought spoils it for me. I look into the faces of crying, adoring fans and know that one wrong move, and they would turn on me.

Where was this love when I needed it most? Off being given to someone else whilst I festered with my demons, alone.

'Thank you,' I say, numbly, my cheeks aching from the forced smile. 'I appreciate it. I hope you enjoy the film. The book is always better...' On and on I go until the faces blur into one.

I'm towards the end of the line when I pause halfway through scrawling my name over a poster with my nipples on display. It isn't that the person holding it is standing out, but more of a deep gut reaction. Like my body is reacting to something my mind still hasn't worked out.

And then I look up into the face of the man who gave me the poster. Into the face of my father.

'Nikos.' His Greek accent is so thick, it should remind me of home. But in truth, the sound bores into my soul and pierces me like a knife.

I can barely move, trapped in his stare. The few people around him hold up phones, filming the moment, not really knowing exactly what this moment is.

My smile falters. I begin to worry the skin on the inside of my lip. I hand back the half-finished signature and go to move away, but a firm hand grips my wrist. No one notices, but I do.

The words that come out of his mouth are just for me. Without context, no one would understand the power. But I do.

'I need more.'

'Yes!' those around him scream. 'We want more. Nikos Ridge. Nikos Ridge.'

Father smiles at me, looking like a feral dog about to bite. I break free of his hold, although the skin around my wrist aches. Part of me longs to reach over the barrier, drag him over and beat him just like he beat -

'Film is about to start,' Selina says, apology written over her face, as she saves me from the moment. 'Better get our darling star inside.'

The crowd continues to react, but I can't help but search it again for my father.

He's gone. Left, like the demon he was, vanishing in a plume of smoke.

'Well done, darling. You've done well. Sold the dream.'

I can't open my mouth to reply to Selina as she guides me off the gold carpet and into the theatre. My mind is fixed on his face, those endless eyes and sinister sneer.

I need more.

It can only mean one thing.

Money. More fuel to feed his twisted sense of revenge. And he knows that I'll give it. I'll do anything to stop him ruining my life, my career.

'I need to use the restroom,' I say, pulling free as I see the glowing sign ahead of me.

'Well, Nikos. There are nice clean, special toilets for the talent. We'll be there as soon as the film begins - '

'No,' I snap, hating how much like my father I sound. 'This will do.'

I hate the look in Selina's face. It's fear, like she's seeing the truth of a person she always believed possible, but never met. Now, she's witnessing it in full force.

'Then I'll wait for you,' Selina says, frowning, her red-painted nails looking as threatening as weapons. 'Or do you have something to say about that too?'

I want to apologise, to beg for her forgiveness. But people are threading around us, and if Selina knows anything, it's keeping up appearances. 'Be quick, darling. The crowd will be waiting for you.'

That pressure on my shoulders is so heavy now, I can barely take the steps towards the restroom. I push the door open, glad for the empty, bright space. I lean against the sinks and bury my face in my hands.

That's when the tears begin.

5
OLI

There's no amount of concealer that can fix the bags under my eyes.

Even if everything had been going swimmingly, the past week would've been a killer. I'm swaying on my feet from lack of sleep, since I've spent every waking minute - and plenty of minutes where I should have been sleeping too - pushing content for the premiere.

I still have a migraine from the hours-long conference calls I'd been on soothing the rightfully terrified author, who was walking her first red carpet. I think I must be severely dehydrated because I'm having a hard time swallowing and breathing and I also think my heart may be about to give out.

Who am I kidding? It's not the work. I *live* for work. I thrive on being busy. It's the heartbreak that's reduced me to a gross-looking shell of myself.

Geoffrey had come crawling back to the apartment two days later, after blowing up my phone with texts and calls, all of which went unanswered. I was too busy crying into a pile of throw pillows while watching the most mindless TV I could find. My diet consisted entirely of Ben and Jerry's Chunky Monkey, which was horrible for both my waistline and my lactose intolerance. He had the gall to actually *get down on his knees* in front of me as I hid in the blankets of the couch, crying and begging me to take him back, swearing up and down that he loved me and he wouldn't cheat again.

I said no. Even if that word was the hardest that'd ever come out my mouth.

I was pretty sure that he was just upset about being caught. And that he thought pissing off the man who did his laundry and shopping and booked his doctor's appointments was his biggest mistake.

His loss, I tell myself, and yet I'm the one who feels like I've lost everything

Geoff had gotten mad, and there'd been a screaming match that I blocked out of my memory, and it ended with him throwing the keys to the apartment at my face and telling me that he was moving out because he couldn't stand all the bad memories *I'd created* here, and that movers would be by the next day to pack up his stuff.

So now I'm standing in a bathroom I definitely can't afford on my own - thank God that Geoff always pre-paid his rent for months in advance in some 'I'm able to deduct it from my taxes' scheme I never understood - trying to fix the mess of my face. My eyes are swollen and red-rimmed, which looks particularly awful in contrast with the purple bags under them.

My phone lights up with a text from Megan.

Are you on your way? - Megan

She's taken to checking in on me every two hours, like she thinks that if she doesn't, I'm just going to collapse and die. Maybe that's the case. Over the last year, she's become more than my boss - she's become my friend, too. Everyone at Sky High has. That's what happens when you put book lovers in a pressure cooker together.

If there's one bright spot in my life right now, it's that the team of people I work with has rallied behind me, all of them bitching with me about what a fucking asshole Geoff is, how no one *really* prefers fucking a twenty-year-old instead of someone with a decade's more of sex experience, and how I'm better off without him anyway.

I'm trying to frame it as a new beginning to my life. A new movie, a huge boost to my career, a fast track to being a celebrity publicist. Money and connections and all that jazz. But my heart hurts and if I'm being honest with myself, I'm deep in mourning a future that I'd seen with Geoff, no matter how imperfect things were. I thought we'd be getting married eventually, that we'd think about adopting a kid or two, maybe getting a dog or a cat. Being a *team*. I was content to be the sidekick to his Armin Wolfe, because like the dragon rider and his fated mate, we were meant for one another.

But I guess not.

I give up on the concealer as I get some of it in my eye. At least when my eye starts to water it's for a reason other than being gutted. I hurriedly shove myself into the tuxedo I'd bought for the occasion, botching the bow tie but not really caring. My feet hurt the minute I get them into the stiff leather shoes that I got to match, and I regret not breaking them in over the last few weeks. Yet another thing that fell off my personal to-do list as my life fell apart.

I call an Uber and get downstairs, thanking God that at least the weather is perfect. It's a gorgeous spring evening, and the sun is setting perfectly on time. It will be golden hour when the stars and my author walk the red carpet, which means that the pictures will be extra stunning.

I just wish I didn't have to go alone.

I distract myself by scanning my news alerts, seeing that press are already reporting on the premiere. I quickly skip through all the posts about the stars - they're not my clients, so I couldn't care less - and find the ones about my author. She's there, smiling in a gorgeous dress patterned to look like dragon scales, and there's no hint of nerves in her confident expression. I play a few clips for myself, and practically burst with pride at how well she's answering the press questions, especially the news about the new six-book deal she just signed with another major publisher, and about the *Age of Dragons* spin-off she'd committed to write for Sky High. All of the hours I'd spent practicing interviews with her had clearly paid off.

When the Uber drops me off in Trafalgar Square, I thread through the crowds and flash my ID for security, which lets me into the press pen. I start shaking hands and answering questions for the media, those that weren't important enough to ask the author and the actors, but which will flesh out a story. There's a tall, stunning Italian woman holding court with some of the reporters at the edge of the crowd, and I can tell that she's probably representing one of the leads by the way the reporters are all shouting questions at her. Besides the two of us, there are a few other publicists working the crowd, and I get lost in the rhythm of answering questions while keeping an ear out for what everyone else is saying.

And then it's over in a flash, and the red carpet is emptying as ushers start to let people into the massive theatre where the movie will play.

I hesitate as I find Megan in the crowd. She makes her way to me. 'Are you coming in, Oli?'

I bite my lip, thinking of how I need to be professional and don't want to break down in tears during all the parts where Armin and his fated mate-slash-fellow dragon rider Gwen confess their undying love to each other. There's even a damn proposal scene in the movie, and I'm wondering if I'll be able to make it through.

'I just need a minute,' I lie. 'Bathroom. Bad stomach and all.'

'If your bad stomach is a result of more ice cream, you get no sympathy from me,' she says, her eyes crinkling in suspicion.

I narrow my eyes, giving her my patented 'I could kill you with just a look' glare. 'I hate how well you know me.'

It's probably going to be more like an hour, which I'll blame on my steady diet of only ice cream. That will get me through the worst of the early declarations of love and fidelity. And then I can dip out to get a drink during the proposal scene. I know exactly where it is, having fast-forwarded through it many times over the last week.

'This is what you've been working towards, Oli. Don't get lost on your way to your seat,' Megan says, squeezing my arm and clearly not buying my bullshit. She's always been able to see straight through me.

'Save me a seat.'

She eyes me nervously, knowing the chances of my actually watching the film are slim.

'It sounds like you're bowing out before the curtains rise,' Megan says.

'You know me, the book is always going to be better than the film.'

She smiles but it doesn't quite reach her eyes. Then Megan turns on her red-bottom heels and leaves.

I breathe a sigh of relief as she doesn't put up more of a fight and make my way up to the second level of the theatre, where I'm sure there's a quieter bathroom that I can hide in.

But when I open the door and slip inside, I realise I'm not alone.

There's a man hunching over the sink, gripping the edges. He's wearing an expensive looking suit, but it's ill-fitting, like he rented it from some shop that didn't even make adjustments. That and there's a faint hint of alcohol under the smell of his cologne. His thick brown hair is falling out of its gelled style and into his eyes, which are beyond tired looking. They'd probably be hazel in the sun, but in the industrial light of the bathroom, they're just a muddy brown. His cheekbones are high, but his face is hollow, like he's just lost a lot of weight.

He's gorgeous, in a faded kind of way, like he'd once been stunning but had let himself go.

He's also very clearly having a panic attack.

'Hey,' I say, because I've been there and done that, and there's no way that I'm going to leave someone to suffer through an anxiety onslaught alone. 'Are you ok?'

The man gives a harsh laugh, almost like he's choking, and grips the edge of the sink even harder. His knuckles show through the skin, and I hope he's not about to start throwing punches. Maybe he thinks I'm coming on to him. I take a half-step back, but then the laugh gives way to a ragged inhale that sounds like it *hurts*.

'No,' he croaks, his voice so quiet I almost can't hear. 'I'm not.'

It looks like the admission costs him, his shoulders curling in and his breathing getting even shorter and sharper. I go into triage mode, stepping up to him. 'Is it alright if I touch you?'

The man nods, and I put my hand on his back, rubbing soothing circles over the ridges of his spine, which I can feel through his jacket. 'I want you to breathe in for a count of four, then hold it, and then we'll let it out slowly.'

It's a trick my therapist taught me, controlling breathing to short-circuit panic attacks. I hope it works for this stranger, because I can't stand to watch someone in the kind of pain I know personally. My medication works well enough that I haven't had one of these in ages, but that doesn't mean I don't remember the feeling of it all too well.

The man nods again, and I count out the numbers slowly, feeling his ribs expand and then contract against my hand. We do it again, and again, and after a few cycles the shaking in his hands starts to ebb.

'That's better,' I say soothingly, switching to what I always wanted on the come-down from a panic attack - a good shoulder massage. It's hard through the jacket, but even with layers of fabric between us, I can feel just how tense and locked-up this man's muscles are.

'Thanks,' he says. His voice is still ragged, but it's a little better now. He's pushing back into my hands, like a cat eager to be pet, and I keep going, digging my thumbs into the tense lumps along his shoulder blades. 'I'm so sorry. This is so embarrassing. I just - I think I need to get out of here.'

'It's not embarrassing,' I counter. 'Plenty of people, myself included, have anxiety that becomes unmanageable at times. But I agree with you - I'm not interested in being here anymore either. But responsibilities and all.'

'Yes,' he replies, eyeing me cautiously, as if I'm about to steal something from him. Clearly, this man distrusts new people just as much as I should've with Geoff, before I was blinded by the high life. 'Do you…'

He stops himself, which makes me lean in. 'Do I what?'

His rich brown eyes, which are more the decadent colour of chocolate than I first noticed, drink me in. From stiff leather shoes to the dramatic pink bowtie I matched with my tux.

I get the odd feeling that he wants to get as far away from me as possible. Is it the bowtie? Maybe I should've gone with boring black after all. 'Never mind. I should go.'

I busy myself by washing my hands, over and over, aware he is still looking at me expectantly. When the question finally comes, it almost knocks me forwards. 'What responsibilities are you hiding from in here?'

A nervous laugh bubbles up my throat. 'Where do I start?'

'Sounds ominous.' I notice the strange accent the man has. It's American, kind of. But there's something else beneath it, the roll of a tongue that transports me to a warm beach in the Mediterranean. Italian maybe? Or Spanish, I can't place it.

'What about you?' I ask, pumping more soap onto my fingers.

'I'm not one to enjoy a crowd, to be honest.'

'Ditto.'

'Ditto? Isn't that a Pokémon?'

I snap my head around, amused by the fact this tall man even knows what Pokémon are. 'You're not wrong.'

He shrugs, tugging nervously at the knot of his tie as the bustle beyond the door dies down. 'Sounds like the movie is about to start.'

I wince, and he notices.

'Can I ask why you're here, if you clearly have no interest in watching it?'

I turn off the tap and notice just how silent the room is. 'Again, you're asking me another question that *you* could do with answering.'

'Well,' the man says, finally tugging his tie off. He pulls it through his collar with careful hands, before discarding it over the basin of the sink before him. 'Let's just say, that my responsibilities are fulfilled for the night. Is that something else we share in common?'

He's not wrong in his assumption. My work was done the minute the red carpet ended, and now all that's happening is people watching a movie that I've screened dozens of times before to get my marketing copy and social media assets just right. There will be afterparties, but Megan and the rest of my friends know full well that I'm not in the mood for a huge crowd of people in a club with pounding music. Not tonight.

'They are.'

He steps forwards, driven by a confidence I could only

wish to have. 'Then there is nothing stopping either of us from escaping?'

Are you suggesting - ' I venture, hesitant. I'm not normally like this, but the guy is practically arching into me, so there's a good chance he's thinking along the same lines I am. 'What I'm trying to say is…Do you want to get out of here? Together?'

Maybe all I need is a distraction. A hot, sad distraction that looks like he could use one too. Something to overwrite the memory of Geoff fucking a twink. Maybe getting railed will wipe that right out of my head, replace it with a good memory for once.

The man looks at me through devilishly long lashes, and the look in his eyes sends heat straight to my core.

'Yes,' he says, licking his lips, the vestiges of panic leaving his expression. 'Let's.'

6

NIKOS

I SIT NEXT to a stranger in a black cab, watching out the window as Central London blurs outside. And I thought traffic in New York City was bad. London takes the cake when it comes to standstill traffic and bad-mouthed drivers.

My initial worry was that the cab driver would recognise me, since my face is plastered on the side of his car, bare chested and with nipples on display as my character rides his dragon. But like the man beside me, the driver doesn't blink. It seems he's far more interested in sticking his head out the window and shouting profanities at every car we pass - at a snail's pace, that is.

'I'd say we decide on a location, because driving circles around London in a black cab is going to empty our pockets quicker than a shop around Harrods.'

I watch the man in the reflection of the fogged-up window as he speaks. 'What on God's green earth is Harrods?'

His pale brow lifts into his hairline, pulling a face of mock horror. 'You're American, right?'

'Is it that obvious?' I retort.

His laugh is as sweet as honey. I like it. He smells like it too, no doubt the kind of man who wears perfume meant for women - not that I care. I mean, who decided that a man couldn't wear Ariana Grande perfume if he wanted to?

'No. I mean - yes. I'm just trying to give you a comparison. Harrods is like one big…mole, like you Americans call it, just filled with designer items.'

'Mole?' I chuckle, which soon becomes a belly laugh at the man's obvious confusion about what has me in hysterics.

'What's so funny?' he asks, his tone an audible version of scowling, crossing his arms over his chest.

'It's a *mall*, not a *mole*.'

'Fuck you,' he says, but with a smile. 'It's the accent. I know what it's called.'

I turn from the window to face him. There's barely space between us, the glass partition separating the back seats from the driver dripping with the moisture in the air. Is it criminal to use the air conditioning in a car in London? I'm sweating a little, the collar of my shirt sticking to my neck. Part from the heat, but more so from my nerves that the man at my side will finally recognise me.

'I'm not familiar with the best places to frequent in London,' I say, offering him a distraction from his obvious embarrassment. 'You decide. I'm just happy for the distraction.'

I expect him to ask me what I'm being distracted *from*,

but he doesn't. There's something easy about his company. I think the fact he helped me navigate an anxiety attack in the bathroom helped break down the barrier between us as strangers. Or the fact we both made a connection from the enjoyment of pocket monsters - now *that* was a fact I was ready to explore when the time was right. I was a secret nerd, and no one knew it because it didn't fit with the leading man image.

'Well, we could hit a club?'

My reply comes out too quickly. 'No, thanks.'

'Crowds, oh yeah. I remember. Sorry'

I nod, trying to hide my nerves. I hardly imagine that I could walk into a club in the heart of London and keep up this luck of not being recognised. Being anonymous like this hadn't happened in so long that toying with the man at my side was a thrill.

'Well, then we could go get food?'

My stomach rumbles in response, but again, restaurants seem to be out of the question. Sadly, I can't say no, since he heard the growl too. 'I could eat.'

'Any requests?'

It's obvious he finds this more awkward than I do, like he's never picked up a person for a night. He fidgets with the material of his jacket, picking the threads from the seam until they fray. 'I'm not in London often, so how about something quintessentially British?'

My purposely bad rendition of an English accent makes him smile. And what a nice smile it is, all lips and a hint of teeth. It's the type of grin that stretches from ear to ear, warming the cheeks and putting sparkles in the eyes.

'Be careful what you ask for - ' He stops himself, fumbling over the fact that a name would fit in his sentence, but he doesn't have one. He bites his lip. 'If I told my friends I just got in a car with a stranger whose name I don't even know, they'd kill me.'

'I could say the same.' I waggle my eyebrows. 'But to really make them cross, how about *you* give *me* a name. Just for the night. Go for it.'

This is the test. A way to work out if this man does, in fact, know who I am.

He narrows his eyes, roaming his gaze over my face. I feel every inch of skin he passes over, as though he's trailing a feather over it.

'Hmm, I think I need to think about that.'

'Don't think too hard, you might hurt yourself,' I reply in jest.

'You don't know my name either, so I think the trade is only fair.'

I lean in, taking a deep inhale of that honey-kissed perfume. I wonder if he tastes as sweet as he smells. I suppose we might find out.

'How about this,' I begin my proposal, just as the cab comes to an abrupt halt. The driver slams his palm into the horn, and his string of *fuck you, prick, bastard chops, dick head* comes spilling out. 'If you can successfully distract me from my responsibilities tonight, then I might just tell you my name come morning.'

Because come tomorrow, I'll be on a flight heading out of London, and it won't matter if he knows who I am. The least I can do for tricking him is give the man a good story to sell to the gossip news sites - the fact that he spent an evening running around town with Nikos Ridge.

His eyes brighten. 'Okay, deal.'

He extends a hand, which I take. Following his lead,

we shake on the agreement. His palms are so soft I almost melt into him. I can tell from the sheen of his nails that he paints them with a clear gel. They're extremely well-manicured, whereas mine look brutalised because I've bitten them to stumps.

'Deal,' I reply.

He leans forwards, and for a moment I think he's going to kiss me. I don't know why my mind goes there, but I'm actually disappointed when he knocks on the plastic window between us and the driver to get his attention. 'Drop us off here, please.'

The driver doesn't complain. Clearly glad not to have to drive any further through London, he pulls up to the curb, takes the cash from my companion, and lets us out.

As I climb onto the streets, I leave the little trepidation I had in the back seat of the car. No thoughts of the film, of my father, or the kittens Selina must be having right now as she works out how to cover that I'm missing.

I'm not a monster. I texted her as I left the bathroom, letting her know I was safe and heading back to the hotel, not to be disturbed, to which she replied with a string of angry face emojis.

Tomorrow, we have a short flight to Paris for the final press interview - she can berate me then. But tonight doesn't belong to me, or the film. It belongs to the man who threads his soft fingers in with mine and drags me into the side streets of London.

'WHOEVER CAME up with the idea of mushy peas deserves a lifelong sentence in prison, no chance of parole,' I say as I watch my distraction scoop up a glob of green mush on a piece of battered fish.

'Don't knock it,' he says through a full mouth, which I would find gross on anyone else, but which is endearing on him, 'until you try it.'

'No thanks, you can have it.'

My stomach is full of fish and chips which apparently, he claims, is 'the most English meal you can eat'. When in London and all that. I scarfed the entire portion down.

My stomach aches from the overload of carbs, which I'll need two extra sessions in the gym to burn - or I would've, if I was still trying to be in shape for the movie. The habits of the last year will die hard. But I try not to care. The bottled beer he brought for us certainly helps wash it down. As does the view of the Thames.

'It's really peaceful here,' I say, leaning back on the stone steps, a cool breeze caressing my face. I close my eyes, listening to the sounds of the rushing water.

'It fucking *stinks*,' he replies. 'But it was the only place I could think which wouldn't have a crowd.'

He isn't wrong. The river certainly stinks - of fish and shit. But the quiet makes it all better. As does the way the lights from the buildings on the other side of the river twinkle as they reflect across the dark waters. In the distance we can hear horns and cars, the chatter of people as they experience London after dark. But here, there's only us and the water.

I've always loved the water. Growing up in a small town back in Greece, I would wake and hear the lapping of ocean waves, and fall asleep to the sound too. When life got dark, there was always the water, offering me a lullaby.

My Mama once told me that the sound of the waves against the shore was her whispering stories to me, no matter where she was in the world. That stayed with me when she died.

Sitting here, on wet stone steps, with a stranger at my side and the water singing in front of us, I don't care about the smell. Nothing has the power to ruin this moment. It's by far the most peaceful I've felt in years.

'How did you find this place?' I ask, peering at him out the corner of my eye. 'Seems like a hidden gem that you can only find when you really need a place to hide from the world.'

The stranger smiles at me, a corner-lip grin that warms me from the inside out. 'It's near the offices I work at. I found it the day I got my job offer. There was so much going on in my mind, a list of endless possibilities of how my life was about to change. I got lost walking out the offices and found myself here. It seemed that this spot found me, to be honest. Since then, whenever I've felt the need for some peace, I come here. It's my special place.'

'Well thank you - ' It was my turn to stumble on the lack of his name, ' - for sharing your special place with me.'

He shrugs. 'You're welcome, I guess.'

I look at him, really look at him, as he stares longingly over the water. He takes a deep breath in, as though he can absorb the peace of his hidden gem. I see something in him that I share. A need for escape, a need for quiet and contemplation.

'It would be nice if the night stretched on forever,' I say, breaking the sudden quiet between us. 'I like this, existing in a place where the only thing I worry about is the name of the man I'm sitting beside.'

It's been almost three hours since we left the premiere, and he's still a mystery to me. I thought I could last the night without caring to work him out, but alas I find myself craving answers.

But answers would lead to the truth, and I don't think I'm ready for that to ruin the moment. Not yet. And the fact that he hadn't told me his name either only proves to me that he feels the same.

'I have an idea,' I say, sitting up, almost knocking over the Styrofoam tub of mushy peas I've left untouched.

'Should I be worried?' he replies.

'Maybe.' I wink. 'But tonight we both wanted to escape from something, right?'

Right...'

'Have you ever watched Cinderella?' I ask.

'I'm gay,' he replies with a laugh. 'I could recite any Disney film word-for-word. Of course I know Cinderella, although I'm more of a Little Mermaid kinda man.'

To be honest, I haven't even contemplated his sexuality, the same way I never really think of mine. I mean, I guess I've never *allowed* myself to really think about my own sexuality before.

'Well,' I say, quickly diverting the topic before I could say something that crosses the line. 'We're both like Cinderella, fleeing the ball and leaving lives behind us. Our crystal slipper is currently back at that premiere, and with it our pasts. We exist only in this moment. So, instead of swapping names and stories, why don't we make them up for each other?'

My perfect stranger ponders this for a moment, taking

a swig of beer as he contemplates. 'Ok. You start. Give me a name.'

It was easy. 'Honey.'

'Excuse me?'

'Honey. Because you smell like it. You're sweet and sticky - sticky, I mean, because you've stuck yourself to me with ease. Hold on, that came out wrong. I mean it in a good way, of course. I like honey and I just think you're - '

Honey silences me with a hand on my knee. The moment he touches me my entire body erupts in shivers. Even with the material between his hand and my skin, I still feel as though he's imprinting himself on me.

'Okay, no need to dig your hole any deeper.' He smirks. 'Honey, I like it.'

I smile, running a hand through my hair nervously and pushing the strands off my face. 'And what are you going to call me?'

'Adonis,' Honey says with confidence.

I laugh. Really laugh. The type that builds in a person's stomach and is almost forced out, breathless and rushed. 'I suppose I can cope with that. How did you work out I was Greek?'

'I didn't,' Honey replies. 'It was more from the way you look.'

I smile harder, which makes Honey's cheeks stain red. 'I'll take that as a compliment then.'

Honey rubs his hand on the back of his head. 'I'm not flirting, you know.'

'That's a shame,' I say, nervous bubbles popping in my stomach. 'I wouldn't mind if you were.'

'It's just straight men often think a gay person being

nice to them is for ominous reasons. I was simply pointing out that you're hot in a no-homo kinda way.'

'Who said I was straight?' I say without thinking.

Tonight, I can be anything. As I said to him, there *is* no past. No Nikos Ridge. No responsibilities. I can be anything tonight, and Honey's presence certainly makes that possible.

'Well, whatever you are, it doesn't matter.'

'No, you're right, it doesn't.'

I hold Honey's stare a beat longer than friends would. I read his embarrassed expression and can't help but find it endearing.

'So,' he says nervously. 'What do you want to do next?'

Who do I want to do would've been a better question. 'The night is young. Anywhere else you want to take me? I'm all yours, Honey.'

I see it then, a glint in his eyes. I know without a doubt he's thinking the same thing as I am. Where else can we exist where there's no crowd, a place we can continue to hide away and play the part of strangers without questions?

A room. Preferably, a bedroom.

'Well, I have beer at my house, Adonis.'

I swear the way he uses that nickname makes me want to show him just how fitting it is. 'I like beer,' I reply.

'I can tell,' Honey replies, looking to my empty bottle.

'Do you know what,' I say, standing and offering him a hand to pull him up. 'I think I've got room for something sweet. I do like to follow up my meals with a dessert.'

'Really?'

I love the way his voice cracks when he's nervous. I lean in, breaking the last wall between us. My mouth comes so close to his face that I can smell the salt and vinegar on his breath. It doesn't repulse me, not even the slightest.

Nor does he pull back.

'I have a taste for Honey,' I say.

'You - do?'

Nothing is stopping me from pressing my mouth to his. Only myself. I know, if I do this, then the story Honey can sell tomorrow morning would really be juicy. Nikos Ridge, fucking a man instead of a leading lady. But maybe that's what I want. A way to sabotage myself, my career - a way to sabotage my *life* until it's no longer beneficial to the man who I once called father.

And maybe it's even more than that. Maybe I just want Honey for myself.

'Shall I book an Uber, or do you fancy a walk? I ask.

Honey sheds the nervous glint in his eyes and smiles, as though he's finally come to terms with what's about to happen. 'Whatever gets us there quicker.'

I pull back, noticing how he leans in a little more. 'I like the sound of that.'

My phone is in my hand in seconds. I pay no mind to the screen full of missed calls and texts and open the Uber app. Honey recites an address and in two minutes our car is booked. Another five minutes and it arrives. In twenty minutes we're scrambling into his townhouse, greedy hands all over each other.

I was right. Honey is exactly what I need. And from the way his mouth crashes into mine, the feeling is mutual.

7

OLI

I DON'T KNOW how I got this lucky.

Eight hours ago, I was standing in front of the bathroom mirror, crying over Geoff, of all people. Now, I'm wrapped up in a literal Greek God, straddling him on my couch.

Adonis's hands are roaming all over my body, from my shoulders to my waist and down to the curve of my ass. His hands are strong and huge and I can't wait to feel those thick fingers inside me.

But for now, he seems content to devour me. We haven't even taken off our jackets or shoes, and I can't bring myself to care. Not when he's kissing me more thoroughly than I've ever been kissed before, not even when Geoff and I were still in the honeymoon phase, if we ever had one. Our tongues slide against each other, and his teeth nip my lower lip, making me moan into his mouth.

'Oh my God,' Adonis growls. He's rock-hard - and *huge*, if what I'm feeling underneath me is any indication. He threads his fingers through my hair and tugs my head back, drawing a breathy whimper from me. How did he know I like to be manhandled? 'Look at you.'

I flush, because this man is gorgeous, far more gorgeous than anyone I've ever been with. My hands are splayed on his chest, and I trace down his impressive pecs to the ridges of his abs, which are well-defined enough to make my mouth water. He's lean, but in a way that clearly shows he spends a lot of time at the gym. 'Look at *you*.'

'I'm nothing to look at, Honey.' I almost start to argue with him, because he looks like he means it, like he genuinely doesn't know how handsome he is. But then he leans forward and bites my neck hard enough to bruise. I want him to bite me all over until I'm black and blue. 'But you? You're the most stunning creature I've ever had my hands on. I'm going to *ravish* you.'

Adonis brings his hands back to my hips and flips us so that I'm underneath him. My legs wrap instinctively around his waist, which grinds my aching cock against his. I close my eyes and moan.

He's all over me, around me, his cologne filling my nose and intoxicating me. His hand finds the waistband of my pants, and for a moment I think he's about to unbutton them and finally get a hand around my dick, but he just gently tugs my shirt out and slides a warm, broad hand up underneath and across the ridges of my ribs.

It's nearly as good. His thumb brushes over my nipple and I arch up into him, totally unable to control myself. This man is driving me feral, and I'm so here for it. This is doing more than any amount of alcohol and ice cream to wipe the memories of the last few horrible days straight out of my mind.

If you can't get over Geoff, get under someone else.

Adonis is nipping at my ear now whilst continuing to tease me with his thumbnail, pain and pleasure mixing in just the way I like it. I'm leaking so much there's no way I haven't ruined my pants - God knows what the dry cleaner is going to say when I take this tux in - but I also have a sense that when I come, it's all going to be over. And I don't want the clock to strike midnight. If I'm Cinderella, and this is my ball, I never want it to end.

The man above me is panting, grinding into me so slowly that I wonder if he's even aware he's doing it. I let my hands wander and undo the buttons of his shirt, slipping my hands inside to find warm, taut skin. I wonder how he's gotten this fit, if he's gotten this body by doing something dangerous, like extreme sports or MMA or something like that. It makes him even more appealing, the thought that he's a person who lives on the edge.

I want him to take *me* to the edge.

Adonis' pupils are blown wide, his cheeks painted with colour. There's a sheen of sweat gathering on his chest that I want to lick off with my tongue. His lips are swollen from kissing. I can't wait to make him come completely undone.

'Bedroom?' I rasp, hoping it's not too forward. Because while I wouldn't mind being fucked right here on the couch, I really could do with re-christening the bed. I don't want the last person to have been fucked in it to be some anonymous twink by my cheating ex-boyfriend.

'Yes,' he growls, and then he's off the couch and *picking me up* like I weigh nothing, which makes me harder than I've been since I was a teenager.

New kink unlocked.

I point him up the stairs, down the hall, and to the

bedroom and let him dump me on the bed and pull off my shoes for me. I lift my hips as he unbuttons my pants, making it easier for him to slide them off me. My socks are next, and then my jacket and shirt, until I'm left in my underwear, which he drags off too.

There's something about lying there, laid out like a meal for a man who's still fully dressed, studying me in the dim light coming from the windows, that makes me dizzy with want.

'Are you just going to stand there?' I snap, motioning to him.

'Don't worry,' he says, shedding his jacket and unbuttoning the rest of his shirt. He's moving slow, like this is my own personal 'James Bond coming to strip for Oliver' fantasy come to life. 'I'm not a tease. Not when I have you waiting for me.'

As he sheds his layers, I get a look at the well-honed muscles on his frame. He's got a fading tan, like he used to spend a lot of time in the sun. But they doesn't make him any less breathtaking, and then I don't care at all when he steps out of his underwear and his fucking huge cock springs free. It's totally perfect and looks hard enough to cut diamonds, and when I can't help myself and reach out, raising a brow until he nods his consent, I draw a finger down his impressive length. He gasps and steps forward, resting a knee on the bed, leaning down to kiss me with a hand on my ribs and another in my hair.

I pull him completely on top of me, the bed springs groaning with the added weight. Our hips slot together perfectly, the skin-on-skin feel of it beyond incredible. We're both clearly ready, and I'm just about done with the extended foreplay now that we're both naked and he's on top of me.

I fumble with the drawer pull of the nightstand, wrenching it open and pulling out a bottle of KY and a condom. I think if his cock isn't in me in the next ten minutes, I might die.

'Go on, then,' I say, shifting my hips and nudging his hand downwards.

Adonis freezes.

All of a sudden, he looks less like he's into this and more like he's a deer in the headlights of a car, about to get run over. His mouth opens, but then closes again. He doesn't make a move for the lube, even though I pick it up and hold it in his face.

'Do you...' I bite my lip, wondering where I misread things. 'Do you want me to prep myself?' Some men get off on watching their partners do it, I know. It's not that I *can't* - it's that I was looking forward to having his fingers inside me, stretching and exploring.

'Prep?' His brows draw together.

Oh my God.

It hits me then. He's never done this before.

'Oh,' I say, my eyes wide. I can see him start to pull back, his eyes shuttering, but I grab his wrist and lock my legs back around his waist. He's not going anywhere.

'I'm honoured to be your first,' I say. 'It's a bit more complicated than with a woman - wait, *have* you been with a woman?'

This man doesn't kiss like a virgin, but I don't want to make assumptions.

Adonis is as red as a beet, but he nods. 'Yeah, a few.'

The way he said *a few* sounded more like *loads*.

'Alright.' I've never walked anyone through this - my first time was with a guy who'd already been there and a done that. 'It's not too hard. You just need to loosen me up before you go for it. I mean, you're *huge*, I don't think I could take you with no warm-up. Even if I could, it would hurt like a bitch.'

He bites his lip, but he's breathing more steadily now. His hips meet mine again, sparks flying up my spine. 'I don't want to hurt you.'

'You won't.' I reach up to run fingers through his hair. He arches up into my touch like a cat being pet. 'I promise. I'll walk you through it. Are you ready?'

I hope he says yes. I'm gagging for it. Not even the idea that I'm about to be fucked by a guy with no clue what he's doing dims my excitement.

Adonis nods. I grab his hand, making him shift his weight onto one forearm. I pop the cap on the lube and drizzle a generous amount onto his fingers. I change positions, hooking my legs over his shoulders, opening myself up. 'Start with one. I'll tell you when to add another.'

He sucks in a breath, and the way he's wide-eyed and tentative shouldn't be as hot as it is. I don't care if this isn't the world's greatest fuck - it's worth it, just to see the expression on his face. I'm going to wank to this memory for the rest of my life.

The blunt tip of his finger presses against my entrance, and I focus on relaxing as he presses inside, so slowly that I think I might die. 'Keep going,' I urge, 'just like that.'

My body gives way for him, letting him in. He pulls back and then pushes in again, and completely by accident he hits the *exact* right spot inside me, making me yelp.

'Did I hurt you?' Adonis freezes.

I push back against his finger, causing another burst of pleasure to race through me. I moan so loud that I'm sure the posh neighbours are hearing and having heart attacks. 'The opposite,' I pant. 'It's - That's *exactly* where you want to hit. Keep going like that and I'm going to come untouched.'

'You can do that?' His mouth drops open, but he makes the tiniest circle with the tip of his finger. I clench around him.

'Oh, love.' I roll my eyes. 'You've clearly never met a prostate before, have you? You can add in another finger.'

I'm far more interested in continuing with the delicious stretch and burn of his fingers dragging in and out of me than I am in giving him an anatomy lesson. That can wait for later. I breathe in as he nudges another finger alongside the first, then urge him to pump them in and out, warming me up for his enormous cock.

I pull his head down to mine again and kiss him, wet and filthy, our tongues battling for dominance. He's pressing forward, bending me in half with his weight, and I want this man to snap me in two.

At my urging, Adonis adds a third finger, pulling them apart like I tell him to relax my muscles, all while grinding against my cock and testing the limits of my self-control. I can't believe I haven't come all over him already. But no way am I going to let this night pass without the ultimate prize.

'I'm ready,' I gasp into his mouth when I can't take it anymore. I reach down and fist his cock, my hand barely getting around it. I know I'm small, but he's a monster. I stroke him a few times, but he hardly needs the help, rock hard and throbbing against my palm. I grab the condom with my other hand and rip open the packet with my teeth, rolling it on and then chasing it with a healthy drizzle of lube to make this easier. 'Just go slow. I'll tell you when to push in more.'

Adonis lines the blunt, broad head of his cock up with my arse and nudges his hips forward such a tiny amount that nothing happens. I giggle. 'Harder than that, darling.'

He tilts his forehead to mine and fists my hair in a hand. 'Alright,' he growls.

His hips move, his cock slowly nudging against me, more insistently this time. I bear down against him and then he's in. I deliberately even out my breathing, telling my body to relax as I adjust. He's far bigger than anyone who's ever fucked me - and far, *far* bigger than Geoff was - but I can take it with just a bit of concentration.

'Are you ok?' He's panting with the effort of holding back, his shoulders shivering under my touch. I rake nails down his back.

'Yes,' I gasp out. 'More.'

I urge him on until he's buried inside me, filling me up until I'm sure I can't take another inch, but then his hips meet my arse and my eyes practically roll back in my head.

'Move,' I order, and sure as fuck he *does*.

Adonis may never have fucked a guy before, but now I wouldn't know it. He withdraws and then slams back in, and with the smallest tilt of my hips I adjust so that he hits me just right, making me cry out. He gets the idea, putting his hand on the back of my thigh and bringing my leg closer to my chest, continuing to thrust in and out and leave me breathless.

Sweat is dripping from his skin and his muscles are standing out from the motion. I'm torn between letting my eyes close and my head drop back onto the pillow so I can take it all in and memorise every sensation, and studying the exact way he's moving so that I can remember what he looks like in this moment for the rest of my life.

I'm never going to top this. Too bad this was a one-night deal.

His abs are perfect as I run a finger down them, counting every ridge. I work my hand down and around to his ass, feeling how perfectly firm it is as he moves in and out of me. I want to ride this man like a horse, but I'm also not stopping him for a second, even to change positions.

Adonis bites his lip, his eyes screwing shut, and I can tell he's close by the way his hips start to stutter, the motion growing less and less fluid. I release the chokehold I have on my pleasure, feeling the orgasm building at the base of my spine until the feeling is overwhelming.

'I'm going to come,' I warn, sliding down into the all-encompassing, overwhelming sensation of bliss. He hasn't even touched me, my cock leaking between us. It doesn't matter, because three more thrusts of his hips have me spilling over, crying out as my inner muscles clench him tight.

My orgasm sets Adonis off, and he roars as he comes, slamming into me with so much power that my hips come off the bed, my climax drawing out until I'm almost sobbing with the pleasure. I can feel him pulsing inside me, and it goes on and on until he's finally collapsing on top of me in a sweaty, shattered mess.

'Oh my fucking God,' he pants. 'Holy shit.'

I'm loathe to be left empty, but I reach down and guide

him out before he can soften, pulling off the condom and tossing it onto the floor. I nudge at his shoulder and he rolls off of me, wrapping me in his strong arms as I snuggle into his chest, my leg thrown over his abs.

This is perfect. I never want this moment to end.

I thought that maybe Adonis would fuck me once and then get up to leave, like maybe he has somewhere better to be. But he just lies there, carding a hand through my hair.

If he's not going to go, maybe I'm still Cinderella and have a few more hours until midnight. I'm going to make the most of every second.

'So,' I say as we both catch our breath. 'How long until round two?'

8

NIKOS

I CAN'T TAKE my mind off Honey. Even my body refuses to forget him. His touch lingers on my skin, his taste on my tongue. I can see my swollen lips in the reflection of the oval plane window at my side. If I tug at my collar, it will reveal a faint bruise Honey left as he sucked and nipped at my neck.

I fight the urge to lift a finger and touch the tender skin, knowing Selina is watching me with keen interest.

'Late night?' she asks, finally breaking the silence I was being punished with since she picked me up this morning. I had to pin her my location so the driver could find me. And as I slipped into the leather seat beside her, I could see from the shadows beneath her eyes that she'd not slept a wink.

Neither did I, but my exhaustion is justified. My night had been spent buried deep inside a man I didn't even really know. My little secret - my dirty distraction.

'So we're talking now?' I ask.

Selina's lip curls and she swears at me in Italian.

'*Vaffanculo*, Nikos. Did you expect hugs and kisses this morning, after you've single-handily driven me to the brink of insanity with your little disappearing act last night?'

I've opened the floodgates of her fury. Like dominoes, one falls, and the rest follow. 'I spent most of last night, not celebrating the film's release, but having my ear chewed off by the production company. *Where is our star? Where is Nikos?* Four hours I spent putting out fires. *Hours*, Nikos. I was on the phone with the studio representatives in LA until three AM. Do you understand what kind of trouble you're in?'

'I can guess,' I reply, knowing now isn't the moment for a retort that would piss Selina off more. The best thing to do, when she gets like this, is let her get it all out. No point apologising until the balloon of her tension has completely deflated.

'Well.' She snatches a small bottle of gin from the lavishly stocked table of the private jet, flicks off the lid, and practically downs the entire thing in one. 'You can blame yourself for the extension the studio has arranged. They're not satisfied that you broke one of your contractual obligations. And because of that, we're heading back to London after Paris for more interviews, TV appearances, talk shows… you name it, Nikos Ridge, and you earned it.'

I look towards the vodka and cranberry I'd made on instinct which I'd left untouched. For the first time in a long time, I hardly notice the alcohol before me. I know why I don't want to drink it. If I do, it will wash the sweet taste of Honey from my lips and tongue. I'm not ready to forget him just yet.

'Could be worse,' I say, leaning back on the leather seat, arms folded.

'Could be worse?' Selina repeats. 'Could be worse?!'

Oh, I've really done it now.

'This is coming from the man who has spent the last three months whining and moaning about going back to New York. Everything you've worked towards, and the moment that is taken away, you say *'could be worse'*?'

'What do you want me to say?' I ask, pinching my eyes closed as if that will help with the exhausted headache I'm dealing with.

'It wouldn't hurt for you to apologise to me, Nikos. We could start there.'

I wince. Apologising is never something I'm good at. But Selina is right, and she deserves it. Opening one eye, I offer her what sounds like a weak apology, when in fact it's the best she's getting - and she knows it. 'I'm sorry for disappearing last night, but needs must.'

'What needs?'

'Anxiety,' I offer, which isn't a lie. 'I had a moment in the bathroom. All the people and the expectations. I couldn't face anyone in that state, so I left. I thought it was better that then the studio punishing me for having a mental breakdown in front of an entire crowd.'

Selina leans forwards and I think she's about to scratch me with her red-painted nails. Then she lays a soft hand on my thigh and sighs. 'I know this is hard for you.'

'Do you?' I can't stop myself.

'I do. When do you think you'll understand that my care for you goes far beyond my percentage in payment?'

I shrug, looking out the window at the rolling white

clouds. It's easier to face the world beyond the jet than the hurt and pain in Selina's eyes.

'Nikos, I'm not going to ask what kind of trouble you got yourself in last night, but we'll need to come up with a solid excuse to tell the people holding your final payment. Sadly, Hollywood doesn't have a heart, so singing a song about your anxiety isn't going to be good enough.'

'Tell them I met someone at the event, got drunk and ended up having the best sex of my life in a posh townhouse in London.'

Selina chokes back a laugh, but quickly stops herself. 'Tell me you're joking.'

'I'm not.'

Selina buries her face into her hands and screams. 'Fuck me. The *risk*. What we don't need right now is some trashy UK article about how Nikos Ridge left his own premiere to fuck some random fan. Since when do you do that? I mean, *come on*, Nikos. Do you really need me to explain the complications and risks of having sex with some random woman? The scandal. I swear you'll kill me before I get the chance to quit.'

I hold my tongue, stopping myself from correcting her. *Who said it was a woman?* Revealing that I'd fucked a man last night was certainly the straw that would break the camel's back. Even *I* didn't really understand how it happened, just that Honey had been there, the right person at the right time.

Honey may have been a stranger, but for the first time in a long time, I was a stranger too. I'm confident he didn't recognise me as Nikos Ridge, but then again I'm sure that illusion will break soon.

Will he tell the press? Maybe. It's possible. It would

certainly net him a huge payment. Do I care? No, I don't think I do - but I don't want him to, all of a sudden. Not for myself, but for Selina - I couldn't do that to her.

It's my turn to lay a hand on her knee. 'I'm only joking, S.'

I'm not an award-winning actor for nothing. I feign honesty, letting the emotion shine through my fake wide eyes.

'Really?'

I nod. 'I booked myself into a hotel away from the premiere. I knew you'd head back to the other room first, and I wasn't ready to face your disappointment. I got drunk on the mini bar, ordered room service, and was knocked out before the film even finished. I promise, it was a one-time thing. If the studio wants to extend the promotional campaign, then so be it. I deserve it. Nasty, horrible, childish Nikos.'

'Oh, shut up,' Selina says, huffing out a laugh, relief plastered across her face.

'Gladly,' I reply. 'So does this mean we're friends again?'

'Friends?' Selina laughs. 'You'd be lucky. And you've got some making up to do.'

'How many croissants will it take for me to make it up to you?' I ask.

'Make it five, and I'll *think* about it. Although our stop in Paris is short. Our plane has been booked back to London tonight. It's a quick turnaround.'

Back to London. A day ago the concept would've irked me. But now, it doesn't. And I know why. Because Honey is in London. This morning, when I'd snuck out of his apartment, leaving him sleeping soundly in the bed on tangled sheets, I was confident I'd never see him again.

Just as I'd tiptoed to his front door, ready to make my great escape, I'd paused in his kitchen when I saw that his fridge was covered in multi-coloured post-it notes. I hadn't needed to read them all to know that each of the post-its had affirmations scrawled on them in messy handwriting. One of them is in my suit pocket now, folded neatly, with Honey's writing on it.

You are enough.

It wasn't meant for me, and yet it had struck home. I feel as though the message - although written by Honey, for Honey - is a message the universe wanted me to read. So now I've brought a little piece of Honey with me as my life goes on.

But I'm not a good thief, so I'd made sure to replace the affirmation with one of my own. I'd taken the pen from the sideboard, and a new post-it, and written a message.

As sweet as Honey, you are certainly enough.
- Adonis

I'd almost written *thank you*, but that felt like a cheap way to end the night we'd shared. Although the thanks were certainly justified. What Honey had taught me in such a short period of time was a lesson I'd never forget.

How long until I see a photo of that post-it note on the front page of a newspaper, next to my name?

I suppose in time I'll see.

'Selina?' I start, knowing she is seconds from finally getting some sleep.

She jolts up, as if the plane had just nose-dived. 'What now?'

'How long are we in London for? You know, as my punishment?' I ask.

'A week.' Selina closes her eyes again, crossing her arms and leaning back in the reclining seat. 'Why?'

I stare out the window again, the alcohol still untouched. I don't know the direction England's in, but I find my eyes drifting out across the sea of clouds, wondering about Honey. I haven't stopped thinking about him. He haunts me, distracting my thoughts from anything else.

I wonder how long his spell will last on me, and if I'll be able to cope with reality once it catches up.

'No reason,' I say, catching my smile in the reflection. It's calculating as a plan forms in my head.

'Then let me sleep, damn you,' Selina complains. 'We land in half an hour.'

'Have you ever tried mushy peas?'

'Nikos, I will kill you.'

I laugh to myself as I reach my fingers into my pocket and feel the edge of the post-in note bite into my skin. 'Please don't do that. I'd like to explore London as much as I can when we return.'

'Then stop talking.'

Selina doesn't see me do it, but I zip my fingers over my lips.

The rest of the flight passes so quickly. I'm lost to the memory of Honey, while looking forwards to the chance to make a few more before I actually have to return to my normal life.

Maybe it's selfish, but I crave him. His touch, his distraction. Regardless of the risks, I can be careful.

He's worth it, after all.

Because last night, I hadn't thought about the real reason I'd left the premiere from the moment I exited the bathroom with Honey. The second the thought of my father comes back to me, I want to pry open the door on the plane and throw myself out, just in hopes the winds carry me back to Honey.

At least with my little secret, I can pretend to be someone I'm not. No expectations, no past or future.

The present with Honey is safe. I crave him more than alcohol.

You are enough. You are enough. You are enough.

'Yes,' I whisper to the window, breath fogging over the glass. 'Yes, you are.'

9

OLI

I FLOAT INTO WORK. It's practically like I'm levitating.

I'd woken up that morning to cold sheets next to me, and for a minute my heart had sunk. It had almost completely negated the incredibly delicious way my arse was aching with the memory of the night before.

But then I'd dragged myself out of bed and seen the post-it note on my fridge, standing out amongst the affirmations I'd been steadily adhering there in the hopes that they would perk up my mood.

As sweet as honey, you are certainly enough.

There had been a plate of fruit waiting for me on the counter, expertly cut up, along with a coffee in a to-go cup from the shop down the street and a muffin that I'd actually eaten instead of picking at. It had been my second full, non-ice cream meal in weeks, after the fish and chips we'd shared by the Thames. As I walk through the doors of Sky High, I'm feeling like a real human again.

I caress the edge of the post-it note I'd taken down from the fridge and stuck into my pocket. It's even better than writing it for myself - the knowledge that even if Adonis had to leave early, probably to get on with whatever job he was in town for as he was clearly just visiting London, he'd taken the time to let me know that he'd cared.

I know it's a one-time thing. I don't know the man's real name. I know nothing about him other than that he was at the premier of *An Age of Dragons*, and that he's American, and that he fucks like a god.

If I could write him a post-it note message in return, it would say: Adonis by name, Adonis by nature.

He hadn't left a phone number, no email, no social media profiles. And it's almost a relief, because last night had been perfect, and it's going to stay that way. There will be no relationship where Adonis will prove to be the kind of man who never washes the dishes, who has terrible morning breath, who wants to sit and watch boring sports games all day every day.

There's no way that Adonis can turn into the kind of man who cheats on you for six years straight.

No matter how much I would love to see him again, it's not going to happen. It's disappointing, but it's freeing too. It was the best night of my life. And I'm fine with it being a memory.

I keep telling myself that as I sit down at my desk.

'Hey,' Megan says as soon as my arse hits the seat. I haven't even had time to turn on my computer before she's at my shoulder. 'So where were you last night?'

I realise that most of the rest of the office is empty. Everyone must have been spending time recovering from the afterparty. I hit the button to turn on my computer, and it whirs to life. My email inbox is overwhelming the minute it flashes on the screen, and I minimise it before I get nervous heartburn.

'Out,' I say evasively.

'Out…being attacked by a suction cup?' Megan blinks at me innocently. 'Because it sure looks it.'

She points at my neck. I do my best not to raise my fingers up to touch the bruise that Adonis left under my jaw. I tried to cover it with makeup, because a scarf would have been amiss given the gorgeous early spring weather. But I guess I didn't do a good enough job.

'Honey,' she says, and I literally jump at the nickname, even though she calls me various terms of endearment all day, every day. 'There's no amount of concealer that could have done away with a hicky that incredible. Dish the dirt.'

She collapses into the empty desk chair next to me, blinking expectantly.

I chew my lip. She *knows* something happened with a man last night. And why not give her the truth? I steal a look around, and the only other people in are one of the editors, sitting clear across the room with massive headphones on, and the janitor slowly circulating around the room to empty the bins and wipe off the desks. It's not like there's anyone here to listen who would possibly care what I'd done the night before.

Maybe sharing the memory with another person will help me remember it better. I need to etch it into my brain so that I never forget.

I sigh. 'Honestly, I went into the bathroom before the movie started because I needed to collect myself. I was pretty convinced that if I had to sit and watch all those scenes where Armin professes his undying love for Gwen, that I'd start bawling in the theatre.'

'Understandable.' Megan's face creases with pity and she leans forward to pat me on the shoulder. 'I figured it was something like that, and it's not like you needed to be there after handling the media, so I decided to give you your space. I'm sorry you're having to deal with this in the midst of that wanker breaking your heart.'

I shrug. 'It's ok. Because...' I draw out for dramatic effect. 'In the bathroom, there was this guy.'

I pause, figuring out how to tell the rest of the story, and Megan makes an impatient *keep going* motion with her hand.

'Mmm,' I hum. The janitor is getting closer to us, and I lower my voice a tad just in case. 'He was practically having a panic attack over the sinks. And it was just so sad - I couldn't leave him like that. So I helped him through it, and then we were talking. We decided to get out of there, and he hadn't been to London before, so I took him to my favourite fish and chips place, and then we sat by the Thames and ate. You know, my spot by the office?'

Megan's eyes narrow. 'You're saying this man *also* decided not to sit in the theatre? And that he wasn't from London?'

'Don't look so suspicious.' I swat at her. 'It wasn't like I picked up a vagrant. He was at the premier, so he was on the list of cleared guests. And so when he suggested we... take things further, I took him home, and we. You know.'

Megan is looking at me strangely, now. 'You what?'

'He fucked me.' I roll my eyes. 'Do you want the play-by-play? He's got a massive...'

She's not looking at me now, though. She's thrown her body practically over my lap to reach my keyboard and is clicking into the internet and pulling up one of the entertainment sites. There's a livestream going on the front page, and it's about *An Age of Dragons* from the headline. I panic for a moment because usually I get notifications about all the press conferences, and I make sure to watch them. It must have come through early this morning, in the mess of emails I've not sorted through yet.

But I don't have time to panic about my lack of professionalism, because Megan is pointing one glitter-painted nail at the screen.

'Is this him?' Megan asks.

I freeze. I stare.

I literally cannot believe what I'm seeing.

There's Adonis. He's sitting at a table with a microphone in front of him, camera bulbs flashing, the scary looking Italian publicist I'd seen at the premier in the media pen standing off to the side.

He's flipping something small and folded up and hot pink between his fingers. *It's my fucking affirmation post-it.*

Adonis is regaling the crowd of reporters with a story about how it worked, filming the dragon riding scenes when the dragons had to be done in with CGI. He's got that deep, raspy voice. The voice that told me last night *I'm not a tease. Not when I have you waiting for me* as he stripped.

Right before he took me to pieces in the best sex of my life.

'Oli,' Megan says in a dramatic stage-whisper, a huge-ass, shit-eating grin spreading across her face. 'Darling. You just fucked Nikos Ridge.'

My cheeks heat as my stomach completes summersaults that would land me on the Olympic gymnastics team.

'Well actually,' I say, numb to the world. 'Nikos Ridge fucked *me*.'

THE REVELATION that I'd had Armin Wolfe's cock up my arse the night before sends me into a tailspin. I'm literally dizzy.

We've taken refuge in Megan's office, because it at least has a door. Once I've told her everything about the night in gripping detail, the two of us huddled under her desk like it's a bomb shelter, we sit for a moment and I try to catch my breath.

Adonis is Armin is *Nikos fucking Ridge*.

I'm screaming incoherently inside my head.

When I'm done with the story, having told it twice because Megan says her mind is so overloaded she can't grasp all the details with just one run through, she crawls out from under the desk, leaves the office, and comes back with two enormous, steaming cups of tea. I take one from her gratefully, my hands shaking, and wonder how the actual fuck this happened.

'So,' Megan says, back to the calm, cool, collected editor-in-chief. 'There's one really obvious thing we have to talk about. And that's that you absolutely cannot out him. You can never talk about this again.'

'Oh my God.' I nearly choke on the tea I've got in my mouth. 'I would *never.*'

I'd told Megan because I hadn't known who it was. Adonis was an anonymous fantasy. Never for a moment would I have disclosed all this if I'd know he was an actual *public figure*.

An actual Hollywood star, who had made a career on being the brooding, sexy, *extremely heterosexual* leading man. The one Hollywood hadn't seen in years until he reappeared to film his big comeback.

The one who always got the girl. Except now I knew he'd just as likely want to get the boy.

'It's going to be our secret,' Megan says. I'm grateful for how steady she's being as I slowly panic. I gulp down another hot mouthful of tea, hoping it works its magic on me and washes away some of the adrenaline coursing through my limbs. 'He clearly doesn't want anyone to know that he's into men, and that's fine. He's entitled to his privacy for whatever reason.'

'Yeah,' I agree. 'I know. I mean, look, I have no idea why he'd want to have sex with me, but it's going with me to the grave, I swear it. Not only would I never do that to another person, I'd also not do that to the cast and crew of the movie. It would send the entire premier into a total tailspin. The hunky action hero isn't straight? He's some variation of my-sexuality-includes-sticking-it-in-guys?'

'Always the publicist, you,' Megan says, blowing on her tea, smiling faintly again. 'Well, this is a hell of a memory, Oli.'

'Yeah,' I breathe out, wondering just how I got so lucky. I got my one night with Armin Wolfe. With Nikos Ridge.

I was his first.
I just wish that it hadn't also been our last.

10

NIKOS

IT'S BEEN thirty-six hours since I last saw Honey, and I can't stop thinking about him. I don't bother trying to, either. Because of this, it has also been thirty-six hours since I last had a drink.

I haven't once thought to open the minibar now that I'm back in the luxury hotel in London. Not once.

Selina is down in the spa, enjoying a well-deserved morning off. She's tried to entice me into a few treatments to 'loosen me up', but the thought of having another person's hands on me, whether sexual or not, makes me shiver.

Honey had touched me last. I want to keep it that way.

I check my watch and read the hands pointing close to midday. As per the schedule in my calendar, in twenty minutes a driver is coming to collect us for an afternoon of filming content at the book publisher. My punishment for leaving the premier is haunting me, the studio filling our schedule with as much press as possible - literally squeezing the lemon dry.

The only thing I want to do is make it through the day to five pm. Because, according to Google, the average London work hours finish at five. Which means Honey will be leaving his job and heading home.

I may not know his name, his number, even his favourite colour - but I know where he lives. Creepy or not, I need to see him. To explain myself, but also to ask him not to tell anyone about what happened between us.

I'd be lying to myself if I wasn't worried. Even now, as I stand waiting for the next twenty minutes to pass, I'm checking socials for any mention of *Nikos Ridge one night stand*, a steamy night of passion with a fan...etc, etc. Every time I check, my heart is in my throat, until I find nothing but film reviews and the countless messages calling me *daddy* or asking me to *mount them like a dragon*.

There's only one person I wish to mount, and even I know that ship has sailed. Regardless if Honey has worked out my true identify or not, I can't afford to act so carelessly. It isn't only my reputation on the line, but Selina's and my entire team's.

Not to mention the most common message I'm seeing is about a petition for a second film. That idea alone is enough to make me feel sick.

My contract with the studio was for one film and one film only. Regardless of the demand from fans, the money offered, I can't do it. I won't. Because the more money and fame I'm offered, the more I have that can be taken away from me again.

I shut off my phone screen, pocketing the phone as thoughts of Honey quickly melt to my father.

It's been almost two full days since I saw him at the film premier. The silence that followed has been long and excruciating. It's only a matter of time until he worms his way out of the woodwork and explains what, exactly, his ominous words meant.

A wave of anxiety breaks over me. But before I'm swallowed by it, I take out the post-it note and fiddle with the frayed paper. The feel of the dull edges against my hands stills the worry enough to think straight.

I don't release the post-it note until Selina texts me, letting me know she's in the lobby and that the car is waiting outside for us. I adorn my mask, leaving the scared child behind me as I step out of the hotel as Nikos Ridge - the man whose life is perfect, until you look close enough to see the fucking cracks.

———

I DON'T KNOW what I expected to find at a book publishing office, but what waits for me in the main entrance was not what I could've ever imagined.

A front desk is glowing with string light spelling out Sky High Press. Behind it is a wall framed with books, the most recognisable being the original cover of *An Age of Dragons* beside the new movie-tie in editions which I'm on, unrecognisable as Armin Wolfe, dressed in leather pants with nipples on full display.

But that's not what captures my attention.

'Honey?' I exhale the name, eyes fixed on the man half-stood, half-leant up against the front desk. He's inspecting his nails as Selina and I enter. No, not his nails - a post-it note.

My post-it note.

I can see from his stare that he's lost to a memory, no

doubt the same one that has haunted me for every second of the day since we parted.

It takes him a moment to hear me, or register the name I used. But when Honey looks up, his eyes flaring wide and mouth parting, I swear my groin aches.

Selina is shaking the hand of a beautiful woman who introduces herself as Megan. If not for being so focused on Honey, I would pay more attention to the way their handshake lasts longer than it needs to. Or the glittering interest filling my manager's stare.

'Welcome to Sky High Press,' Honey says, his voice devoid of emotion. He hardly looks at me, even though I cannot take my eyes off him. My body refuses to move forwards a step and take his outstretched hand.

We greet each other like strangers.

'Nikos,' Megan says, eyes looking between me and Honey with a hint of expectance. 'It is so lovely to have you stop by. Thanks for taking time out of your - no doubt busy - schedule for this.'

It's rude of me to ignore her, but I just cannot take my eyes off of Honey.

Honey still has his hand outstretched. He's seconds from lowering it before I strike out and take it. 'Hello.'

'Nice to meet you, Nikos Ridge,' Honey says, his reaction suggesting this interaction is not a surprise to him, as it is to me.

So he *had* worked out my truth. A spark of distrust ebbs into me. Maybe he always knew, and he was playing me, using me like everyone else does. But then I see him shoving the the post-it note in his other hand into his pocket, and I know he's angry.

'And you,' I reply softly. Selina is staring daggers into

the side of my face, and I can tell she's trying to work out why I've left my confident bravado back in the car. 'Can I have your name?'

Honey actually contemplates this. I see the wheels turning behind his eyes. I almost expect him to refuse me, but when he speaks, I feel as though I've just been handed the secrets to the universe.

'Oli,' he says.

'It's lovely to meet you, Oli.'

I long to lean in, pull him to me and inhale his scent. I have to bite down on my tongue to stop myself from telling him that, as much as the name is lovely, I still prefer Honey.

'Well,' Megan says awkwardly. 'Shall we get on with preparing the content? I'm sure you don't want to be hanging out with us all afternoon, not when you have all of London to explore.'

'Good idea,' Selina adds, equally noticing the tension hovering around the reception. Even the worker behind the desk is peering over the tip of her rounded glasses, thin lips quirked into a grin.

'There's no rush,' I add, finally releasing Honey's - Oli's hand. 'There's nowhere else I'd rather be then here.'

Selina barks a laugh. 'Ever the charmer.'

'Indeed,' I say, hoping Oli knows my comment is for him and him alone.

There is so much I want to say but can't. Not with the audience. But I also know I cannot go an entire afternoon wading in this sea of tension. I have to speak with Oli. I just need an out which won't make Selina and Megan ask questions.

Apparently Megan can read minds, because she offers

one. 'Oli, do you mind taking Nikos straight to the audio department? Selina, if you don't mind, I would like to run over the schedule for the afternoon with you before we begin.'

Oli snaps his attention to his colleague, clear annoyance evident in his eyes. But before he can refuse - and it's clear he wants to - Selina speaks up. 'Sounds like a plan. Although, for fear I will sound like a demanding diva, can I ask that some refreshments are brought to the room? I fell asleep on the massage table this morning and missed lunch.'

I know Selina well enough now to hear the flirtatious tone in her voice. That and the way her hand lays itself on Megan's upper arm, gently guiding her and the conversation down the path she desires.

'I can do that,' Megan says with a smile, before shooting Oli a look. 'I'll meet you in room A10, okay?'

Oli nods hesitantly, before turning on his heel and beckoning for me to follow him. I do as he gestures, chasing his heels like the desperate puppy I am. Selina doesn't even pay me mind as she heads in another direction with Megan, both engaging in conversation as if nothing else in the world matters.

This is my chance.

Oli stops before the entrance to a lift, pressing the call button until it lights up with a red glow. I stand at his side, aware of the countless people watching on from a distance. But nothing else seems to matter when his arm is inches from brushing my side.

'You're angry with me,' I accuse as the metal doors slide open and a crowd of surprised people walk out.

Oli doesn't reply until everyone is out of earshot. He

steps into the lift, lips so tense that they're practically white on his face. I follow in, and Oli presses yet another button. The doors slide closed, locking us away.

Only when they seal closed does he reply. 'So, you're Nikos Ridge.'

I laugh because it's easier to fall into humour when I'm feeling awkward. 'I am, although I'd prefer if you still called me Adonis.'

'Why?' Oli bites out.

I gape like a fish out of water, unsure how to explain that the hours I spent as Adonis were the easiest of my life for as long as I can remember. No expectations, no past or future. As Adonis I'm allowed to exist only in the moment.

'Because I prefer it,' I reply, pathetically.

'Well, I prefer not being tricked and lied to.'

My hands wring together, giving them something to do. 'It wasn't my intention.'

Oli exhales a long breath. I wait for him to say something, but he doesn't.

'I gather you already knew,' I say. 'So what's the issue?'

He turns on me. We're so close I'm forced to look down at him. His pale hair is swept back with product, his knitted cardigan practically slipping off his left shoulder. I notice how his shirt - which is more grey than white - is likely a result of him not separating his clothes out when washing them. I like that. I like that he doesn't care. Most of all, I like how I see my warped reflection in his round glasses.

'I'm not annoyed at you,' he says with a tone that suggests he's definitely lying. 'I'm annoyed at the situation.'

'And the situation is...?'

Oli steps in so close I can smell the light perfume he wears. I take a deep breath in, hoping to etch the smell across my bones.

'That two nights ago I had one of the best nights of my life, and it was with...you.'

'That sounds an awful lot like regret.'

'Not regret,' Oli adds. 'I just know it can never happen again. So imagine my surprise when Megan shows me your face on an interview, and I find out it was the same face buried in my arse the other night.'

'Is that why Megan sent us away, because she knows?'

Oli hesitates, reading the panic that no doubt shines in my eyes. 'Don't worry, she won't tell anyone.'

'And what about you? Are you going to let the world know of my dirty secret?'

I regret the words as soon as I say them. Oli rocks back a step, pressing himself as far away from me as the lift allows. I step forwards, reaching out to grab his arms. 'I didn't mean that - '

'You don't need to explain yourself,' Oli says, turning his back to me, arms crossed. 'I get it.'

I don't know what makes me do it, but I reach towards the wall of buttons and press the one that reads *emergency stop*. Just as I intended, the lift comes to a halt.

'What are you doing?' Oli snaps.

'Apologising,' I say before I close into him, turn his body so it faces me. I lean my hips into his, press his spine into the metal wall. And then I kiss him.

My hands thread on either side of his face, tangling in his hair. He tastes as I remembered, sweet as his nickname. I feel myself growing hard against his body, his warmth. I know he can likely feel it too, the way my body pins him to the wall, my tongue working to open his mouth and explore him.

I regret not shaving this morning as my coarse hairs brush across Oli's soft chin. When I finally pull back, I brush my thumb over his pink lips, clearing away the spit I left behind.

The way Oli looks up at me, cheeks flushed and eyes blinking, I swear I want to tear his denim jeans off and bury myself in him. 'What...what was that for?'

'I didn't mean to call you a dirty secret,' I fumble over my words. 'It's not the *you* part which is dirty, more the *secret*, and I...I don't know how to say it without sounding like a prick, but - '

Oli leans up on his tiptoes and silences me with another kiss. This one is harder, more frantic and desperate. He threads his arms behind my head and holds me to him. My hands reach down for his thigh and lifts it up. I've almost got him hooked around my hips when he's the one to pull away.

'I get it,' Oli says, breathless and lips swollen. 'Your dirty little secret is safe with me.'

'Is it?' I question.

'Don't you trust me, Adonis?'

'Should I, Honey?'

With the back of his sleeve, he wipes his mouth and then reaches and does the same for me. 'I suppose you'll just have to find out.'

He presses the button to get the lift moving again, and I almost fall to my knees to plead for just a few more moments of this existence. But alas, life must go on.

We both gather ourselves, straightening our clothing

like we're in some kind of rom-com movie. I have to reach into my boxers and shift my hard cock to the side. I don't think there is anything that is going to make it soft, not when I can still taste Honey lathered across my tongue.

'If it is any consolation, I had plans to come to your flat tonight and explains myself,' I say as we shoot up to the upper floors of the building.

'You were?' I can tell he's surprised from the pitch of his voice. 'And how were you going to do that?'

I had a plan, and although the outline has shifted with this revelation, I still must see it through.

'I want to wire you some money,' I say. 'If you can send me your bank details, I'll put the money into your bank by morning, enough that it should see you over. It's the least I can do for keeping this between us.'

'Excuse me?'

I peer at him, wondering what I'd said that caused the growl beneath his words.

Oli's eyes are wide, his hands balled at his sides. He refuses to look at me, but I can see he's shaking.

'Money,' I repeat, trying to work out what was wrong. 'Hush-hush money you could say. Enough that any newspaper or online site would never be able to - '

'Fuck you, Nikos Ridge,' Oli splutters as the doors slide open. '*Fuck. You.*'

His voice breaks slightly, enough that the sound works at the web of cracks imprinted across my skin. I feel myself break apart as the sadness echoes around the barren lift. I go to call out for him, but notice the countless heads peaking over desks and around doors. It's natural for me to put my mask back on, but as I watch Oli disappear in the maze of the office, I want nothing more than to stop him.

I don't even know what I've said that upset him. I thought I'd made up for referring to Oli as a dirty secret, and now he's not only angry, but sad. Hurt. And I did that.

It takes me a moment to understand that whilst everyone else expects money from me as Nikos Ridge, Oli doesn't. Because the Nikos Ridge I'm used to is not the person he knows.

I am Adonis in his eyes, and Adonis doesn't pay his way out of his problems.

Adonis, apparently, has to grovel. And for Honey, I will do just that.

11

OLI

I'M SO mad that I'm shaking.

I know that Adonis - *Nikos* - doesn't know me, but what kind of utter asshole does he think I am, that I need to be paid off to keep a secret that any decent person would know needed keeping?

What an arrogant fucking prick.

I haven't been able to concentrate from the moment we heard from the movie's PR team that they wanted Nikos Ridge to come film social media with some of our books, maybe doing a cute Q&A with the author. I ordinarily would have an entire schedule plotted out, down to the minute, to maximize the time we got with the star. If this were a normal day, a normal job, I'd have researched the hottest trends of the week and made sure to plot out reels and TikTok videos that matched.

I've done none of those things, worrying over meeting Adonis and ensuring that I don't accidentally spill his secret. I've literally bitten my nails down to the quick, which drives me even more wild. I'm chewing so much gum to try to avoid further nail biting that I'm surprised my jaw hasn't fallen off, and my fingers are twitching for a cigarette.

Except now all of that has been redirected from anxiety to full-on *rage*.

I stalk through the maze of desks to room A10, one of the small studios that's equipped with camera equipment, good lighting, and soundproofing tiles on all the walls. I assume Adonis - *fuck me*, Nikos - is following me, but I don't care to look over my shoulder to check. If I look that man in the eye at the moment, I'm liable to slap him across the face. I don't know what I did to give him the impression that I was a total piece of shit.

I yank the door to A10 open so hard that the handle flies out of my hand and whacks the wall. I get myself inside and pull more gum out of my pocket to stuff in my mouth. Maybe it will help me not say something that's going to get me fired.

Nikos walks in a second later looking like a dog left out in the rain, all puppy-dog eyes and pleading looks. His lips are slightly swollen from our kiss.

'Shut the door,' I snap, hanging onto the threads of my anger. Just because he's hot, doesn't mean he gets a pass on being rude as fuck. I'd done that with Geoff, made myself small because it was easier than standing up for myself, and now I'm just seriously not in the mood for any more of that type of behaviour from men who think they're rich and handsome enough to look down on other people.

'Honey - ' he starts, but I cut him off with an upraised hand.

'We're here to work,' I remind him. 'Sit.'

I point to the stool sitting in the middle of the room. Nikos obeys, shrugging off the blazer he's wearing to reveal the soft grey t-shirt he has on underneath. His jeans bunch up around his still-obvious hard-on when he sits down, one foot propped up on the stool's crossbar.

'I didn't mean - ' he tries again, but I *ah ah ah* him until he shuts up again.

'We. Are here. To *work*.' I hiss. I head over to the camera and power it on. It would be easier if I could use my phone, but then again, privacy concerns.

I almost laugh.

I get the lights on, making sure that he's well-lit, and then scroll through my mental list of video ideas, searching for the most humiliating ones. There's a copy of *An Age of Dragons* sitting next to me, and I toss it at him. He catches it with totally infuriating grace.

'Read the fifth paragraph on the second page of chapter 51,' I order. It's a particularly filthy sex scene, in which Armin and Gwen do it in the mud. Not precisely the kind of mud wrap that I'd appreciate getting in a spa, and it's the only part of the book that fans mocked online.

'Oh?' His eyebrows shoot up to his forehead and I can tell right away that he knows *exactly* which scene I'm referring to, which infuriates me even more.

Of course he'd be the kind of person to *actually read the fucking book*.

'Yes,' I say flatly. 'Go on. We have a whole list to get through.'

It's a lie, and I think from the tilt of his head that he knows it. But he just purses his lips and cracks open the book, flipping to the right page. I count him down and he starts to read, and I thought this would be humiliating but *of course* he makes using mud as lube sound hot instead of incredibly disgusting and UTI-inducing.

Listening to his rich, deep voice reading about things so much like what we did that night in my bed makes my head spin. I'm mad at him because he was a dick in making assumptions about me extorting him for money, and I'm mad at him that he didn't trust that the night meant something to me like it did to him.

I wouldn't keep the post-it note of a man I was planning to betray to the media for money.

But I'm watching him do this, and when he gets to the end of the passage and gives me a few seconds of smiling silence to edit in an ending, he slumps down. He literally, physically gets smaller. The transformation is incredible, and excruciatingly sad. Because I can tell that he just put on a mask for the camera, and now that he's not being filmed it's been taken off.

Adonis - *Nikos Ridge* - is showing me his exhaustion, and his anxiety, and I don't see how I didn't realise before that *those* were the emotions written all over his face.

My anger starts to ebb away, and I'm powerless to keep a hold of it.

'I'm not going to sell you out to the media, and I don't need to be paid money to do so,' I say quietly. I can't meet his eyes. 'I was offended because you implied I wasn't trustworthy, that you thought I needed to be paid off to do the decent thing. I don't. But I can see why you might think that.'

Because maybe a man who wore a mask did so because he'd learned the hard way that it was necessary.

He clears his throat. 'I'm sorry, Honey. Oli. I didn't

mean to. Look, I'm in town for a little while. I want to make it up to you.'

The sound of my name on his lips sends a jolt of arousal through me. I lick my lips 'And how are you going to make it up to me?'

'It depends,' he replies, his eyes searching my face. 'I can wine and dine you. I can take you shopping. We can spend all night with take-out and Netflix. I can make it up to you in other ways.'

He drops his gaze down to my belt at that last suggestion, and the final scrap of my resistance is gone.

'Well,' I say, my voice husky. 'I can think of some other video ideas that we can practice sans camera if we go back to my place. Special things, for your biggest fan.'

'Oh?' The hope that crosses his face is almost unbearable. 'And who would that be?'

I take one step towards him, then another, until I'm standing between his legs, our eyes level as he's sitting down. He puts his broad, warm hands on my hips as I rest mine on his insanely muscular thighs.

'Me,' I say. And then I lean in and kiss him.

———

IT TAKES a Herculean amount of effort to make it through the rest of the day. The filmed Q&A with the author goes off without a hitch, and she's even confident enough that we do an impromptu Instagram live with the two of them together. I'm so proud of her and how far she's come with her ability to manage PR and public speaking that I feel like I'm going to burst. I give her a long, tight hug before sending her off. I catch Nikos smiling at me from the corner of my eye, and it's all I can do to not react in turn.

Even if we're going to end up at my flat together again, I need to make sure that no one realises there's more to the two of us than a publicity manager and an actor. I don't like being made to feel as though I'm - as he put it - a dirty little secret, but right now what's between us is different than that.

It feels like being *trusted*. It feels like helping someone else feel safe. It feels like something private that's just for the two of us and no one else. An extension of that special bubble we were in after the premier, when we were just Honey and Adonis.

I'm alright keeping that feeling going for just a little bit longer.

Because I'm going to take what I'm being given, I think to myself as I turn off my computer and wave goodbye to Megan. Nikos left an hour ago and said he was going back to the hotel to freshen up, and then would have his driver wait outside my flat. The anticipation builds as I dash down the stairs of the tube and shove myself onto the train just as the doors slide closed.

I really don't want to keep waiting.

True to his word, there's a big black SUV waiting in front of my building. I head up the steps to the front door, and I feel Nikos join me. I don't look back, just soak up the heat of his body. But when I reach into my bag for my keys, my fingers just brush empty air.

'Fuck,' I curse. I turn to him, because I have no choice. I'm looking around like there are paparazzi everywhere, but my street is nearly empty. 'I must have dropped my keys somewhere in the office. They're not here. I'll have to call a locksmith.'

I had spare keys, but they're with Geoff. My mother has another set, but she lives an hour away, and I'm not going to ask her to make that drive so I can fuck a movie star. I'm not *that* depraved.

'It's ok.' Nikos reaches out and brushes the backs of his fingers against my arm. His eyes are fixed on me, two pools of molten desire. 'I can still make it up to you. What do you say we go out for a bit and then head back to my hotel?'

My keys are probably at the office. I'll have to search for them, but I can do that later tonight after I'm done with Nikos - or, more accurately, when he's done with me.

'Alright,' I breathe, and let him usher me into his car.

'I'm ready to grovel,' he pronounces, and I flush with heat. 'However you like best. I say we start with Burberry and work our way to Chanel.'

I go a bit breathless as he leans across the arm rest to nip at my ear.

'Ok,' I say, and he leans forward to give the driver directions. 'Do your worst.'

'Oh,' he growls. 'By the end of the night, I assure you, I'll be forgiven. Even if I have to spend the whole night on my knees to get there.'

And that's when I realise there's no way I could ever stay mad at this man. I'm well and truly fucked.

12

NIKOS

IF I COULD PROVE to Honey that I trusted him, giving him my credit card and sending him into Harrods was certainly one way. I told him to buy himself a new outfit - something that was smart but casual, essentially reading off the dress code for the private dinner I had quickly booked from the back of the car for later that evening.

Honey refused me at first, as I knew he would. His hesitation was cute. Endearing. But what wasn't cute was the obscene amount of money sitting in my current account. Money that deserved to be spent by someone *good*.

If I could've gone in with him, I would've. I hardly imagine a baseball hat and sunglasses would be a sufficient disguise in a place like Harrods. And as I'd put it earlier - in bad taste - Oli is my dirty little secret. So I wait for him in the car, my driver taking the opportunity for a quick nap in the front. The main streets are packed, so I keep the blacked-out window rolled all the way up.

If anyone was to notice Nikos Ridge waiting outside of Harrods in a parked car, it would elicit questions.

For the next forty-five minutes, I scroll social media, learning more about the man I've put all my trust into. It isn't hard to find him. After searching Sky High Press's about me page, I find out Oli's surname. Oliver Cane. I can't help but chuckle. Cane, like the sugar variety. He really was as sweet as Honey.

Sweet enough to rot my teeth and make me thank him for it.

Typing his name into Instagram doesn't pull him up. Instead, I resort to searching Sky High Press's followers, putting together different combinations of his name until, ding ding, I find him.

@Oli.Loves.Books.4.Life.

My chuckle becomes a full-blown laugh that spreads a warmth across my chest and down my limbs. I open up his page to find a handful of pictures, all mainly - as I could've guessed - about books. Reviews, recommendations, and aesthetic mood-boards of his current reads.

His page gives nothing else away about him. Carefully curated, I get the impression that he cares about his appearance both online and off. But as I'm about to close the app, I click on his tagged photos.

I've struck gold the moment the screen changes. Instead of pictures of books, these photos are more real-life action shots of Oli with friends. I recognise Megan instantly, her bright smile and glittering eyes the very same as what she used on Selina today. I quickly check her page, see she's posted a story, and view it.

There she is, my Selina, smiling into a camera. I pocket the knowledge that Selina and Megan are out tonight, knowing I'll ask my manager more about it tomorrow.

Going back to the tagged photos, I scroll, drinking in the photos of Oli. He's attractive in every single one, no matter the angle or filter. There's even a photo of him with what must be cream on his nose. He's holding two strawberries up on either side of his cheeks and pulling a ridiculous face.

My first thought is how I want to lick the cream off him and make him feed me those very strawberries. My second thought is *who posts such an intimate photo?* I click on the name of the account - @GeoffBigRacks, and it takes me to a private account. No information to glean. I go back again to the tagged photos and notice lots of images further down of this Geoff and Oli.

Something uncomfortable stirs in my gut, like jealousy maybe? No doubt this is some old boyfriend, although the most recent photo of them is only three months ago, and the oldest goes back almost six years.

A boyfriend. Or an ex.

I'm highlighting Geoff's name, ready to stalk the internet for more information, when my driver straightens and the door to my side clicks open.

'Miss me?' Honey says, breathless and straining against two large orange bags he's hoisting into the middle seat.

'I did,' I reply, pocketing the phone with a half-typed-out name in my search bar. 'How did you get on?'

'Hell on earth.' Oli practically flops onto the seat, quickly closing the door behind him. He brings a waft of perfume with him. It is not as sweet as he usually smells, but still alluring. Although I realise then that I prefer the

Oli *before* he is spoiled by vendors selling rich scents to rich people. 'Never ask me to do something like that again.'

He hands me back my card, which I hardly care for. 'Well, next time don't forget your keys.'

'Are you suggesting there will be a next time, Adonis?'

Back to the nicknames then. I see.

'As I said, that depends on if you forget your keys again.'

Honey pulls a contemplative face. 'I really don't forget things though. I'm sure I had them in my bag pocket. I'm usually fastidious about putting things into the same places every time. I've never done this before. It's all the excitement of the...situation, I think.' He bites his lip.

I lay a hand on his knee because he's clearly distressed, and I hate to see him like that. 'No worries. That's an issue for tomorrow. Tonight, we have fun.'

'If what you have planned is anything like what I've just been through, I think I won't make it through the night.'

I squeeze his knee, wanting to do more than that but hyper-aware of the driver waiting for my signal to drive to the next stop. Luckily, the car is soundproof. All my driver knows is I'm taking out a long-distance friend out for dinner. Unless I fuck Honey in the back of the car - which is certainly something I *want* to do, but won't - the driver won't know any different.

'Do you trust me, Honey?' I ask.

'Do I have a choice, Adonis?'

I shake my head, eyeing the bags of clothing he'd just brought. 'Traffic depending, we have twenty minutes until we reach the next stop. I'd start getting changed if I was you.'

'Here?' he squeaks.

I gesture to the door. 'If you'd like, you can step outside and strip off. Although, I'd prefer if you do it for me and me alone to see.'

Honey narrows his eyes on me as his lips quirk into a smirk. 'Are you going to be a respectful man and turn away?'

'Sure,' I say, turning my back on him, but catching the near perfect reflection in the blacked-out window. I catch eyes with Oli, whose smirk is so delicious I want to clean it off with my tongue. 'Better?'

'You're a fucking nightmare, Adonis.'

'You have no idea.'

―――

THE WAITRESS GUIDES us through the kitchens to a small room at the back of one of London's most prestigious restaurants. Under the guise of a 'meeting with my publicist', she doesn't question why Nikos Ridge is out having a meal with another man. Nor do I sense any second thoughts in her eyes. Clearly, she's far too enamoured with me to even contemplate the possibility that I would fancy a man.

Plus, the light dose of flirting certainly throws her off the scent. Flirting that doesn't go unnoticed by my date.

'She was so red I thought she was going to explode,' Honey says as I pull back his chair and beckon for him to sit.

'What can I say? I have that effect on people.'

Honey scoffs to himself, making the chair creak against the floor as he tucks himself in. 'I hate to pop that arrogant bubble of yours, Adonis, but you don't have that effect on me.'

'Are you jealous?'

'No,' he says too quickly.

'Then you're a liar,' I reply, taking me seat opposite him. 'Because your cheeks are practically on fire right now.'

Honey lifts a hand to his cheeks, fumbling for an excuse as to why he's now the red-faced one. 'I'm warm, that's all.'

He isn't wrong. The small room we're sitting in only has enough room for the both of us. The round table is set in the heart, surrounded by walls covered in Italian memorabilia. I imagine this is some museum showcasing the owner's love for their Nona. Portraits of a stout looking woman with white hair and a toothless smile are waiting beside fake lemon trees in pots and bags of pasta.

Selina is the one who spoke favourably about this restaurant, saying the food was as authentic as you'd get if you ate in Sicily itself. With two Michelin stars, the family who runs the restaurant has kept the love and pride in what they do for over twenty years. It only took five minutes to call in a favour and get a private table for the night.

'I hope you don't mind, but I've pre-ordered the food.'

Honey's brows raise into his hairline. 'Arrogant, and a control freak, that's what that says about you.'

'Careful,' I say, leaning over the table as if I could make it vanish and kiss him. 'If you continue stroking my ego, I might be forced to stroke something of yours.'

'Are you trying to make me forget about your comments earlier?' Honey asks. 'Because it's going to take more than meatballs, limoncello, and tiramisu to make it up to me.'

'We have all night,' I reply. 'I think I'll be successful come morning.'

Oli takes a moment to silently study me, drinking me in just as I am with him. He bought a black velvet blazer, a loose white shirt, and fitted jeans with my credit card. He looks handsome, yes. But not like Oli - nothing like the man I find endearing in his knitted jumpers and faded Doc Martins. I'm not sure I like this dressed-up version of him - he doesn't seem like himself.

The first course hasn't been brought out yet, and I'm already contemplating taking the clothes off him, burning them, and forcing him back into the clothes he actually wanted to wear, not what he thought I'd like him in.

Truth is, I'd prefer him with nothing on.

'What are we doing, Nikos?' Oli's question comes out of almost nowhere.

'Having fun,' I reply as if that's good enough of an answer. 'Enjoying each other's company.'

There's a faint hint of sadness in his tone as he asks the next question. 'Whilst we can?'

'I'm in London until the end of the week. I thought we could…get to know each other. Make some memories, before I go back to reality and you…'

'Stay behind in my reality.' Oli shuffles in his seat. 'So this thing between us is simply to pass the time.'

There's a sinking feeling in my stomach that I don't quite understand. 'Why, did you expect something more?'

He shakes his head, hair falling over his eye. I long to

reach over and brush it back, not wanting anything obscuring his beautiful heart-shaped face. 'No. No I didn't. I guess it's just good to set some boundaries, right? To... protect ourselves.'

'Protect ourselves from what?'

'Feelings.'

A shiver passes over my skin. 'Yes, ok. I think that's smart.'

'I'm not saying you're even *capable* of catching feelings, and I know I'm not ready to either. But if we just lay out the groundwork, set the parameters of what this is, then it will make things clear cut. Black and white. No risks.'

I lean back in my seat, already hating where this conversation is going, but knowing it's necessary. 'I've never been one to follow rules, so please, take the lead.'

I swear I can hear Honey swallow. 'Ok. So, tonight is an exception, but no more dates. No more doing nice things together that might jeopardise our feelings.'

'Are you feeling... jeopardised now?'

I hope you are.

'No. This meal... is a business meeting, right? I mean, that's what you told the waitress.'

'It can be whatever you want.'

'No, it can't.'

I stop for a moment, noticing the clear hurt in Oli's eyes. I want to ask *why* he's hurt, but he diverts his gaze away to the knife and fork in front of him and starts to fiddle with them.

'I have an idea,' I start, which makes Oli look back at me. 'Why don't we fuck the rules. We don't need them. We're two men enjoying each other's company for a few days. If you don't want to see me again after tonight, you simply need to say the word. I'll respect that. We both know nothing will work between us anyway, and I don't want you to feel used.'

He looks at me through those devilishly long lashes and I swear his next words make me instantly hard. 'What if I want to be used? If only for a few days?'

'Why?'

'A way to take my mind of my reality, whilst you are clearly escaping the responsibilities of yours.'

'Touché,' I reply, spreading my knees out beneath the table to allow for more room between my thighs for my *very* hard dick.

'So we have a plan?' Oli asks.

'Sounds like we do.'

In what I swear is an attempt to prove that he isn't overthinking something, Oli looks me dead in the eye, picks up his fork, and drops it on the ground.

'Oops,' he whispers.

The fork clatters to the floor and slides to a stop beneath my boot. His chair screeches as he pushes back and crawls under the table to retrieve it.

I don't even have it in me to stop him.

Because as he disappears beneath the white cloth draped over the table, he sees my hand, grasping my cock, trying to ease the blood out of it.

'Are you...hard?' Oli's muffled voice comes from beneath the table.

'You caught me,' I admit. 'Whatever you're doing, I'm here for it. Go on."

I can't see him, which only entices the excitement to burn hotter. I half-expect Oli to pick up his fork and climb back onto his seat despite my entreaty, but what happens next makes me call out.

Oli replaces my hand with his. In seconds, the button of my trousers is undone, and the zip pulled down. With the ease of a trained professional, he pulls out my throbbing member and places his wet lips around the tip.

'Fuck me,' I groan as the sudden pleasure overwhelms me. I lean back in the chair, head falling back so I'm looking at the ceiling.

I feel his lips pull off my cock. 'Is this the type of fun you were expecting?' Oli asks.

I can't see him, but I can already tell his eyes are glittering with mischief. His cool breath works against the moisture on my cock, his tongue likely half an inch away from it.

'Yes,' I mumble, threading my fingers in his hair. I pull enough that he must feel the tension across his scalp whilst I blindly guide him back to my cock. It's in his mouth in moments, his tongue swirling circles around my length, his hand cupping both my balls.

I haven't cum in days, and I swear I'm seconds from bursting. It isn't going to take much for me to finish if Oli continues like this.

His spare hand wraps around my cock, moving up and down as he follows the rhythm of his mouth. His breathy moan tell me that he's enjoying the dribble of pre-cum that seeps out of my tip.

So much for an appetiser.

In the spirit of appetisers, the door swings open and in walks the waitress. She pauses at the door for a moment, noticing the empty chair Oli had sat in. She's carrying two bowls of the lemon-infused consommé I ordered.

'Oh, sorry, Mr. Ridge. Would you prefer I come back when your friend returns to the table?'

My 'friend' is currently under the table, sucking my cock. The little devil doesn't even pause his sucking at the waitress's entry. He continues to ravish me whilst she stands before me, completely ignorant of what's going on two feet away from her.

'You can - leave them here.' I say, gasping as Oli grazes his teeth down my shaft. 'I'll be - he'll be finished in a moment.'

She smiles, clearly assuming Oli's stepped out to take a call or something of the like, and quickly deposits the bowls on the table and leaves. By the time the door closes, I burst in Oli's mouth, depositing days' worth of cum into his cheeks. This time I'm confident I hear him swallow, but for a completely different reason.

By the time he takes his seat, hair dishevelled from my grip on him, lips pink and cheeks flushed, I swear I could go again.

'That was... you are... Honey I'm - '

'I'd say spit it out,' Oli interrupts, laying the dropped fork on the table and picking up a spoon for the consommé. 'But I think the comment would be in bad taste, considering...' He widens his eyes at me as I'm sat, utterly immobilised, my cock still left out of my trousers like some forgotten toy.

'Hmmm,' Oli moans. 'This is delicious.'

I stare at him, utterly dumfounded. 'Yes, yes you are.'

———

We stay in the restaurant for hours, laughing and eating, stealing kisses between courses. It becomes a game, playing and then pretending, whenever the waitress comes in to check on us, that we're nothing more than business associates. By the time we leave, Oli is yawning. It's no surprise he's asleep with his head on my shoulder as my driver takes us back to my hotel.

I truly believe nothing can ruin the night, until my phone vibrates in my pocket. I draw it out quickly, not wanting the noise to wake him. He's so peaceful when he sleeps, with the light smile that's plastered across his face.

I cancel the incoming call before checking the number. A few moments later another buzz warns me that I've received a voicemail. It isn't until then that I noticed the withheld number and know exactly who's just tried to call me.

My father. Haunting me in the moments of my life when I've found the most peace. The shadow that never leaves me alone.

Dread slips down my spine at what his voicemail could say. I wish I was strong enough to ignore it, pretend he never just tried to call, put this off until tomorrow. But I'm weak. I can't ignore it.

I click on the icon for the voicemail, lift the phone to my ear, and listen.

'Hello, son.' His voice is deep and gravelly, a result of years of smoking. For as long as I can remember, he's sounded like this. It's a voice that should make me calm and happy, and yet it only creates dread in me.

'I'm disappointed you have not reached out to me yet, after seeing each other all those nights ago. I've been patiently waiting for you to get in touch regarding what it was I need, but I can't say I'm surprised that you are choosing this moment to ignore me. You are on a high in life right now, and as your father I'm so very proud to see. But more so than ever, you have a lot to lose, which is why I'm so surprised you've not called or texted. So, since I've been the one to reach out, I think it's safe to say that you know exactly what I need. I'll give you a couple of weeks to arrange the necessary details, but if you want me to keep quiet about what you did, another hundred thousand is going to need to hit my bank account. Otherwise, I'll talk. And with so much on the line for you, I imagine you really don't want the truth getting out. Just think about what it would do to you. I'd really hate to see all your hard work… jeopardised.'

I feel the sudden urge to vomit. I can't breathe. With the phone held to my ear, my father's breathing sounding through the voicemail, I long to open the car door and throw myself out.

It takes a few seconds for my father to speak again.

'Two weeks, son. I'll give you time. I still love you, even after what you did. Remember that.'

The message ends with a beep.

I lower the phone, my body and mind numb to the world. Oli stirs on my shoulder, his breathing pattern shifting. I'm desperate for him to wake up so I can take my mind off my father's threat.

That was what it was. A threat and a promise.

All my career he's held my secret over me, like the blade of a guillotine. I'm completely powerless to fight against him. But I knew this was going to happen eventually. Deep down, I knew he would never be satisfied.

That was why I took on this film. To get the money to

pay him off, and hope he's satisfied enough that he stops asking for more. Because when I return to New York, I have no desire to ever work again. No *need* to work for more money that my father could chase after me for.

I pocket my phone, knowing this isn't a game I'm going to play for much longer.

He can tell the world my secret for all I care. By the time they find out, I'll be long gone. With no career to speak of, I won't have anything for him to threaten.

Two weeks. Two weeks to pretend. To play this game I've fallen into. Then it will all be over. For Oli, for me, for my father - for everyone.

If I had the ability to call my father back, tell him to fuck himself and fuck his threats, I would. But that isn't how this works. The only means I have to contact him is putting a message in the transaction notes from the bank when I wire money to him. Shame, then, that in two weeks, he won't be getting what he wants. He'll never be hearing from me again.

13

OLI

Even after staying up for half the night, Nikos fucking me in every conceivable position in his massive hotel suite, I'm wide-eyed and totally awake when I walk into work the next morning. The fact that Nikos had me buy clothes at least helped with avoiding any walk of shame which would have given us away - I'd purchased a cashmere jumper which felt like heaven, but at least looked like something I'd conceivably have in my own closet, tossing it on over the new jeans and slipping back into my normal Doc Martins.

Of course, I'd done it in full view of Nikos, still lounging on the bed like a Greek god, his head propped up on a hand, the rumpled sheets slung low over his hips.

I'd looked him dead in the eyes as I'd slipped on the underwear I'd purchased just for him. He'd looked like a starving man seeing food for the first time in weeks.

We've agreed to meet up tonight, back at my flat. The tight silk rubbing against my cock and arse are going to make it hard to focus on work today, but I've just got some mindless tasks editing the videos we took yesterday. The oversized jumper covers the fact that I'm still half-hard in my jeans, despite the multiple orgasms I'd had last night and the ache I'm still nursing from Nikos railing me.

I can't believe I'm doing this.

It's the singular thought running through my mind as I get to my desk. I don't *do* stuff like this - I'm cautious and boring and I love books. I'm not meant to be the one getting swept up in a whirlwind romance that I know will break my heart. Despite what we discussed last night at the restaurant, I know there's no way that I'm going to be able to escape from this without being heartbroken at the end - even if it's just grieving that the best sex of my life has come to an end.

But the way that Nikos had held me as we'd drifted off to sleep, the way that he'd run his hands through my hair - it let me dream, just a little bit, of doing this every night.

I want to slap myself but settle for shaking my head hard. No way do I want everyone thinking I'm insane, going around hitting myself until I see reason instead of gorgeous brown eyes. I sit down in my chair and shift through the piles of papers I've accumulated over the last day. Relief floods through me as I find my house keys, tucked under a printed-out stack of analytics from our last social media campaign. I make sure to tuck them into my bag carefully and take a picture of them just to remind myself that yes, I'm not crazy, I did put my keys away this time.

As a precautionary measure, I tidy my desk, junking most of the papers and sweeping up croissant crumbs. I throw a few empty paper cups with the dregs of tea into the bin, and then nod appreciatively at the janitor who scoots over on his rounds to collect the bag and then wipe down my desk with antiseptic cleaning solution. It's vaguely embarrassing that I've become such a slob, but once my desk is clean, my brain feels just a little bit better. Other colleagues are way messier than me - the man doesn't even blink when he walks away with my crumbs and cups and odd papers.

My phone lights up with a text. I almost break my wrist I reach for it so fast.

Holding it under the edge of my desk so that no one can see, I open the message from Nikos - saved in my phone as Adonis, of course - to find a selfie that takes my breath away. It's nothing lewd - it could have been posted on his own social media, the kind of picture that shows his gorgeous face and just a hint of bare chest, not a thirst trap but a thirst tease. The sunlight from the window is hitting his face and turning his eyes more hazel than brown, gilding his olive skin so that it looks like he's cast in bronze.

He's a fantasy come to life. I shift in my seat, tucking one leg underneath me and sliding down to accommodate the way my dick hardens.

> ADNOIS
>
> Really could have used some honey with my tea this morning.

The message is simple, discreet, meaningless if anyone looked at it. No one would know it was meant for me.

But I do.

I hover my thumbs over the keyboard to start typing a reply, but my phone rings instead. It's from a blocked number, and I roll my eyes. Sometimes journalists insist on using them, and it makes it hard to know whether I want to take the call or not. I sigh and answer.

'Hello?' I put on my consummate professional voice. 'Oliver Cane speaking.'

For a moment, there's only raspy, heavy breathing on the other end of the line. I almost hang up, considering it a wrong number or one of those annoying spam calls, but then the caller starts speaking.

'I know what you did with him.'

My blood freezes instantly. 'What?'

'With Nikos Ridge. You kissed him in the elevator.'

I feel like I'm going to be sick. Who could have possibly known that? The voice doesn't sound like anyone I've ever spoken to, so it's not someone in the office. I know them all. We're not a big team. And we were alone in the elevator too.

'I have the pictures,' the voice continues when I don't say a word. 'And I'll show them to everyone, unless you get something for me.'

'What?'' I manage to croak out. I don't know what's going on, but I feel like I'm going to vomit. I'm actually full-on shaking.

'The watch that he wore to the movie premier,' the caller says. 'I need it by the end of the weekend. Leave it at *your* special place along the river, in a coffee cup, by 9am on Monday. Or those pictures are being sent to the Daily Mail. Tell anyone about this and the same thing happens. I'll know. Trust me. If you tell Nikos, the photos will be plastered across every news site by next week. I'm not fucking around, Oliver.'

Today is Friday. That's less than three days from now.

Are we being stalked? He must be following us, because how else would he know that spot? How else would he know that Nikos and I had been there?

Before I can ask any questions to try and get answers, there's a click on the other end of the line and the call ends. I toss my phone on my desk like it's made of spiders and wrap my arms around myself.

This has to be some insane fan. I know that actors sometimes struggle with stalkers, with fans who take things way too far. This person has to want some memento of the premier, or they're going to try to sell it at some auction for a load of money. And they're going to ruin Nikos' life unless I steal from him.

Nothing bad is going to happen to me if those pictures are revealed. They must be from the security camera and it's not like people don't know I'm gay. No one at work will care if I snogged someone in the elevator. They'd all clap me on the back, probably.

But it would ruin Nikos' career. And he's been very clear that he's not out and doesn't want to be. It's why I'm his secret.

It's why whatever this is between us has a two-week expiry date.

I can't tell Nikos. I just have to do what the caller says. It's not like he's going to notice a missing watch. He's probably got a million watches. And I'd be doing this to protect him.

'Oli?'

I blink at the sound of my name. I look up, and Megan is standing there, a cup of coffee in her hands and a wrinkle between her eyebrows.

'Are you alright? I said your name like three times.'

I wonder if I can speak without throwing up. 'I must've eaten something bad. I'm not feeling good.'

'Poor thing,' Megan murmurs, but I don't stop to talk to her. Instead, I get up and dash to the bathrooms, where I lock myself into a stall and proceed to throw up my breakfast - the breakfast I'd eaten in bed with Nikos. I'm a sweaty, dishevelled mess when I emerge, but I have to act like everything is alright. If I don't, I'm putting Nikos at risk.

Megan is still sitting on my desk when I come back, and she takes one look at me and mother hens all over, pulling me into her office and then going to fetch a bag of ice from the fridge and a cup of peppermint tea.

'Here.' She shoves the tea at me and I grasp the mug in my clammy hands. She sits down on the couch next to me and puts the ice on the back of my neck.

'Food poisoning is the worst,' she says as she motions for me to drink the tea. 'Hopefully it's out of your system now. Do you need to go home?'

I shake my head, miserable. I'm not going home to my empty apartment to stew over the shit I've gotten us into. The ways in which I might hurt Nikos despite desperately not wanting to.

'No,' I sigh. 'I'm good.'

―――

Spoiler alert: I was not good.

I'm actually not sure how I made it through the day. I spent a lot of time tapping idly at my keyboard whilst not producing any real words. When I don't text Nikos back, lost in the panic of the call, he sends another message through.

ADONIS

Meet you after work like we agreed?

I bite my lip hard enough to bleed when I see that. I want to see him badly enough that my whole body aches with it, but I'm clearly putting him in danger. Still, if I want to avert the disaster that is this anonymous caller, I need to nick his watch.

Then, I should probably tell him that we should stop seeing each other. If this is what happens after just a few days of knowing each other, what would happen after a few weeks? There are an untold number of batshit insane fans out there. I like Nikos far too much to risk him.

But that doesn't take away from the issue at hand. This stalker wants his watch, otherwise career-ending photos will be leaked.

I'm on the tube, and my mind keeps flashing back to the way he'd looked so sad and lost during our filming. The gentle, caring, vulnerable side he'd showed me on our date. The way he'd let me fall asleep on his shoulder in the car.

This must be why he's so guarded. Shit like this must happen to him all the fucking time.

It makes me sick enough that I want to throw up again.

One more date. One more night. I'll tell him while we're out that we're going to fuck one more time and that's it. I'll tell him I've changed my mind. I'll get the watch and he'll never see me again. I can't handle the pressure of keeping this a secret. It will be close enough to the truth.

Except when I see Nikos sitting on the steps to my building, his head in his hands, I feel a physical pain in my chest, bad enough that I wonder if I'm having a heart attack.

It's the way he smiles, genuine and unguarded, when he looks up and sees me.

'Hey,' he says as I walk up the steps to meet him. 'I missed you.'

I don't touch him until I unlock the door and we step inside. Then I fall into his arms, letting him hold me tight. Being this close to him makes me feel safe, like everything is going to be alright.

'I missed you too,' I mumble against his chest. Even the smell of him steadies me.

How the fuck am I going to let this go?

'Are you alright?' He pulls back and looks at me, frowning. 'You're really pale.'

I shake my head, trying to act normal. 'I didn't have time for lunch. It was a wild day at work. I'm starved.'

That excuse works, because his frown rights itself into a grin. 'That, luckily, is something I can help with. Do you think you can wait about an hour? I had a plan for tonight.'

'Yeah,' I say, because honestly, I'm not sure if I can eat at all. 'I can wait.'

'Good.' Nikos smiles at me. 'Drop your stuff in your apartment and we're going out. We need groceries.'

'Huh?' The power of words has honestly deserted me. 'What for?'

He flicks me on the nose, grinning impishly. 'I'm going

to cook for you. A special family recipe. I hope you like Greek. And I'm even dressed for the occasion.'

Nikos gestures down to himself, and I notice that he's shed his normal high-end wardrobe. He's wearing a worn-down hoodie and broken-in jeans, a baseball hat on his head and sunglasses tucked onto the neck of the hoodie, running shoes on his feet. I've never seen him look this casual - I wouldn't know he was a celebrity if I didn't know *him*.

'That's in public,' I say stupidly. 'Is that safe?' The only thing filling my thoughts are the threats that the caller made this morning.

'That's the trick,' he says, giving me a wink. 'No one expects a celebrity to be in Aldi.'

If he's not worried, I determine not to be worried. 'We're coming back here?'

'I'll even stay the night.' Nikos smirks.

It's perfect. He's got a watch on - I can see the flash of it under the cuff of his hoodie. I can't tell if it's the same one from the premier, but who the fuck cares. This person just wants something that touched Nikos Ridge's skin. He'll stay with me, we'll get undressed, the watch will conveniently get lost, and the next morning I'll call it quits. We don't have to speak ever again after that.

The thought is wrenching. I smile anyway. 'Let me drop my stuff.'

I practically fling my bag into the entryway of my house. I make sure I have my keys this time, and my wallet - although I doubt Nikos would make me pay for anything.

'Come on then,' he says, holding open the front door for me. 'Let's go.'

I take a deep breath and join him, my eyes darting around. Nikos pops the sunglasses on and takes my hand. I'm instantly hyper-aware of the surroundings, but the people walking by don't spare us a second glance. We're just two men walking down the street after work.

It feels too normal. It feels too much like something I *want*.

I should let go of his hand, but instead I just hold it tighter.

The shop is only a five-minute walk from where I live, and every minute of it is simultaneously a nightmare and a dream. I'm afraid of paparazzi or fans jumping out from behind the bushes, but I also can't stop myself from imagining what it would be like to spend each and every day like this.

Aldi is packed, the after-work crowd at full swell. Nikos grabs a basket with his free hand and tugs me along to the produce section, picking up herbs and onions and shiny red bell peppers, sticking them in the basket. He never once lets up on his grip, like he's afraid that if he releases my hand I'll run away.

Maybe he's more perceptive than I give him credit for.

But still, I relax the more we shop, not trusting myself to speak but leaning greedily into Nikos' side, enjoying his warmth. It's all fine until we stop by the butcher counter.

Oh fuck no. Fuck me.

My entire body tenses until I'm stiff as a board, and Nikos gives a little yelp of pain. I look down and realise I'm gripping his hand so tightly that his skin is turning red from the pressure.

'Oli.'

Two male voices saying my name at the same time.

Nikos, easing his hand out from mine to put his arm around my shoulders, his eyes wide with concern.

Geoff, standing behind Nikos, his face etched with fury.

I whimper. Nikos turns, tucking me into his side, to glare at Geoff. He must have heard him say my name.

'You fucking little *slut,*' Geoff hisses. He looks terrible - his beard unshaven, his hair too long, his eyes bloodshot. He's standing there with a basket full of generic products. Geoff *never* bought generic, the snob. 'It's been what, two months? And you're already sleeping with someone else?'

I open my mouth to defend myself, to say *you were the one having sex with other men in our bed*. But my face is flushed with humiliation, and I know that if I start to speak, the angry tears building in my eyes will overflow.

Thank God Nikos comes to my rescue.

'Do *not,*' Nikos practically growls, 'speak to Oliver that way.'

'Be careful of him.' Geoff barks out a harsh laugh. 'Lost my job because of that one. He broke my heart enough that it wasn't in my work anymore either.'

There's a strong smell of alcohol coming off Geoff, and I have a sneaking suspicion about what precisely he was doing instead of working.

'Frankly, that seems like a *you* problem.' Nikos dips his head down to press a kiss to the top of my head. 'He's treated my heart just fine. And my cock even better.'

Nikos glares at Geoff and it must scare the crap out of him - Nikos is bigger and broader and looks like he could take Geoff out in a heartbeat - and I feel just a little bit better when Geoff sneers, but then turns on his heels and leaves.

I curl into Nikos, grateful that he's holding me. I didn't think I'd ever run into Geoff again, although I'd stood in the shower enough nights thinking about what exactly I would yell at him if I did see him again. But it turns out that when faced with him, I was just a coward.

Which is how I know that I'm not going to be able to let Nikos Ridge go.

14

NIKOS

I FORCE us to stop in a park on the way back to Oli's house. We sit down on the grassy lawn, staring out at a small pond with mallards and a swan - majestic as fuck, but as deadly as I feel inside.

We're shaking for different reasons.

Oli hasn't said a word since we left the supermarket. It's like he's been floating in a stasis state, unable to form words or even stop himself from shaking. I hate seeing him like this. If we weren't in public, I would've punched the man - who was clearly an ex-boyfriend - for making Oli feel like this.

The man had looked like shit warmed up. Dark circles, the scent of alcohol tainting his breath. And whether Oli noticed it or not, there was the remnants of a faint white powder dusting his jacket.

Drugs. His dilated pupils as he was glaring at Oli proved my theory right.

I dig my hand into the bag and pull out the bottle of white wine. Luckily it's a screw-top, so it's easy to open. I take a quick drink to still the fury that's etched itself into my bones, then offer the bottle to Oli.

'Drink this,' I say. 'It will help.'

Without taking his eyes off the swan, he grabs the bottle and downs a quarter of it without breathing. A dribble of wine slips down his chin. I catch it with my thumb, sticking it into my mouth to suck clean.

'Are you ready to talk about it?' I ask.

'There's nothing to say.'

I shuffle closer, but not without pulling my baseball hat down and searching the area around us for any onlookers. Luckily, we're alone. 'That's the biggest lie that I've ever heard, Oli. Clearly that man means something to you, to cause such a reaction.'

'Geoff means nothing to me.'

'Not anymore, maybe.' I lay a hand on his knee and squeeze. If he looked down, he'd see my fingers trembling. 'Come on, Honey. Talk to me. Off-load your worries on me. Let me help.'

Slowly, he turns and looks at me, dead in the eye. The severity of the emotion in his face knocks the breath from my lungs. The whites around his pupil are red, not from crying, but from stopping himself.

'I was in a relationship with him for too many years.' Oli admits what I'd already worked out, based on what the man had said and Oli's Instagram. My first instinct is to walk back, find him, and pummel the man for ever hurting my Honey.

Then reality sets in and I know that this Geoff likely recognised me and was now walking around London with the story of how Nikos Ridge said Oliver Cane treats his cock and heart well.

Shit. I wasn't thinking. I just saw Oli hurting and acted on instinct. But I can't bring myself to regret it, not with how scared Oli had looked when the man started yelling.

Burying that worry down, I focus on what matters and that's Honey. He needs consoling, and I'm not prepared to leave this park until he's smiling that brilliant smile again.

'And let me guess, you were too good for him, so it broke off and clearly he is suffering for it.'

Oli buries his face in his hand, the bottle of wine almost tipping over in the grass. 'Actually, I came back from work early and found him fucking someone else in our bed. It... it broke my heart.'

Geoff had set the timeline when he mentioned Oli moving on in two months. So this breakup was fresh. Which meant the pain would be as furious as it had been the day Oli found his boyfriend in bed with another person.

'He never deserved your heart,' I say, the anger seeping into my tone. 'It's men like that who deserve to have their balls removed. Love should be coveted, protected. Geoff was never worthy of it. He wasn't worthy of you either, Honey.'

'How can you say that?' The tears fall freely now. I want nothing more than to pull him into a hug and let the tears soak into my hoodie. But before I move, a couple walking a well-behaved Labrador stroll past. 'You don't even *know* me. We're strangers. And in a matter of days you'll leave me and my life will go back to the misery it was before you entered my orbit, whereas you get to go back to your big home, in your big city, with your big ambitions and big future - '

Fuck if people see me.

I drag him into my side and wrap my arms around him. 'You're right. We're strangers. So let me be the one to tell you that I'm well versed in love and its parameters. In fact, Selina - my manager - once sent me on a two-week intensive course of therapy. And I'll never forget the first thing my therapist said to me, after I off-loaded my trauma onto her.'

I talk his face in my hands and make sure he's looking at me and no one else. 'We take out our hurt on those we care about the most.'

Old sniffles, the tip of his button nose red as a certain magical reindeer. 'Is that supposed to make me feel like Geoff's actions are justified? That fucking someone in our bed, in our home, was all because he cared about me?'

'No,' I say, brushing a strand of his blond hair out of his eye. 'I was actually talking about how you just told me off and accused me of leaving you behind... as if that's ever a possibility.'

Oli is shocked into silence. I see his mouth part - lips wet with wine and tears - and I want nothing more than to kiss them dry. 'I'm sorry.'

'Don't you ever apologies to me, Honey. You don't owe me that.'

'Then why are you doing this?'

'Because I like you,' I reply. 'I find you interesting, endearing, kind, thrilling, seductive. I could go on, but I fear if I make your head too big, you won't be able to stand up right, so I'll have to carry you back home.'

I almost choke on the last word, realising that it was the first time I've used it, not to speak of Greece, or New York... hell, even some luxurious hotel room I'm camped out in during press or filming.

Oli draws back and clears his wet eyes with the back of his sleeve. 'I'm such a mess. One interaction with a toxic ex and I can barely function. I think pathetic is a word you missed out on when you listed my qualities.'

'The only person I can call pathetic is Geoff. How could he hold the most precious thing in the world in his hands, and ruin it?'

Oli slips out a small gasp. The sound pierces through my gut and out the other end. He penetrates me - heart, soul and body.

'You think too highly of me,' Oli says, again trying to dismantle the possibility that a person could actually respect him. Which, after meeting Geoff, is clearly pain and trauma left over from their time together.

'Perhaps I do, but that's the beauty of it. Those are *my* opinions, and you can't sway them with your lack of self-esteem.'

'Lack of self-esteem?' Oli repeats.

'What would you call it?'

'Heartbreak, pain, grief over a man I thought I'd end up marrying, who ruined my life instead.'

'Ruined your life,' I try the words out with a soured expression, telling Oli how wrong they are. 'From the way I see it, your life is pretty much put together and solid. Whereas Geoff is suffering. Did you hear him? Because of you, he lost his job, he looks like shit, smells even worse, and clearly has a nasty habit for drugs and booze.'

I can see from Oli's face that he's worried about Geoff, even after everything the man did to him - or didn't do, like actually treat him the way Oli deserves. 'Geoff had everything. The high-paid banker job, the money, the looks. I've never seen him so...'

'Pathetic,' I answer for him. 'As I said before, it's certainly a word that works best for Geoff.'

Oli takes the bottle of wine and has another swig. 'I don't want to think about him. Just when I was beginning to forget him, he stumbles back out of the fucking sewers and ruins everything.'

'No, stop.' I stand up and offer Oli a hand. 'Geoff can only ruin what you give him power over. Unless you're going to continue pitying him, worrying about him - '

'I'm not worried about him!'

'Say that to the line between your brows, Honey. Now, up you get.'

He takes my hand, and with some force, I heave him up to standing. 'I know you had grand plans to cook for me tonight, but the thought of going back home isn't as pleasing as it was earlier. I'll walk in and just see Geoff everywhere.'

'Little fucker's haunting you, is he?' I go for a joking tone. 'Maybe I should call a priest to come and visit for an exorcism.'

Oli cracks a small smile. I return one, knowing I got him to do that, even as he's clearly still miserable.

'It's going to take more than sage and a few prayers to cleanse the flat of Geoff's presence.'

A spark of an idea comes to mind. It's so enticing that I hope it catches into an inferno. 'Then I have another suggestion.'

'I see the devil in your eyes, Adonis.'

I narrow them, doing my best 'evil mastermind' impression. 'If I'm honest, I'm a shit cook and was only trying to impress you. How about we get back... home, and I'll order some Greek food instead?'

He wrinkles his nose. 'But it's peak time in London, the food will take hours to arrive.'

'Good.' I take his hand in mine. 'Because something I can do, which sage can't, is fuck you in every corner, on every counter, in every room of your house, so that you'll never think of Geoff again.'

Oli's eyes light up from within, his cheeks flushing a rich crimson. 'On *every* counter? I have so many.'

I lean in, the thought of Oli's naked body already making me hard. 'Every single one.'

———

THE DELIVERY DRIVER rang the bell almost two hours ago, and the moussaka, stuffed peppers, and chicken gyro wraps have been left outside the front door, likely now cold and completely inedible. I have no desire to stop myself long enough to retrieve them. And from Oli's display of Olympic-level stamina, he's not going to take a break either.

I'm practically dying for food, but feel full to the brim after feasting on every inch of Oli's skin. His house, for all intents and purposes, is completely ruined. The kitchen is a mess, items strewn across the floor from where I'd brushed them off to make room to lay Oli on his back.

I made a mental note to buy him a new kettle, because the one he had is now in pieces on the floor, shattered and forgotten. But for now, my focus is on his body, making him smile and laugh, while giving him the best orgasms of his life.

'Honey,' I exhale his nickname, breathless as I carry him from the kitchen towards the bathroom on the second floor. His legs are wrapped around my waist, clinging to me like a monkey to a tree. I'd only just withdrawn my cock from his tight arse. It now rests between my legs, cum seeping from my tip. 'I could keep going all night and all day, but at some point, you'll need a break.'

Oli dips his head and kisses the words from my mouth. 'I'll be the one to tap out when I'm ready, unless this is your way of telling me you're finished.'

Considering I'd finished twice already, I'd usually need a few bananas and high-sugar foods to create more cum. But it seemed Oli was some rare medicine that could continually fill my balls.

'Believe me, Honey. I can go again, and fully intend to.'

'But there are no rooms left,' he replies as I walk us into the bathroom. But then he pauses, looking around. 'Oh, I stand corrected.'

I place him on the edge of the bathtub, reach over him, and turn on the shower. It's one of those bath-shower combinations, so this is going to be the most complicated place to fuck in his apartment.

'I'm a man of my word,' I say, testing the water to make sure it's not scalding. 'Now get in.'

Oli swings his legs over the tub's edge and gets in. I'm about to follow, like hypnotised mice trailing the pied piper, when Oli reminds me that I'm still wearing my watch.

'It looks too expensive to break now,' Oli says, his brow twitching with genuine concern. I find it cute that he cares about my belongs, considering I just broke many of his during our hours of crazed sex.

'Selina *would* kill me,' I say, flipping the catch and removing the watch. I wouldn't notice if it disappeared, frankly, not when Oli's in front of me. It's just a Patek Philippe. But I'm sure that losing it would mean some kind of insurance paperwork that my manager would roll her eyes at.

I plop it precariously on the edge of the toilet. Then before any more talk about my watch ruins the moment, I climb into the bath after Oli.

Water falls down over us, attempting to wash away our sins. The bath has filled to our ankles, the pleasantly warm water sending shivers across my skin.

'Turn around,' I command, keeping my tone soft.

Oli doesn't need to be told twice. He turns so his back is to me. I love how soft his skin is. I brush my fingers over his shoulders, wanting nothing more than to count the freckles across his skin and memorise the number.

Not that I could ever forget this moment - or him.

Oli may be my secret sin, but it's a sin I'd happily have worn into my bones.

I lower my mouth to his shoulder and kiss it. Oli moans, leaning his head to the side in a wordless request. I move my lips up to his neck, dragging my tongue over the salty skin, nipping with teeth when I get to the base of his neck.

'I wish I could pause time,' I say into his skin. 'So that this lasts forever.'

It's a risk, talking about the fact our time together will soon come to an end. But I feel like I have to say it aloud, so Oli knows how I feel inside.

'So do I, Adonis.'

Before I give into the sadness, I reach for the bottle of soap and drip some over my fingers. I kneel down, dragging fingers down Oli's spine until I come to the curve of his arse. I lather my hands up until they are frothy with suds, then I rub it across every inch of his arse until it looks like Father Christmas's beard.

I never realised I had a Christmas kink until now.

'I could eat you for breakfast, lunch, and dinner,' I admit as I slip two fingers into his stretched hole, delighting in the breathy cry that exits Oli's mouth. 'Not to mention the snacks and treats between meals.'

'You'll… get bored - ' I slip a third finger in. 'Fuck, Nikos.'

'When we're together, you don't call me by that name. Do I make myself clear?'

I want to preserve the illusion that we're different people. That I don't have to leave. That I could stay here forever if I wanted.

'Yes,' Oli practically screams. As I work my fingers in and out, Oli has to lean against the tiled wall just to keep himself upright. His back arches, his hands splaying out across the wall. I want nothing more than to stick my tongue between his cheeks and devour him, but my cock is hard again and I just can't wait.

'Yes, what?' I ask as I stand up, position my cock, and rub the enlarged tip over his entrance.

'Yes, Adonis.'

'Good boy,' I growl.

Oli can't reply as I bury myself eight inches deep in him. The noise he makes is one of pure pleasure. I grip my balls as I begin to thrust. I wrap my spare hand around his chest, forcing him to lean onto me.

Water cascades down on us, blinding me and filling my mouth. Oli is reaching back, greedily grasping at my arse, begging me to move faster, harder.

'My Honey,' I say, using his nickname as a means to claim him. 'Next time you shower, you think of me. You cook a meal, and you think of me. You sit on your sofa, and you think of me.'

'Yes,' he exhales, spluttering as water fills his mouth. 'I will. I will. I will always think of you.'

Hearing the pure, undiluted honesty of his admission has me slowing my thrusts down. I want nothing more than to kiss him, but in this position I can only lay my mouth on his neck. But it's not good enough. I need him, his intimacy, his soft and gentle nature.

'I want to see your face,' I say as I withdraw myself. Gently, I turn him around until his wide eyes land on mine. Droplets catch in his lashes, clumping them together. I'm jealous of the water that gets to coat him and touch every part of his body. I want nothing more than to have him, all of him, all at the same time.

'You're looking at me, Adonis.'

'Yes, yes I am.'

I lift Oli up, lay his back on the wet wall, and position his legs around my waist. He's so light I can move and manipulate him into any position I want. But I do it softly, with gentle hands.

'You're so beautiful, Honey.'

I mean every word. I hope he hears it in my tone beneath the splattering water.

His hands are free, so he lays each palm over my cheek and kisses me. I melt into him, delighting in the sudden softness of the moment. I have no desire to fuck him anymore - but that doesn't mean I don't want to be inside of him.

As I enter him, I do it to reflect the moment. Soft. Languid. Calm.

This is different now. Something shifts between us, an intensity that's so high it can only come from two people who have nothing to hide. Even though I do, my secrets buried deep, for a second I exist as a man without a past or future.

With Oli, only the present matters. And that is a place I would like to be in forever.

As I take him, I do it slowly. We kiss, all lips, tongues, and hands. The passion of the moment is boiling over, and yet I take my time. I don't rush. I don't - fuck.

I make what could only be understood as love to Oli.

Lust, maybe. How could I love someone I hardly know, or who hardly knows me? And yet, that's how I would explain this moment. Two souls, two bodies, existing as one.

'Don't look away from me,' I say in between kisses.

'I'll never look away from you, Adonis.'

God, the way he uses that name, just as I asked. It's like I truly am the person he sees me as, not the mask I wear.

'I think... think I'm about to come, Honey.'

I'm hardly moving inside of him, and yet the feeling comes thick and fast. It's the connection, the intensity of our silence, our touch. I can't control myself.

He pulls my head down to his mouth again, stopping just shy of a kiss, so when he speaks his lips tickle over mine. 'Fill me up. I want it, I want you. All of you.'

'I wish I could give it to you,' I reply.

'Then do it,' Oli says - no, he *demands*.

'What... if I'm not deserving... of you?'

Like Geoff. Like any man you'll ever meet. Like the man you will love when I go back to my life, and you stay in yours?

Oli kisses me as if it's enough of an answer. And it is, although I long to hear him speak it. When he draws back, he puts his mouth next to my ear and answers me. The moment the words come out of his mouth, I'm spilling the last dregs of my cum inside of him, completely emptying my balls and soul simultaneously.

'I deserve you, and you deserve to *exist* as you, too. Yesterday, today and tomorrow. Adonis and Honey. Fill me up, baby. Mark me as yours.'

15

OLI

I WAKE up sore and satisfied and desperately hungry.

There's a hollowness to my chest that doesn't feel awful, for once. Instead, I feel…lighter. Like Nikos was able to pierce my ribs and remove all the damaged parts of my heart that Geoff had stomped all over.

Seeing him last night was like a slow-motion wreck. I could tell that something awful was moments away from happening when I saw him out of the corner of my vision, and I was powerless to stop it. But then Nikos stood up for me, and I'd been a mess but I'd been a mess that someone *cared about*, the way that I'd always wanted Geoff to protect me.

It healed something in me that had broken. The idea that I'm not worthy of anyone standing up for me at all. That I'm worthless.

With Nikos, I feel like I'm worth everything. Even if this new inner worthiness has an expiry date.

It's half past seven when I get out of bed, leaving Nikos sleeping soundly where Geoff used to lie. It's so satisfying, looking at the way his golden-kissed skin contrasts against the sheets, more gorgeous and fit than my ex ever could hope to be. I throw on a pair of joggers and a sweatshirt and make my way down to the first level, starting to tidy up the place. We wrecked the house, which is exactly what I wanted. Living here has been like living with a ghost, Geoff haunting me at every turn. Now, every time I move to a new room, I have an image of Nikos instead.

Nikos grabbing my hair as he guides my mouth onto his cock.

Nikos between my legs, his tongue teasing my entrance.

Nikos holding me up against the window, so deep in me that I'm screaming his name.

Nikos and I in the shower, the water coursing over both of us, something far more dangerous than simple lust passing between us.

Make me yours.

My own words are echoing in my head as I pick up cushions from the couch and rearrange blankets, sweep up shards of the teakettle I always thought was fucking ugly that somehow got smashed to the floor. I grab cleaning spray and a cloth and start to clean all the surfaces we fucked on, removing streaks of cum and lube and picking up what seems like an infinite number of used condoms.

Nikos took his job seriously. He truly did fuck me in every room in the house. On every surface. It's the only time in my life I wished for a bigger house, because I would have begged him to keep going until I was so used I couldn't even speak.

But it's more than that. I want the illusion that I'm his.

I want the illusion that he's made me his, that he's claimed me, that he's never, ever going to let me go.

I get to the bathroom off the kitchen, where we'd showered. I right the bottles of soap on the ledge, collect the used condom from where it's lying next to the drain, and then something glints in the corner of my eye.

Nikos' fancy watch is hidden between the toilet and the shower. It must have slid off and dropped into the crevice, and it's not easy to see. Almost like it was meant to be there.

It makes me sick, thinking of it. I'd put the caller's threats out of my mind after the shock of seeing Geoff, letting Nikos take over for the night. But here's a golden opportunity that I'd half intended when I'd told Nikos to get rid of his watch the night before so that it didn't get ruined in the shower.

It's fate, right? That it's so easy for me to take it and hide it in the bathroom cabinet, wedging it behind a box of plasters. If Nikos notices it there somehow, I can claim that I'd just put it there for safekeeping while cleaning. And if he doesn't, it's going to be even easier to do what the caller had asked me to. Even if he asks where it is, we can look for it on the bathroom floor and not find it. The toilet lid was open - I can convince him it had probably fallen right in.

His manager Selina will just have to fill out that insurance paperwork that he'd mentioned last night. I'm sure they've seen stranger claims than that.

My hands are shaking just a bit as I finish straightening up. I head back to the kitchen where I've stashed my phone. There's still no sign of Nikos - the poor man probably needs his rest after fucking me like a machine for hours last night - and so I open my email to see how bad the damage is after a whole night of not paying attention.

But what I see there is so much worse than a pile of work missives going unread.

It's an email from an address I don't recognise, a random string of numbers and letters that's clearly made up just for this email. The subject line is 'Dirt.'

When I click it open, nausea seizing hold of me, I find a single line of text.

GKNAOBFAJS124JRNOAA451@WOOPWOOP.COM

> Now that I have more dirt on you and Nikos Ridge, that watch better be left for me today, otherwise these pictures are the ones that the world will see.

And underneath are dozens of pictures.

I go...totally blank.

My vision blacks out before coming back into focus, and I think that I'm going to pass out, or vomit, or both.

It's Nikos fucking me in every conceivable position. Grainy and taken up from on high, like they're from security cameras. Which they are.

My house is full of them.

The house has a top-of-the-line security system. There are cameras wired to look at every window, ever since we had a break-in a few years ago. I was the one to insist on it, because I was home alone so much. And fuck, there was no way that I was going to be able to take on a burglar, even if it was just stupid kids wandering around the posh parts of London looking for expensive electronics through left-open windows.

We'd gone all-out, every room connected to the

system, so that at the push of a button on the wall or my phone the police would be called. Just in case, because it made me feel more secure. It took some of the anxiety away, too, of worrying that I'd left the door open or the fire going in the fireplace when we were out, the rare times the two of us went away over the years.

Well, now it had fucked me. And worse, it had fucked *Nikos*.

There is one other person who ever had access to this system, even though he's never once used it, to the best of my knowledge. I'd had to install the app on his phone, and when we'd been out together and I'd asked him to check the cameras to make sure I hadn't left the stove on, he would roll his eyes and tell me it was too hard to get into the app, with the two-level authentication. So I'd do it for him.

I changed the password when he left, I'm almost sure of it. But what if I didn't? What if he'd gotten into the system?

What if he was just waiting for the right time to use it to hurt me?

It all made a stupid, awful kind of sense. My ex, bitter and vicious because he thinks *I* was the one to fuck up his life. He always was good at that, putting blame on someone else. *It's your fault I have to work so late, you have expensive taste. It's your fault that I had to go out with the guys without you, you're no fun. It's your fault I had to cheat on you, you're frigid in bed and it's like fucking a piece of wood for all you participate.*

You know when all the puzzle pieces fit into place? Like cogs in a machine, clicking as they connect? I felt that now, the whole thing playing out in my head. Geoff, drunk and out of a job, maybe even on some of the "performance enhancing powders" he claimed everyone took at work, although I was sure it was just cocaine. Stalking me through the pictures I'd posted online through a burner account I hadn't noticed. Seeing that I was at the premier. Probably following me, trying to get a moment to pull me aside and berate me, maybe even publicly humiliate me so that he could ruin my job like I'd supposedly ruined his. Meeting in Aldi had seemed like a coincidence, but maybe it wasn't.

It hadn't been his voice on the other side of the phone, but he'd probably just used one of those voice warping apps, knowing that if I recognised him there was no way that I'd let him get more than two words out of his mouth before I hung up.

I should have realised when the caller mentioned my special place. I'd taken Geoff there, even though he didn't appreciate it. He'd just complained about the river smell and the fact that he didn't want to sit on the stone ledge in case he'd ruined his pants.

He hadn't treated it like it was a haven, the way Nikos had that night.

This is fine, I tell myself. I have the watch and I can give us an excuse to go walking by the Thames, if Nikos even wants to stay with me today. I didn't ask if he'd had any plans. If he doesn't, I'll head there myself.

I'm dizzy from the anxiety coursing through my system, but I keep telling myself that it's all going to be ok. It's just Geoff being a dickhead. I've got this under control. I know how to handle men like him. Nikos never, ever needs to know.

I swallow down bile as I go into the security app and

quickly change the password. Then I go back to the email and wonder if I should delete it, or if it's potentially evidence in case Geoff doesn't quit and I need to involve the police.

The stairs creak, and I look up from my phone to see Nikos standing there, only wearing the boxer briefs he'd had on the previous night. He's practically glowing. I quickly swipe out of my email app and try my best to hide the guilty look on my face.

Geoff just wants this one thing. He just wants a fancy watch to sell to make up for losing his job, or he's just after a way to make me feel horrible and like he still has control over me even though we're no longer together.

That's all it is.

I'm not sure if I feel better or worse now that I've realised it must be Geoff behind this. On the one hand, it's better because I know how to deal with him. I'm going to leave him the watch with a note to fuck off, that he got one over on me and now we're finished for good. If this happens again, I'll call the police on him. On the other hand, it's worse because someone close to *me* is threatening Nikos. It's because of me that his privacy and his career are at risk.

'What's wrong, Honey?' Nikos' brow crinkles in a way that makes me think I'm not being as good an actor as I thought.

I fan my face, because I'm actually hot. There's sweat on my forehead, which I wipe off with the sleeve of my hoodie. 'I'm honestly just famished.' My voice is steadier than I thought it would be, and I mentally pat myself on the back. 'I cleaned everything up, but I realised we didn't eat dinner last night, and now I feel a bit woozy.'

'I'd make you tea... but I...' Adonis flickers his eyes towards the kitchen.

'Broke it, yes.'

'A new one is already on order, should be arriving in a couple of days.'

I lower my eyes. 'Thank you.'

Nikos buys the lie, because he comes over to me and wraps me in his strong arms, bracing us against the countertop. At the feeling of his solid chest behind me, his chin on the top of my head, his arms bracketing me like iron bands, some of the peace comes back to my mind. Nikos has got me. I'm going to fix this. Nothing bad is going to happen.

'Well,' he says, his voice rumbling in his chest and into my back. He puts his phone in front of us, and opens a delivery app. 'I'm not very good at cooking, but I *am* good at hitting buttons.'

He orders us an obscene amount of food, and when it's done and he's checked that the ringer on his phone is on so we actually catch the delivery person this time, he picks me up and puts me on the counter, stepping in between my legs and staring into my eyes.

'Are you ok?' He reaches up and brushes a curl out of my eyes. 'After last night?'

He doesn't know, I remind myself. *Everything's fine.*

'Yes,' I breathe, leaning forward so our foreheads are touching. 'Thank you for standing up for me. You didn't need to do that.'

'Always,' Nikos growls, his broad palm cupping the back of my head, holding me close. 'And I did, and would again.'

I wish it was true. I feel like I'm going to cry, sitting

there, because he's famous and gorgeous and rich and he's *leaving*. He's never been mine, no matter how he'd looked when we were fucking. No matter if I'd sworn that there was something else in his eyes beyond just passion.

There's never going to be anything else in his eyes when he looks at me. We're not going to have a lifetime of these mornings. This is just a little gift from the universe to get me back on my feet. A little test, to see if I can stand up to Geoff for good and make him get the fuck out of my life.

I don't correct Nikos, though. I just throw my arms around him, and let myself be held until breakfast comes, and Nikos unwinds my grip so that he can answer the door and keep indulging in our little fantasy, where we're together and eating breakfast and spending a quiet weekend with each other.

Even if the watch currently hidden in my bathroom cabinet tells a totally different story.

16

NIKOS

I HATE LEAVING OLI. The more we spend time with each other, the tighter the band holding us together gets. I fear it will break soon enough. It's going to snap and sever when I get back on that plane to New York and leave this pocket of peace behind.

It's early afternoon and the weather has taken a turn. Outside the radio station's narrow window, early spring rain is lashing against the glass. Although the room is soundproofed, every time Selina comes in and out, I catch the tell-tale rumble of thunder.

'And that is it, ladies and gentlemen, our delicious dive into Nikos Ridge.' The presenter speak with the cadence of someone constantly high on life. It's both infectious and rather annoying. 'Before we sign off on Radio Unlimited 404, can you give our listeners one bit of advice that you wished someone told you sooner?'

I sit in stunned silence, wanting nothing more than to leave the building, clamber back into my driver's car, and forge my path back to Oli. But alas, I have a job to do. And if Selina is going to let me enjoy my final days in London, I need to be in her good books.

'Um...Well...'

'Nikos Ridge may slay dragons in his personal time, but he is utterly lost for words. Is this a first? I think this is a first?'

He is a man in his mid-forties, with a balding head and tired eyes. He's dressed in something I'd imagine a teenager would wear - an over-sized basketball jersey and faded jeans. His headphones balance on his head, one ear covered and the other exposed.

Right now, I'd like nothing more than to reach over the small desk and throttle him.

'It's called thinking before you speak, Jim. You should give it a go.'

Selina shots me a sharp eye, but I deliver my retort with a brilliant smile and a bit of a laugh so Jim, the radio DJ, can't complain. In fact, he rocks back in his chair and gives the most obnoxious laugh I've ever heard.

'Careful, Nikos. Or was that Armin speaking through you?'

'All I will say is, be thankful I'm not a method actor.' Otherwise I'd be using a huge-ass sword to cleave his head off.

Jim raises his hands in surrender and tells his audio listeners exactly what he's doing to create the scene. 'Now, about that bit of advice.'

I've never been any good at being put on the spot. Hell, I don't even like being in the spotlight. But I close my eyes and imagine the question coming from another mouth - I imagine it's Oli asking me, and the answer comes quickly.

'When life gives you honey...' I pause, smiling at the image of his face, and what I did with that face last night. 'Lick the entire pot clean.'

The studio erupts in cheers and claps, and the show is taken off the air. The moment the red light on the 'live' box turns off, Jim sheds the over-the-top attitude and slumps in his chair. A cigarette is in his mouth in seconds, the small space filling with the acrid smell of tobacco and smoke.

'That'll be our cue to leave,' Selina says, pinching her nose as she guides me to the door. As we leave, she hands me back my phone. I flick the screen on, hopeful that I'll see a text from Oli telling me he had listened. He'd said he was going for a walk when we finished breakfast, and that he'd tune in. I hope he missed the rain. But my phone screen shows nothing from him. Only one missed call - from that unknown number again.

Father.

If it wasn't for Selina, I would've walked into a wall. She takes my elbow, guiding me through the shabby offices until we reach the street beyond. I hear her speak about no more engagements, and how we can spend our final five days in London in the spa. I'm sure she even mentions something about Oli's colleague Megan. But all I can think about it the missed call.

As if starring at the screen conjures my father into existence, the phone buzzes in my hand and a new unknown call fills my screen.

'I need to take this,' I say, pulling away from Selina as she begins to climb into the car.

'Do it inside the car,' Selina says. 'As the Brits would say, it's pissing it down. Raining cats and mice - no, cats and dogs. Something like that.'

I haven't even noticed. But now she says it, I'm wet through. My hair is plastered to my head, my smart casual outfit of a jumper and jeans clinging to my body.

'No, I'll just be a moment.'

There isn't room for Selina to complain as I step aside, accept the call, and hold the phone to my ear.

The first thing I hear is thunder, both above me and through the end of the phone. Father is close.

'I thought you were ignoring me, son.'

'I was working.' I don't know why I bother to offer an excuse. But there is something about hearing his voice that turns me into that seventeen-year-old boy all over again. The rage is the same too. Destructive, dangerous…

'Well, haven't you been busy. It's as though everywhere I look these days, I see your face. Imagine what that's like for me. Being haunted - *taunted* by you. It isn't nice.'

I bite back the urge to tell him to fuck off, look the other way, pretend I don't exist just like I wish I could do. Instead, I steady my breathing and ask the question I know this call is about. 'What do you want, father?'

'Peace. But my money is drying up.'

'We had a deal. I did what was asked of me. I owe you nothing more'

'What's the price of a life, son?'

I want to vomit. I lean against the soaked wall of the radio building, making sure my back is to the car so Selina can't read my expression - my horror. 'One point five million. Which, may I remind you, is the price you set yourself. And you have it. It's all yours.'

'There's something called inflation.'

'Fuck inflation.'

My father doesn't reply straight away. His breathing is uneven, heavy and rasping from years of drinking and smoking. When I inhale, I can smell him. It's like being back in the radio station, with Jim puffing on his cigarette as though his life depended on it.

'I need more,' my father finally says.

'That's obvious. But it's not going to happen. I have nothing else to give. In fact, I give up. Fuck this, fuck your threats, fuck - '

'Do you know the time, son?' His question stops me in my tracks.

I look down to my wrist on instinct, but my watch isn't there. I always wear one, because I need to be able to check the time during interviews without turning on my phone. I noticed as much when I was late for Selina's pick up this morning, but I was already in the car by that point and couldn't go back into Oli's apartment to get it. 'What does it matter?'

'Ah, what a silly question. Here, let me tell you. It's almost half-past four in the afternoon. Nice watch, by the way. I'm sure this will fetch me some money to keep me going until you can gather another five hundred thousand for me.'

'What?'

'Your watch. Patek Philipe, solid gold, is that a pearl face? Must be one of a kind. You really should be more careful where you put your things, son. When you care about something, when it holds value, I really wouldn't take my eyes off it. Do you know what I mean?'

My head is reeling. I can't make sense of what he's saying, or maybe I don't want to. I can't even begin to understand how my father has got access to my watch - the watch I left at *Oli's* house during our night of passion.

Father has always had a way of reading my mind. 'Check your phone.'

As he says it, the phone buzzes against my ear. I draw it back, seeing that an exposed number I don't have saved into my contacts has sent me an image. I open it, my thumb trembling. As the picture fills the screen, my knees go weak.

My watch is on the wrist of a man. My father's wrist, with an angry scar that I'd recognise anywhere - a scar I gifted him myself all those years ago. But that isn't the only thing the photo shows. The way my father is holding his wrist up to take the photo, I see a figure walking away in the distance.

'Oli,' I breathe, drawing the phone back to my ear.

'That's right, son. Now, need I remind you that I know and see everything. Call it 'daddy's intuition'. So, about that five hundred thousand. I need to see it in my bank, otherwise your watch won't be the only thing I take from you.'

The world tilts on its axis. Thunder crashes ahead, followed by a spear of lightning. Selina is calling for me to get into the car, but her voice is muffled by my heartbeat. It's as if I exist in this moment, while also being in a void, watching on through a body that no longer belongs to me.

'How did you - why would you…'

Father's laugh triggers something feral inside of me. A

beast wakes, swallowing my fear and panic in a jaw full of pointed teeth, leaving only the urge to destroy. I see red, look at the wall, and smash my first into it.

'Now, now, Nikos. Calm down. Nothing bad needs to happen if you do as I ask. Give me the money and I will disappear.'

'You promised that last time,' I say through clenched teeth. 'But you came running back for more like the mutt you are.'

'Pretty boy, that Oli. You should really tell him how dangerous stairs can be... one wrong step and he'll have a nasty fall. And his house has so many of them. If I was you, I'd be very worried. Considering Mr. Cane has a nasty habit of losing his keys, I'm surprised you keep him on such a loose leash.'

'If you *fucking* touch him,' I growl, no longer caring for who hears, 'I'll - '

'Nikos, do you really want to play this game again?'

I close my eyes and the scar on my father's arm is imprinted in the dark of my mind. No matter how I try to calm my breathing, I fail.

'Five hundred thousand. You have my number now. Contact me when you have the funds.'

The phone call ends, and I'm left clasping the phone to my ear. I can't remove it, not knowing that my father has just threatened Oli. I don't care about the fucking watch, but Oli - how my father even knows about us is beyond me. As I lower the phone, I see the photo again, tracing my finger over the figure of Oli in the distance.

This is my fault. I've put him in danger.

You should really tell him how dangerous stairs can be... one wrong step and he'll have a nasty fall.

His warning is clear as day. And I know my father - he's a man of his word. His threat of stairs and falling is history repeating itself. He has done it before, and he would do it again.

'Nikos, get in the damn car!'

I turn to Selina, numb to the core. All I can think about is getting to Oli and taking him somewhere safe. My father is a dangerous man - why else would I have played this fucking game with him all these years? But I'm also my father's son. An apple fallen from the same tree.

'What was that all about?' Selina snaps as I climb in next to her on the back seat. She takes my hand and lays it on her lap, inspecting the torn skin across my knuckles. 'Punching walls. What are you, a brute?'

'I'm fine,' I lie, and she knows it.

There is a compartment between our seats which I lift up. A light glows inside, cool air slipping out, revealing a collection of water bottles and snacks. But it's the mini bottle of vodka that I reach for. Before Selina can snatch it away, I've unscrewed the lid and downed the entire thing.

She just stares at me, helpless. Her sadness rocks me to the core. 'I want to help you. But I can't do that unless you tell me what's wrong. You've been cagey for months, Nikos. Years. I want to *help*.'

I'm onto my second bottle before the car engine starts. 'I need to get away.'

Run away, but I can't admit that.

'You need more than a holiday, Nikos. You need to talk, actually talk to me, or someone. Anyone. Whatever is going on, you have to share it.'

I know she's right, but the only thing I can think about is her mention of a holiday. It's what I need. I have to get away, with Oli. He isn't safe if my father knows where he lives.

How? Why? So many questions, and yet I feel like finding out the answers would destroy me.

I look Selina dead in the eye, fuelled by anxiety, adrenaline, and two shots of vodka. 'Take me to Oli.'

She doesn't react with confusion, which proves me that she knows about us. Maybe Megan told her, perhaps I made it obvious. Then another thought comes to mind, fuelled by my paranoia.

Was Selina the one to rat me out to my dad? For the right price, would she betray me?

'Do you think that is wise, letting Oli see you like... this?'

Tears well in my eyes. If the door to the car wasn't locked, I'd happily throw myself out. At least that way these threats could no longer hold power over me. But then who would protect Oli?

'I need him.'

Selina chews on my statement and nods. 'I want to be able to help you, Nikos. But I can't do that unless you want me to.'

Do you? Do you actually?

'Please.' My entire body is shaking, my knuckles bleeding, and chest aching. I dare close my eyes in case I see Oli's body laid out at the bottom of a flight of stairs, head cracked and eyes empty of life... just like my...

My phone is in my hand, distracting me from the only thought that can undo me. I pull up the internet. In a matter of moments, all whilst Selina is looking at me, I have the website that I need before me.

'What are you doing now, Nikos?'

'Holiday,' I exhale, unable to form a sentence. 'Just like you said. I'm getting away. I need a break.'

But more so, I need to get Oli away. And there is one place that I know in the world that my father would never return.

The scene of the crime that started this nightmare.

'I'm going home.'

17

OLI

I FEEL like I'm going to pass out the whole time I'm engaged in this horrific deception.

It doesn't quite feel real, like I'm a character in some spy movie who's been tasked with setting up a drop. You know that sense of unreality that sometimes comes along with anxiety, like you're not the one in charge of your body? Like you're seeing through someone else's eyes?

Yeah. I'm feeling that *hard.*

Nikos told me this morning that he was going to record for a radio show, and that it would take him a few hours to get back. I told him that I had errands to run and that I would listen as I did them, and I felt so bad as he kissed me and then walked out of the door that I wanted to die.

I'm not going to listen, and I know it.

I grab a hoodie out of my closet and throw on jeans, fishing out an old baseball cap too. There's no reason for me to be disguised, but I feel like it's armour. Like if I'm dressed this way, I'm not the one who's actually dropping a watch worth tens of thousands of dollars into the coffee cup I get from Costa along the way.

Drinking the coffee gives me instant heartburn. I dump the rest in the Thames.

Sorry fish.

The spot by the river where Nikos and I had sat was so special to me, and now Geoff has ruined it, just like he ruined our relationship and my heart. My stomach lurches as I shake the last dregs of the coffee out of the cup and then drop the watch into it, snapping the plastic lid on top.

When I glance around, I can't see Geoff anywhere. I know he must be watching, though. He probably was following me the whole way here. The thought makes me hunch my shoulders as I turn back towards home. I'm constantly looking behind me as I walk, too wound up to take the tube. Fresh air usually does me good when I'm anxious, but not this time. My stomach just sinks further with every step I take.

It's over, I remind myself. *He got the sick revenge he wanted, and now he's out of your life.*

Geoff is the kind of man who just wants to be in control. He just wants to know that everyone is wrapped around his finance-bro finger. This is like a dog pissing on something to show ownership.

It's the last time he's going to do this to me. I have to believe that.

I stop into the hardware store after the half-hour walk home. It's raining now, and only getting worse. A clock on the wall shows that Nikos' radio program must have ended by now, but I can't bring myself to text him. Not with what I've just done.

THE ACTOR AND HIS SECRET

I pick up a roll of white tape, the kind that you use to section off stripes when painting. I disabled the security system last night, but I don't trust Geoff to not find a way to get back in.

When I walk in my front door, the first thing I do after drying off is grab a chair from the kitchen. The tape held under one arm, I drag it to the first camera by the door. I stick tape over the lens, a small enough piece to be nearly unnoticeable this high up, but enough to cover the lens. I play Nikos' interview through my AirPods while I work, and when he says the part about life giving him honey, my stomach swoops.

If only life had given me him to *keep*.

By the time there's a knock at the door, I'm sweaty and my arms ache, but I've covered all the cameras. I take a moment to compose myself and greet Nikos. He steps in quickly and leans his weight back against the door, turning the deadbolt with one hand and grabbing the back of my neck with the other. He looks me up and down, and only when his eyes have finished traversing my body does he seem to relax.

'How was your interview?' I fist my hands into the soft cotton of his t-shirt. He's soaked through.

'It was ok.'

Is that all? Clearly he's pissed off about something.

'I heard what you said about honey.' I shuffle on my feet. 'It was... nice.'

He doesn't answer me for a moment, and cold washes through me. Does he know? Did he come home to confront me about his watch? Did Geoff contact him too, God forbid?

I step back, out of his grip, wondering if he's about to lay into me for stealing from him. 'Nikos?'

He shakes his head, like he's trying to snap himself out of something, and then he runs his hand through his hair. His shoulders relax, if marginally, and I relax too when he sighs. Maybe he's just tired.

'I'm glad you listened. Pack your bags,' Nikos says after a heartbeat of silence. He smiles, but it doesn't reach his tired eyes. 'I have a surprise for you.'

'I - What?' I don't know what's going on, and for a horrible moment I once again think he caught me leaving his watch for Geoff. 'What do you mean?'

Nikos runs a hand through his hair, and glances out the window for a moment, a shadow crossing his face. 'I need to get away. Selina agrees. This was the last of my media engagements in London, and now I've got some time off. I want to spend it with you. I want to get away from the bustle of the city and spend some time just you and me. If you're alright with that. Selina already checked with Megan and got you some time off as a personal favour.'

It isn't as if I've used any of my vacation days. But as if summoned, my phone buzzes on the counter. It's Megan.

MEGAN

I'm sooooo jealous!! Enjoy Greece! Don't check your email or I'll kill you! Love you xx

It's followed by a load of emojis - palm tree, sunglasses, and then a series of extremely suggestively arranged vegetables.

I suppose there's a very clear upside to the flirtation

going between Megan and Selina. I'm not going to say no to free vacation days, not when the thought of Geoff trailing me makes me want to run away.

'Ok.' I step forward into Nikos' arms, and the moment I bury my head in the crook of his neck, I relax. I feel him relax too, like he was nervous I would say no. 'Let's do it, then. What do I have to pack? When do we leave?'

Nikos holds me close. 'There's a jet waiting for us at Heathrow whenever we're ready. And pack clothes for warm weather.'

'Oh?' I can't get over the fact he's just said he has a jet waiting for us. A fucking private jet. 'Where are we going?'

He pulls back and kisses me on the forehead, and now there's a genuine smile on his face. I give a little shudder at the feeling of our bodies pressing together,

'What better getaway for an Adonis than going to Greece?'

ROLLERCOASTERS HAVE NEVER BEEN my thing, and it's even worse when my emotions are what's going for a ride. I was barely thinking when I shoved clothes into my suitcase at random and found my passport in the safe. Now I'm cradled in the soft leather seat of a private jet, after having been taken directly onto the tarmac in a black SUV.

To the few people that saw us embarking, we're childhood friends, or actor and publicist... the lies are getting hard to keep up with. But I can't feel a way about it, after what I've done to Nikos.

Going from the anxiety of last night, to the tension of dropping off the watch, to the high of being whisked away on a private jet by an actual movie star...my heart can't take it.

What is my *life?*

Nikos is sitting across from me, running his finger around the rim of the glass of whiskey that the flight attendant had given him before we took off. I'm nursing a diet Sprite, which I couldn't believe they had on a plane. But I guess when you're rich, you get anything and everything you want.

Nikos has shed some of the tension that he'd been carrying in London. I don't know if it's being officially away from prying eyes, or if it's getting out of London and away from his obligations. But it hits me that I've not seen him this comfortable except when we were alone together in bed. There were worry lines around his eyes that aren't there anymore.

'You don't like the spotlight, do you?'

The question slips out of my mouth without my permission, and I wince because it's not like we know each other well enough for me to get that personal. But Nikos just makes a thoughtful sound and shakes his head.

'I hate it, actually.' He licks his lips. 'I'd always rather be spending time by myself, or with my few close friends. To be honest, I'm pretty shy in crowds. They make me nervous.'

'Wow.' I can't help but run my foot up and down the back of his calf. 'You would never know.'

He gives me a crooked half-smile. 'Actor, right?'

'How'd you get into it, then? Acting?' He's not tensing up, and he's not deflecting, so maybe he's alright with me asking prying questions. 'If you're an introvert who's not into the spotlight?'

Nikos take as sip of his drink, the ice clinking against the glass. 'I was scouted, first as a model. I'd moved to America as soon as I was eighteen, I needed - *wanted* - to get out of Greece. There...there wasn't much there for me anymore. So I was in New York, working as a barista because I didn't really know what else to do. An agent stopped by for coffee and slipped me her card.'

I nodded. 'And it spiralled from there?'

Nikos slumps down in his seat so our knees are touching. He hooks an ankle around mine, like he's trying to keep me close. 'Pretty much. The money was great, so I fell into it. Modelling gigs turned into acting jobs when my agent realised I could play a part. And the roles got bigger and bigger. It was hard to say no to the money, even if I really didn't like the fame. It felt nice, actually, to put my acting talent to good use.'

I hum. It makes sense. 'You liked the job, but every job has its downsides.'

'Which is why I usually need a getaway after big press junkets.' His smile is soft. I feel like I could drown in his eyes. 'Thank you for coming with me.'

The way he's looking at me melts from soft to hot. Maybe it's the alcohol he's drinking, or the way he opened up to me. But I can tell that there's desire in his gaze.

'They're going to leave us alone,' he says. 'I asked them for privacy. If we get hungry, I'll go back and ask for food. But for now, it's just us.'

My mouth is dry. I take a deep breath, trying to tame the arousal building at the base of my spine.

'Have you ever fucked in a plane?'

The way Nikos says it is so bare, so rough, that I can't help myself. I whine.

I narrow my eyes on him, reading the nuances of his expressions. I see the stress in the lines across his forehead, and beside his honey-gold eyes, but Nikos does well to hide the root cause. 'I get the impression, from the confidence you just asked that question with, that you're already a proud member of the mile-high club?'

'Not yet.'

'Not yet?' I retort.

'Come here, Honey.' Nikos sets his glass down on a nearby table and opens his arms to me. I practically launch myself across the space between us and climb him like a tree. 'Would you like me to fuck you?'

I'm needy, and clingy, and I know it. But right now, all I want is for Nikos to claim me. I want him to use me. I want to be his.

'I want you to fuck my throat.' My voice is breathy and high, and my head is spinning. All the blood in my body has rushed downward, and I'm painfully hard. The idea of stripping down completely when the air stewardess is sitting in the cockpit unnerves me. But discreet blowjobs...yes, that I can do.

'I'd never say no to that mouth. So, if you're so certain,' he says, licking his lips, 'get down on your knees.'

He spreads his thighs apart on the wide leather seat, and when I look down I can see the outline of his hardening length through his jeans. I almost drool at the way they're stretching across his muscular thighs. I scramble back off of his lap and my knees hit the plush carpet of the jet. My knuckles graze the hard ridges of Nikos' abs as I unbutton his jeans and pull down the zipper.

Nikos winds his fingers into my hair as I take in the way his cock is straining against the fabric of his briefs. There's already a damp spot on the cotton where he's leaking, and the breath punches out of me when I realise that *I* did that. I'm the one who got a movie star hard and aching.

'Go on.' His voice is rough, and his hips tilt up, like he can't wait to have my mouth on him. 'Show me how good you can be for me. Show me how deep you can take me, Honey.'

I try to say something but it's just an incoherent moan when it leaves my lips. I abandon any hope of speech and instead bend forward to mouth at his cock, the heat of it against my lips making my stomach clench. It's been a while since I blew a guy this big - who am I kidding, I've *never* had a cock this size in my mouth.

But I'm nothing if not dedicated.

I slide the waistband of Nikos' briefs down to expose his length, and as soon as I do, his hands push me down. I take his crown between my lips and flick my tongue out, tasting him. He's leaking and when I run my tongue over his slit, he arches his hips up and moans.

'God, Honey.'

His accent comes out so much more when he's aroused, like he's losing control. I want to be the one to give him that - to allow him to get rid of the shell that he's built around himself to survive being in the public eye. I want to make him feel like he can be himself. Just Adonis. Just free.

I take a breath and draw him further into my mouth,

relaxing my throat and jaw and digging my fingers into his thighs. Every time the muscles there jump, every time I hear him pant, it encourages me to keep going.

'Honey.' He's saying my name like it's a prayer. Like *I'm* the one who's a god.

I manage to keep from gagging as he hits the back of my throat, filling me up, using me. He stays still, so I draw back, licking my way up his shaft, my tongue tracing the thick veins running along the underside of his cock. His hands tighten in my hair, just on the edge of pain, and I give myself over to him. He pushes my head back down until my throat is flexing around him, my eyes watering and spit coating my chin.

I'm a filthy mess, but I don't care.

I start up a rhythm, working his cock, one hand moving to the base because even when I try I can't fit it all in my mouth. The noises Nikos is making are so hot I think that it wouldn't take much for me to come. I could get off on the way I'm making Nikos pant.

'Honey, I'm - '

I can tell that Nikos is close by the way his cock is twitching and his thighs are tensing, and I hum as I lower my mouth back down over him. The slight vibration sends him over the edge, his cock pulsing as he shoots cum down my throat.

He pulls me off his cock before he's finished, coating my chin like he owns me. Like I'm property.

I swipe a hand across my face, Nikos' come coating my palm, and then stare him in the eye as I lick myself clean.

'You're a menace, Honey,' Nikos pants, his hands tightening around my waist.

I'm whining and practically crying I'm so eager to

come, and all it takes is Nikos hauling me up and grinding a palm against my length before I'm shuddering through an orgasm that feels like it lasts a lifetime. I swear that I black out a bit, sagging against Nikos.

I cry out as I come, not even worrying about the air stewardess hearing.

I wouldn't mind if everyone in the whole world knew that I belonged to Nikos Ridge.

Turns out, my moan wasn't so muffled. Just as I get back to my feet, a pretty face pops around the door to the cockpit. 'Did you require something, Mr Ridge?'

'No, no,' he replies, pushing distance between us, reminding me to play the part of dirty secret, instead of open lover. 'I'm rather satisfied at the moment.'

I offer her a weak smile, hoping she doesn't see the smudge of his cum still on my chin or the wet spot darkening my trousers. She nods, sweeps her eyes over us, and disappears. The moment the door closes, we burst into a fit of giggles, like naughty schoolboys.

I let myself laugh, even if it hurts to remember that us, this–it's nothing more than a lie.

18

NIKOS

We arrive in Thessaloniki airport after a short, but *clearly* enjoyable, three-hour flight. It takes a further hour to taxi the jet, wait for a car to pull up, and get our luggage gathered.

But my sense of peace is shattered as we're greeted by the early signs of press. It's well into the evening already, the sky painted black and speckled with stars. It makes it easier to see the flashing lights of cameras as Greece's media await my arrival.

'There really is no rest for the wicked, is there?' Oli says from behind me. I keep him away from the jet's window, not wanting him to be caught in the crossfire.

'It would seem that way.'

I lean against the wall of the jet, mind whirling with how this was possible. No one knows I've booked a flight to come except Selina. She told Megan so Oli could get time off work. But clearly, news is out. The private jet company wouldn't risk exposing my schedule for fear of being sued, and I trust that none of the air stewardesses were posting on social media about me - they'd be fired on the spot.

For the second time, discomfort swirls in my gut. *Selina*. Had she told someone else besides Megan? Paranoia sings in my ear like a devil on my shoulder.

'Mr. Ridge?' The pilot calls as he walks back up into the jet. 'It's taken a moment to arrange the necessary protocols with the local Greek police, but they've allowed for your driver to collect you straight from the runway. The car is on its way round now and should be ready for you in a few minutes. Would you both like to follow me?'

'*Efcharisto*, Michael,' I reply, allowing the Greek to roll off my tongue. My accent, although weaker than it once had been, still comes naturally. I don't get to practice my mother tongue much more than speaking it at the family-owned Greek bodega on the corner of my block back in New York.

Oli makes a choked noise behind me, and the sound goes straight to my groin.

'*Parakalo*.' The pilot nods, tipping his hat off in a sign of respect.

As he promises, we hear the rumble of an engine and I look out the window to see a car driving towards us. The cameras are still flashing in the distance, and the thought of stepping out of the plane makes me sick.

'It's going to be ok, Nikos.' Oli places a comforting hand on my shoulder. He must have noticed how tense I'd gotten.

Is it going to be ok? My father likely knows where I am already. My attempt to run away from my problems, just like I did when I was eighteen, is proving to be a waste of time. But there's another problem, and he's standing behind me. As much as we toy with the risk of being together, it's one thing convincing professionals that my and Oli's relationship is purely platonic. He's a publicist for the book my new movie is based on - it's not a stretch that we'd be seen in London together.

But the second the gossip sites catch wind that I've flown home with another man? It would be a disaster of epic proportions.

'Honey, I hate to ask this of you.' I reach for the blanket from the chair at my side, imprinted with the private jet's logo on the baby-blue material. 'Do you mind?'

He studies the blanket, his face screwing into a brief grimace. But it lasts but a second before he takes the blanket from me. Oli doesn't need telling in words as to what I want him to do.

Pretending this is ok, when it's far from it, Oli lifts the blanket and drapes it over his beautiful face. It hangs down, perfectly large that you can only see his white trainers. He could be anyone - he's short enough compared to me that no one would think twice assuming it's a woman I've brought to stay with me on some lust-addled getaway.

'You'll have to lead the way,' Oli says, voice muffled by the weight of the blanket.

Alone for a moment on the jet, I lean in and kiss him with the blanket between our mouths. I slip my hand beneath, find his and entwine our fingers. 'I've got you, Honey.'

I'm glad for his touch. It grounds me. As we step out of the jet, cameras flashing and people screaming from inside the closest terminal, we quickly clamber into the blacked-out car waiting for us.

Greek music is playing. An icon of Mary holding baby Jesus swings from the driver's mirror. The air is thicker in the car than outside of it. Even with the air conditioning blasting at full speed, all I want to do is crack a window open, but I can't.

'*Kalos irthate,*' the driver says, his accent thick, reminding me of home. 'Are you ready to go?'

'Just a moment,' I reply, head reeling. Leaning into Oli, I pat his knee. 'I hate to ask this of you, but can you keep that blanket on a little while longer?'

'Yes,' he replies, but with a lack of confidence. 'Although you'll have to deal with me being a sweaty mess. It's suffocating under here.'

'I'll make it up to you soon.'

I can hardly think straight. I've booked me and Oli a private villa in the centre of Halkidhiki. It's on private land, surrounded by miles of olive groves and vineyards. It's perfect, the best place for us to hide away from the world. With its own pool, a fully-stocked kitchen, and a secret path to a private beach, there's nothing more we could need once we arrive.

But. *Big* but. If the media knew I was arriving here, there is a chance they know where I'm staying. I can't risk going, knowing cameras and fans would be waiting behind olive trees to get pictures of me and Oli.

So, I have to think fast.

There's only one place I can go where the press won't find me. Oli wouldn't know any different. He was entirely modest and hadn't even asked where we were staying. Proving his intentions were pure, even though I couldn't wait to see his reaction when we walked into pure luxury.

I lean into the mirror, reaching into my pocket and

withdrawing a handful of euros. Oli can't see me do it, but I hand the money to the driver and give him a new location, telling him in Greek that we're changing direction. One where we will be alone - except for all the ghosts of my past which I've run from.

The ghosts I thought I'd left behind.

Facing them won't be as torturous with Oli by my side. At least, that was what I tell myself as the driver starts the engine and drives off.

'THIS IS...' Oli drawls from my side, yawning as he steps out of the car to get his first look at our destination.

'Plain?' I answer for him, getting me first glance at the view before me.

'Perfect,' he says. 'Completely and utterly perfect.'

Oh, to have Oli's rose-tinted vision. Life would be a lot simpler - and more enjoyable.

We thank the driver, retrieve our suitcases from the trunk of the car, and stare ahead at the walk before us. The dirt track is set on an incline, just outside of a small Greek village. Cars can't make it up to the house at the end of the path, because it was never designed for modern day cars. And in the years since I'd obtained the property, I'd not spent a penny changing it or modernising it.

Because it was my family home, with its familiar once-white-painted walls now faded and dirt-smudged. Unlike the rich memories that assault me as I get a glimpse of it at a distance, which are as vivid as ever. It wasn't luxurious like I'd planned, but it does have access to a private cove at the back of the property.

Crickets play a symphony around us, blending perfectly in with the meows of the stray cats who live in the hillside around us. I look behind me, seeing the glint of the village in the distance. The last time I saw this view, I was walking away from my home, thinking I was leaving the demons behind.

Turns out they followed me wherever I went.

'Shall we?' Oli says, one hand on his suitcase, the other extended for me.

I take his hand, glad for the touch, even though I'd not taken my hand off him the entire two-hour drive here. 'I'm sorry it's nothing special.'

'You're joking right?' Oli says with a smile. 'This is everything I could need.'

'What, a run-down house in the middle of nowhere?'

'Not quite. I mean the privacy, and the fact I get to spend it with you. Plus, I've got all those books to read.'

All the books I'd had an attendant from the private jet company buy him from the airport bookstore in London as I made him hide out before our flight - basically the entire romance section. It was the least I could do. Hell, I'd buy him the entire store if it meant making up for treating him the way I am.

It takes us five minutes to walk up to the house. I check my phone for signal and see it is completely without. I smile for the first time since landing in Greece.

No calls, no messages, no father, no threats.

I don't need to worry if the key to the house was where I asked the estate agent to leave it. Even though it had been six years since I bought the property, there's an element of community and trust in Greece. And, to prove me right, the key - although slightly rusted from time - is right where I'd expected it to be, in the chipped pot beside the front door.

It takes a few tries to get inside, the door sticking from the humidity. Oli waits for me to enter first, giving me a moment. He doesn't know the importance of the house yet, but he can clearly read my silence for what it is. Oli knows me better than I know myself, it would seem.

I'm hit by the smell. Oregano and sea salt. I stand in the foyer, eyes closed and inhaling deeply. If I listen carefully, I can hear the gentle lull of waves in the distance. But if I pretend, really put myself back in time, I can almost hear my mother tinkering in the kitchen. Her soft humming as she cooked *kleftiko* or hung our laundry up on the exposed balcony on the second floor.

I almost break down, right then and there.

Until a presence steps into my side, a soft hand resting on my lower back. 'Are you ok?'

I open my eyes, facing the dark and empty house I once called a home. 'I will be.'

'This place... it's special to you. Isn't it?'

I nod, doing everything in my power not to look in the direction of the staircase. The memories I have of that location are far from kind. Even though I know the floor had been cleaned of blood, and the bottom step scrubbed of my mother's brain matter, I can still picture the scene as plain as day.

'This is my...*was* my home. Where I grew up.'

Arms wrap around my back. Oli leans his face into my spine and exhales. 'Thank you for bringing me here.'

I can't reply. The air is too warm, the memories far too overbearing. Why I even thought this was a good idea is beyond me. In a moment of panic for my career, I'd somehow decided I'd rather face my own living hell than possibly be seen with Oli.

As if that would be such a bad thing.

I tug at my collar, trying to get some air beneath my stuffy clothes. 'Do you want to go for a swim?'

Oli's caught off guard. 'It's like, one in the morning. At least London time.'

'Perfect time for it, then.'

I turn until I face him. I take his cheeks in my hands and bring his face to mine. Our mouths touch for the briefest of moments, enough that the horrible memories are forced to the back of my mind.

'But my trunks are at the bottom of my suitcase.'

I pat his arse. 'Where we're going, you don't need to wear anything.'

He grins crookedly. 'This was your plan all along, wasn't it, Adonis?'

I gift him another kiss, this one breathy and full of need and desperation. 'It was.'

We leave our suitcases in the foyer. With Oli's hand in mine, I guide him out the corridor, towards the back of the house where the small garden - once pruned and well-manicured - is now overgrown. A rickety gate leads to a stone path that takes us down the side of a cliff face. It's so dark I can't see where I'm going, so we take it slow, and I give into my muscle memory to guide me from step to step.

The ocean glows like a blanket of pure obsidian. The moon hangs in a cloudless sky, reflecting off the calm waters below us. Oli's giggles soon become hearty laughs as we reach the sandy bed of the shoreline and begin stripping off. With each piece of clothing, I feel like I'm taking off a part of myself - the illusion of Nikos Ridge that I'd worked all my life to build up.

Completely naked, the waves lapping over my toes, Oli by my side, I feel free. Weightless. The water is warm, but I still shiver from anticipation.

'Ready?' I ask, looking at Oli. His features are hard to see in the dark, but I adore how the moonlight graces the planes of his face. Even clearly tired from the traveling, there's energy in his stare that lights a pyre inside of me.

'If a giant octopus comes and drags me into the depths, I expect you to come and save me.'

'Just as Perseus slayed the kraken,' I reply, ready to completely submerge myself in the waters, allowing it to wash away my worries. 'I'll never let anything happen to you.'

His smile falters, and I fear I ruined the moment. But Oli faces the ocean before I can ask what is wrong.

'Race you,' he says, pulling his hand from mine and throwing himself into the ocean.

The splash covers me. I gasp, watching his lithe pale body slip beneath the waters like a mermaid returning home. It takes but a millisecond for me to follow him in.

Home was once a place I loved, but soon became a physical manifestation of my horrors. Maybe - just maybe - Oli will fix that. Just as he is slowly fixing me.

19

OLI

This is *literal* paradise.

The sun is warm but not overpowering as we lounge on the beach, the both of us stretched out on towels in the sand. Nikos is already getting a tan, and I can tell that with only a day or two in the sunlight, he's going to be a rich, deep gold. I can't see his eyes through his sunglasses, but I'm pretty sure from the steady rise and fall of his chest that he's sound asleep.

Good. He didn't look like he was getting nearly enough rest in London. Plus, the gentle sound of the waves would lull anyone to sleep.

We're touching, his arm pressed up against mine and his ankle hooked over my leg like he's subconsciously stopping me from leaving. But there's truly nowhere else I'd rather be in the world. I could stay here, with him, forever.

There's a small stack of romance novels on the beach next to me, sand sneaking into the pages, and a few bottles of water. I read fast, and I turn the last pages on my second book of the day. Usually romance novels suck me in, but right now? I'm living a romance novel of my own.

Fiction doesn't hold a lot of appeal when you have the real thing right in front of you.

I finish off the book, ensuring that the girl gets the guy in the end, and toss it to my side. I curl over and slot myself between Nikos' arm and torso, my head resting on his chest. His skin is like a furnace, a combination of the heat of the day and his natural warmth. He mumbles sleepily and then brings his arm around me, tucking me closer to him. He's hardly had his hands off me since we arrived at the house, and I can't say I'm complaining.

I doze for another hour or so, until I'm roused by the way my stomach is rumbling. It wakes Nikos up too, and he turns to me with concern. 'Are you hungry?'

'Mmhm.' I'm about to make a joke about how he can feed me his cock, but I stop. It doesn't feel right in the moment. There's been something more tender, more intimate about the way the two of us are orbiting each other since we arrived. Like some of the lust has burned away and left something deeper behind.

'Come on, then.' He gently eases me off his shoulder and gets to his feet, then bends down to scoop me up in his arms, bridal-style. 'You can rest inside where you won't turn into a tomato, and I'll run to the village and get things to cook.'

I don't argue about being carried as Nikos starts to walk us up the steep path, leaving our books and towels behind - which is certainly one perk of a private beach. 'I hope this is a good replacement for the gym.' I poke a finger into his rock-hard abs. 'Carrying me up these inclines.'

'I'll carry you wherever you like, Honey,' he replies, pressing a kiss to my forehead. He smells like sun and the ocean and sweat, and I can't get enough. I tuck my head into his chest. 'This is better than any gym I've ever been to.'

I agree. This is like our own little world. No internet service. No texts and calls. No work or life. Just us.

'Besides,' he continues on, his voice soft and gentle, 'I never want to let you go.'

There's a lump in my throat as he looks down at me, the way that the confession is raw and intimate. Like Nikos has also felt the shift between us since we arrived.

What I would give to make Nikos' desire come true. To make it so that he never has to let me go. There are a million reasons why that can't happen, but I shove each and every one of them to the back of my mind. I'm not going to let the inevitable end of whatever this is cloud the perfection of the present.

I take the easy way out and say nothing that would betray my feelings. Despite the way Nikos has been looking at me, I can't fool myself into thinking that he feels the same way.

Nikos settles me down when we arrive at the top of the path, my feet sinking into the grass behind the house. There's what must have been a lovely garden, and I can't help but think that if I had time, I could bring it back to life. I breathe in, savouring the smell of the lupine growing wild around the house, listening to the crash of the waves.

'Come on inside,' Nikos says, taking my hand and tugging.

I follow and it's a relief to get inside with the shade. I go to the kitchen and run the tap, filling a glass with cool water that I drink down. Nikos comes up behind me, pinning me against the sink with his arms, and turns the water off.

'I'm not going to be gone for long,' he says into my ear. I shiver at the sensation of his breath on my neck. 'When I get back, I'll make us lunch.'

'Something Greek?' I turn my head up for a chaste kiss, which Nikos delivers, pressing his lips to mine.

'Of course.' He winks, and I'm breathless with how handsome he is, and how much younger he seems here away from the stress of his everyday life. 'There's nothing else right for the setting, is there?'

I wave goodbye as he puts on shoes and a shirt and heads out the door. I guess he's not worried about being recognised because it's such a small town - the people here probably don't even look at him differently, if they've known him his whole life. I can imagine there's so much comfort to that, coming back to a place that you know, and where everyone knows you. Stability amidst all the change.

For a moment I wonder if I should take a quick nap to replenish my energy. The jet lag has done a number on me, not that we have anything on our schedule that we have to be awake for. But I can't resist the urge of exploring the house where Nikos Ridge grew up.

The ground floor doesn't have many personal touches, almost like an estate agent had come through and gotten it ready to sell or rent out. There's cookware and dishes in the kitchen, a living room with comfortable furniture in it looking out at the olive trees around the house, and a few other empty rooms that probably once served as bedrooms or maybe a dining room or office. I go up the stairs to the second floor, bypassing the bedroom where we'd stayed last night and looking through the other rooms. One of them has a bunch of furniture in it, like everything personal has been stashed here to make the rest of the house a blank slate.

I slip in, running my hand over furniture in olive wood that looks like it could have been hand carved. There are colourful hand-woven rugs rolled up and decorative pots and vases lined up against a wall. Religious icons hang on the walls - each as intricate and detailed as the next. I've never been one for religion, but I can certainly appreciate the beauty in it. I imagine the way the house must have looked when Nikos lived here with his parents, warm and bright and welcoming.

On a chest of drawers pushed off to the side, there's a stack of framed photos which must have been taken off the walls of the house. I look at the first one, and a pang goes through my chest. It's a young, curly-haired Nikos, no more than three or four years old, sitting on the sand with a shell in his hand, grinning. I trace the photo with my finger, memorising the way he looked as a baby, and then move it aside to see the next one.

It's a posed picture of Nikos and two people who must be his parents. They're wearing fancy clothes, and I wonder if this was some holiday. His father is familiar. He looks just like Nikos - he must have been the same age in this picture as Nikos was now, if not younger. He's not smiling - he looks dead serious, and more than a little humourless - but his mum is grinning. She's beautiful, not just the way she looks but the light in her eyes, and the way that she's hugging baby Nikos close on her lap, beaming with pride.

Nikos never talks about his family. I wonder where they are now - whether they're still living in Greece, or whether they've passed away. I don't want to pry, but maybe being here will get him to open up about what his life was like before he became Nikos Ridge.

I hear the front door open and my cheeks heat - I don't want to be caught snooping. I carefully place the pictures back in order and dash to the top of the stairs, calling out a hello to Nikos.

He takes one look at me, silhouetted against the doorway, and I can tell something's wrong. He looks like he's seen a ghost.

'Nikos?'

'Be careful,' he begs.

'Of what?' I look around, hoping there isn't some kind of snake or massive insect right next to me in the house.

'The - coming down - the stairs.' His voice cracks, like he's really, really upset. I startle at the emotion written all over his face - he looks like he's going to cry. 'Please, Oli. Be careful.'

'Alright.' I speak like I'm trying to soothe a spooked horse, making a show of putting my hand on the banister and slowly making my way down to him.

'Oh, love,' I say as gently as I can manage when I get to him. He's shaking like a leaf when I put my arms around his shoulders. This is clearly something deeper than I realise, maybe trigged by being back in his childhood home. 'Tell me, what's going on?'

20

NIKOS

I'VE NEVER TOLD anyone this story, besides the police who investigated it when I was eighteen. Of course my father knows, and still hangs it over my head like a rotting carrot I'm supposed to chase after.

Just the thought of voicing it aloud is painful, but Oli is persistent, which I find almost calming. Like someone else is taking control of something I've never been able to deal with.

'Sit with me,' Oli pats the rusted iron chair on the veranda at the back of the house.

The sun beats down on me, making me sweat through the white linen shirt I'd put on to go shopping. I rip the sunglasses and hat off, no longer caring if it was a good enough disguise when I popped into the small town and brought supplies. No one seemed to notice me. If anything, the kind-faced Greek woman who'd served me spoke in broken English when talking to me, clearly telling me she had no idea I was one, Greek and two, the same boy she'd last seen over twelve years ago. My new American accent to my Greek must have made me seem like a different person.

I bury my face in my hands, unable to clear the image of Oli standing on the stairs. It wasn't the first time he'd used them since we got here, but it had been the first time without me standing right next to him. Seeing him, just stood there, on the very step that cracked my mother's skull open like an egg was terrifying.

You should really tell him how dangerous stairs can be... one wrong step and he'll have a nasty fall.

'Take your time,' Oli encourages, reminding me I hadn't said a word since he ushered me back here. He places a hand on my back and rubs circles into my skin. 'Did something happen at the shop? Crazed fans?'

I wish it was that easy. 'It's not that. It's...' I look at him through damp lashes, the tears falling freely. 'There's a reason I haven't cum here in so many years. I didn't plan to take you here, but when we got to the airport and saw all the media, I panicked and changed our destination.'

Oli doesn't pause his calming circles. In fact, he lays his other hand on my knee and squeezes. His touch alone anchors me. 'We can leave, if it's easier?'

I shook my head. 'I can't always run away.'

'Run away from what, Nikos?'

His use of my name is jarring. I long for him to continue pretending we're strangers, using the nicknames as a way to keep playing this little game we found ourselves in. But since we arrived here, for two days now, I've been lava bubbling in a dormant volcano, ready to erupt. Seeing Oli on those stairs was the stone dropped into the chasm that broke down my defences.

'My mother died here,' I admit.

Oli takes a moment to take in this information. His silence is so palpable I can taste the emotion in the hot air. 'I'm so sorry.'

Normally people follow up sad news with an apology, but how could they possibly mean it? Except when Oli says it, he's so sincere I swear I believe him.

'We don't need to talk about anything that will only upset you more,' Oli starts.

'But I do,' I reply, the flood gates wide open. 'I - I need to say it and maybe the memories will stop being so overbearing.'

I wonder if Oli realised that we'd hardly spent time in the house. Most of our days had been on the beach, the evenings out in the small garden overlooking the wondrous views. I have done everything in my power to dance around the ghosts lurking here, but all I'd done was push down the inevitable until it broke me from the inside.

'Then I'm here, no judgement. If there's anything I can offer you, it's a safe space. Somewhere for you to put your secrets.' He leans his head on my shoulder, finding yet another part of himself to touch me with. We're practically conjoined by the time the secrets spill free.

'My mother she - she fell. Down the stairs.' It was half a lie. 'Seeing you on them just made me panic. It was a silly reaction. But the last time I saw someone I care about on those stairs, they didn't get the chance to walk down them.'

'Oh my god, Nikos. That's awful.'

'It was. I mean, it is.'

'That must've been really hard for you and your father. Losing the pillar of your family like that.'

I drew back, the glare of the sun punishing me. With a shaking hand, I reach for the glass of chilled water Oli prepared for me. The contents slosh over the rim before the water reaches my mouth. I almost choke just trying to swallow it down.

I could tell Oli everything. What my father did. What he was still doing. But once the story was finished, Oli would go from pitying me to thinking I was the root cause of the evil. I caused it. Her death, although not by my hands, was my fault.

As I sit beside Oli, the rushing waves far below and the chirping of crickets surrounding us, my mind replays what happened in the moments before my mother's death.

I slip into the memory with ease.

———

'Mum, hurry up!' I screamed at the top of my lungs, voice cracking from late puberty. I looked up the stairs, waiting for her to come for me. Our bags were packed and ready at the door. I'd borrowed a friend's car to get us to the airport, where cheap tickets had been booked to get us out of Greece.

She'd gone back upstairs for something. A picture. I saw it in her grasp when she rounded the top of the stairs. 'I'm ready, darling.'

Father arrived home at the worst moment. If only we'd left sooner, then maybe she would've still been alive. Hell, if I'd not made her leave, if I didn't plan this all…

THE ACTOR AND HIS SECRET

The bruise under her swollen eye was black and blue. Courtesy of father's fist the previous night - the last straw. When he hit her, beat her, it was always in places no one could see. But the fit of madness he'd last night was the worst yet. It was a miracle she was still alive.

A door slammed open. I heard father's booming voice as he returned home. He'd seen the car, the bags. Then he caught the two passports in my hand, mother at the top of the stairs - dressed for the first time in weeks. He knew what was happening. We were leaving him. Our abuser. Our monster. The man I'd watched beat my mother bloody for years. The man who terrorized me with threats of the same, which I was only spared from by my mother taking my place.

I was done letting him hurt her.

I placed myself before the stairs, trying to block him from reaching them. His fist was fast and sure. My head cracked back and stars blurred my vision. I was sprawled on the floor in moments. By the time I righted myself, father had climbed the staircase and stood at the top, grasping my mother by the shoulders, shaking her.

'Get your hands off her!' I'd shouted, mouth full of blood.

'Stop this,' mother pleaded, eyes pinched closed, clutching the picture in her grasp as though it was her lifeline. I'd see later what picture it was. One of me and my parents together, happy as we once had been.

'Father,' I begged, 'please don't do this. Just let us go.'

'No,' he shouted back at me, still shaking mother. 'You'll never leave me. Never.'

What happened next was so quick

'Nikos,' Oli pleads. 'Breathe!'

I snap my eyes open, blinking away the memory for a moment of clarity. It's still there, lurking in my mind, ready to sink its claws into me and drag me back into it.

'It was all my fault, Oli,' I pant. My breath is coming short and sharp.

I don't see his reaction.

Instead, I watch as the phantom of my father pushed my mother from the top step, sending her helpless body tumbling down the stairs. Her scream cut short as her skull cracked against the two bottom steps. Blood pooled across the floor, spreading towards where I stood, helpless and afraid. All I could do was look down at the wide, terrified glint in her all-seeing eyes. Hair matted with blood, body bent, hand outstretched towards me, flashing me my first glance at the picture she'd gone back to collect.

She died because I made her run away.

'This is your doing, boy.'

I looked up the stairs to where father stood, breathing heavy, expression the mask of the monster I knew him to be. I didn't think. I only acted. I bent down, picked up a shard of glass from the shattered frame, and ran up the stairs to face him -

ARMS ENGULF ME, finally dragging me out of the memory. I leave it behind, refusing to see what happens next.

'Accidents happen, Nikos. The world is a terrible and cruel place. And sometimes, not everything has a cause.' Oli consoles me as my tears soak his linen shirt. 'It wasn't your fault. It was no one's fault.'

It was there, on the tip of my tongue, to tell him that he was wrong. My father had killed my mother in a fit of panic and rage. But I could never tell anyone that. If I did, it would only invite more questions.

As my father told me that day, his arm bleeding where I'd slashed him, his neck bruised black from the grasp of my hands. *'Your handprints are all over her, and now me. Tell anyone what I did, and* you *will be the one to be convicted.'*

It takes a moment for me to gather myself. When I do, I give myself a few more selfish moments of Oli's hold before I pull away, dust off the emotion, and regain control. 'I shouldn't have off-loaded that all on you. This is meant to be a nice break. A chance to get away. Instead, I'm spoiling it.'

'Nikos Adonis Ridge, I swear if you say something like that again, I will take you down to the beach and drown you myself.' Oli is deadpan when he threatens me, and yet I know he'd never. 'You're allowed to have emotions. I know you're used to being this super-star actor who's more robot than person. But remember, with me, you get to be someone else - your true self. We all have demons. Sometimes you banish them alone, and other times you need a little help.'

'Thank you,' I say, wanting nothing more than to forget this conversation. Yes, it has lightened the load a little bit, but not enough. I will never escape my haunting past - not when my father still uses it like a noose, tightening year by year.

When I ran away from home after my mother's burial, when the police case was closed and confirmed as an accident, I never looked back. My father didn't get in touch until he saw me modelling in a magazine. His demands for money got bigger and bigger the more gigs I got. Then, when the acting jobs rolled around, I was practically giving every penny just to keep him from ruining the life I'd created. Everyone thought I'd blown my money on drugs, alcohol, and women. I hadn't had the energy to combat the assumptions, but it couldn't be further from the truth.

Nikos Ridge, the mummy murderer.

Nikos Ridge, his father's son.

Nikos Ridge, the monster.

'There must be some nice memories here,' Oli says, cheeks reddening. 'I found some family pictures, and you looked so happy. Carefree. Let's focus on those for the rest of the day, shall we?'

I swallow the bile down. The idea of Oli laying eyes on my father, even in a picture, makes me want to burn the house down. But he wasn't wrong. We'd had a good life before father lost his job and turned to drinking, that's when the physical abuse started.

'There were a few,' I choke on a deranged laugh. 'Just so long ago that it's easier to ignore, you know?'

'I get it,' Oli says. 'I challenge you, Adonis, to tell me one memory that you love about your mother. Something you did with her maybe. Let's distract you, and help you remember the good times over the...bad.'

Impossible. But for Oli, I would try.

I clear my eyes with the back of my hand. 'Me and my mother, we used to cook together. In fact, it's thanks to her that I eat more than instant noodles and fried food every day. I'm not the best, but she taught me.'

'See. That's beautiful. What was the one thing you used to cook together that you have fond memories of? Maybe we can do it together, refresh those memories with new ones?'

The answer was easy. In fact, it was almost divine. I hadn't had the connection until Oli asked the question, but as I did my heart swelled in my chest, tripling in size.

'There was a dish, something sweet, that I think you'll enjoy.'

Oli leans in, leaning his head back to look up at me. 'I'm listening.'

'*Loukoumades*,' I say, cheeks pricking at the thought of them. 'They're like donuts, but Greek. But the best part about them…'

'Yes?'

'Is they are drizzled in honey, Honey.'

His smile is bright and overwhelming. I long to imprint it on my mouth and think of nothing else but the curves of his lips. 'That sounds -'

'Like fate?' I answer without thinking.

'Yes,' Oli replies, blinking at me, lost to the connection between me, him and my past. 'Like fate.'

Not wanting to think of anything but this, I take his hand and guide him to the kitchen. When we enter, I don't even contemplate the stairs. I think of nothing but cooking with Oli, making new memories that would last a lifetime.

It isn't until we are covered in flour, our fingers and lips sticky with fresh honey, that I remember that, one day, this memory will also haunt me.

All good things must come to an end, sometimes that end comes sooner than we hope for.

21

OLI

I CAN GET USED to waking up in Nikos' strong arms.

The next morning, the sun is streaming in through the open windows, and the breeze drifting in cools my skin. We'd talked late into the night, with Nikos sharing more memories of his mother and growing up here in Greece. I could tell that it was bittersweet, especially when he'd slipped up and said that he'd always wished that she could meet the person he'd one day fall in love with.

He'd gotten misty-eyed, and I'd done the best to hide the lump in my throat. Not just a reaction to his pain, but to the deep, aching *want* that pierced my chest.

I wanted to be the person he introduced to his family. I wanted to be the man to make Nikos Ridge fall in love.

What I'm not brave enough to do right now is put a name to the feelings that are growing inside my rib cage like the flowers gracing the garden. I've always been quick to fall for people, and I don't want to get hurt - not like with Geoff. And besides, I know full well that Nikos isn't mine to keep. We're on a deadline, not meant to last. All I can do is enjoy the here and now, and not let myself catch inconvenient feelings.

I don't want to break the spell of a sleepy Nikos, enjoying watching him breathing softly, his face completely relaxed. I want to trace the curve of his jaw with my finger, to memorise every line of him, but I try to stay as still as possible so as not to wake him.

I must move, though, or maybe the sun warming his skin is enough to rouse him from sleep. Nikos blinks awake, his golden-brown eyes catching mine.

'*Kalimera.*' His voice is lower than normal, rough from sleep. He squeezes me tighter, and I relax into his grasp. 'Did you sleep well?'

I reply in Greek, the words for good morning rolling off my tongue with forced ease. '*Kalimera, agape mou.*'

Agape mou - My love.

His tired eyes widen in pride. 'You remembered.'

'I did,' I say into his chest. I can't get over the way he smells, especially here - I could drink in his scent forever. 'Did you sleep well?'

'Mmm.' He makes a satisfied noise and buries his nose in my curls. 'How could I not with you by my side?'

My heart summersaults, and I have a hard time pretending that it's a flippant comment he's made hundreds of times with people he's slept with, not with how sincere he sounds. Not when I can feel the beat of his heart pick up as he presses a kiss to my hair.

'What do you want to do today?' I ask, trying to distract myself. I can't catch feelings. I can't.

'I thought we'd go into town for an early breakfast, and I can show you around.' Nikos sounds tentative, and I wonder if it's because town holds more memories for him, or because he's worried about being recognised. 'If that's alright with you?'

'I would love that.' I snuggle deeper into his embrace for a moment, allowing myself the luxury of being held. I had no idea that Nikos was such a cuddler, but he seems even less inclined to get up than me. But eventually I need to get up and use the bathroom, so I reluctantly free myself from his arms and get up.

When I get back from washing up and brushing my teeth, Nikos is in shorts and a linen button-down shirt with the sleeves rolled up, and I have to stop myself from staring. He looks like a movie star on set in Greece.

As soon as I have the thought, I mentally smack myself over the head. Nikos *is* a movie star, and we *are* in Greece.

I'm the luckiest man in the world right now.

'Ready to go?' Nikos raises an eyebrow at me, and I pull out shorts and a light cotton t-shirt from my suitcase, throwing them on.

'Whenever you are,' I say.

He leaves me reluctantly to wash up too, and when he's back I can't resist but kiss him, his mouth minty from toothpaste. He hasn't shaved since we got here, and the stubble on his jaw is tantalising. But for once I'm more interested in going out and doing something with Nikos than in pulling him back to bed.

His hands travel down my back to cup my ass, but he leaves it at that. He must be feeling the same way I am, because he pulls back and extends a hand. I take it and he leads me down the stairs - I'm careful to use the banister, not wanting to give him any anxiety - and out onto the gravel path that leads to the dirt road.

We walk in silence for a few minutes, enjoying the

breeze and the sound of the waves far below us. It's gorgeous and serene and private, and I wonder what it would have been like to grow up here as a kid.

'This is where I got my stage name from.' Nikos stops us when we reach the top of an incline in the winding road. He turns me back in the direction we came and points, and I take in the view. 'I used to climb it as a kid.'

There's a hill - a *ridge* - in the distance, a natural enclosure encircling the area where Nikos' family home is.

'I love that.' I lean into him, relishing how solid and strong he is. 'That even as you started a new life, you kept a bit of your old life with you.'

Nikos rubs a hand up and down the outside of my arm. 'I never thought about it that way. It's...nice, when you put it like that.'

'I'm happy to help.' Because I *am*. I like being the one here with Nikos as he confronts his past and reclaims a part of a place that clearly means so much to him. 'So what's your real last name?'

He doesn't even hesitate. 'Drakos.'

The trust in the confession warms me through. 'Thank you,' I say, and Nikos drops his arm from around my shoulders and takes my hand in his, squeezing. 'Nikos Drakos. It sounds right. It fits you.'

'It's a common surname in Greece. In fact, you'll laugh at this, but it translates to dragon.'

'Dragon?' I gawp.

'Or ogre.'

I can't help but smile. 'If your management finds out about that, they'd have a marketing field day.'

'No one will find out,' Nikos says almost too seriously, as if the mode is suddenly ruined. 'No one can find out.'

Anonymity is important to the rich and famous, but I can't help his reasoning is tied to the trauma of his childhood.

We keep on walking - it's not too far to town to walk, but it's definitely a bit of a hike. When we round a bend, I stop. There's a donkey standing by the side of the road.

'Is that a donkey?'

'Yeah,' Nikos replies. 'They're all over in this area. They're wild, but they're not going to bite, if that's what you're afraid of. Not unless you really annoy them, or you tease them with food you won't give up.'

'No, I love it. I'm not afraid.' I can't help my grin. I love animals, especially the four-legged sort. 'They just... wander around here?'

'Yeah,' Nikos says, his arm slung around my waist. 'They trim the grass and don't bother anyone much. It works out great for everyone. They like to be pet, though. Or at least they did, last time I was here.'

The donkey is, indeed, looking at us with a hopeful tilt of its head. Nikos looks down at me, a smile lifting the corners of his mouth. 'Do you want to?'

'Yes!' My enthusiasm makes him chuckle, but he takes a hold of my wrist with the hand not wrapped around my waist and stretches my arm out.

I squeal as the donkey trots forward and butts its head towards my waiting hand. I touch its velvety-soft nose and it makes a happy noise, so I keep going, stroking its forehead. I feel like Snow White, except in the middle of Greece.

'Do you know they have a button that makes their ears go back?' Nikos asks. I love the humour in his tone, so unlike the sadness in his voice yesterday.

'Huh?' I turn to him, pausing my petting, and the donkey nudges against my hand insistently until I resume.

Nikos looks at me, the edges of his eyes crinkled with his smile, and such a look of adoration on his face that it honestly almost hurts. He picks up my hand again and presses it firmly to the donkey's forehead. I break out into laughter when the donkey's ears go from upright to back behind it like airplane wings. The donkey looks affronted and gives a huff before it trots away to the side of the road to eat some more grass.

'See?' Nikos bends down and captures my lips in a tender kiss.

I wind my arms around the neck of this man who misses his mother, who likes animals, who can cook a mean honey donut, who takes a good five minutes to become coherent after he wakes up. It's like double vision. The real Nikos, versus the one that the rest of the world gets to see. I don't know how many people are gifted with the real Nikos. I'm honoured to be one of them, but in a way that feels like the sweetest kind of pain.

'My *Yiayia* used to sing a song to me, about a donkey with big ears.' Nikos closes his eyes, giving in to the memory. 'I used to remember it, but now, like the other memories, they're lost to me.'

There are tears pricking at the corners of my eyes, and I struggle to hold them back. Nikos notices anyway, pulling out of the kiss and running a thumb beneath my eyelashes to catch an errant tear.

'What's wrong?' He bites his lip.

I shake my head, not able to say much over the lump in my throat. The trust that he's put in me is incredible, the way he's let me *in*. It's a gift, to see the truth of a person, to get down to the heart of them. He's bared his soul for me, but it won't matter.

It can never matter, because he's Nikos Ridge and I'm just his secret, no matter how much I wish that wasn't true.

'Honey,' he whispers, pulling me into a hug. I blink against the linen of his shirt, trying to compose myself. 'I know. I know.'

And I believe he does, because I see the same pain, the same struggle, in his expression too.

'Come on,' I say, drawing in a shuddering breath. 'Let's go get that coffee.'

IT DOESN'T TAKE MUCH LONGER to walk into the small town. We find a café that has seats overlooking the ocean. There are fishing boats tied up at a nearby dock, and the shining sun and lapping waves help to melt away some of my melancholy. When a server drops off menus, Nikos translates for me since it's entirely in Greek, and I order eggs with feta and tomato, sprinkled with fresh oregano and a black coffee - or café. He orders fruit, making a joke about needing to maintain his godlike physique, and a fancy iced frape.

'I didn't think that hearing you speak Greek would be a turn on.' I trace the veins of his inner forearm with a finger. There's nothing more alluring in my book than a man wearing a shirt with rolled-up sleeves.

He laughs. 'If I knew, I'd speak Greek all the time. Maybe when we get home?'

'Yeah,' I say with a wink. 'When we get home.' I ignore

the way that the word *home* feels like a knife slipped between my ribs.

Nikos says a bunch of stuff in Greek as the older female waiter comes back to drop off our food, and she looks scandalised, telling him off good-naturedly as she takes food and drinks off her tray and places them on our table. I flush, wondering what he said, but the wicked humour in his eyes tells me I'd sink into the ground if I knew.

She leaves us to eat, and the intensity of earlier is gone I'm grateful. I can't afford to catch feelings and the light and breezy conversation as Nikos tells me all about the town we're in, how it's changed since he last came here, is the perfect distraction. The food is divine, and the setting is postcard perfect. There are cats sunning themselves on the sea wall, and families making their way to the beach to enjoy the gorgeous morning.

The café fills up, and a man wearing a priest's collar sits next to us and stares at our intertwined hands. For a moment I wonder if this town is small or religious enough that two men showing affection is a problem. But then he meets my eyes and gives me a small smile. 'Are you here on a honeymoon?' he asks in British-accented English. Not someone local, then.

I immediately flush at his question, tongue-tied with how much I want to answer *yes*. But Nikos gets there first, his hand tightening in mine. 'No. Just vacationing.'

'My mistake,' he says softly. 'It's just that you look so very much in love.'

There's a wistfulness in his voice that's unmissable, something deeper than simple loneliness. It makes me ache for the priest, the way that he smiles sadly at us. Like he wishes he was in our place.

Nikos' face goes tight, and my stomach drops. It has to be that the mention of love has made him uncomfortable. It's the reminder I need to get out of my head and back into reality. No matter what my feelings for Nikos may be, they're not what I'm meant to have.

'You're here for Mount Athos?' Nikos redirects the conversation, but at least he doesn't draw away from me. I take some comfort in that. I recognise the name of the holy mountain that Nikos told me about earlier, where religious men would go to make pilgrimages.

'Yes,' the priest says. 'My boat leaves tomorrow. I'm here to atone for something I've done. Or, well, in truth - I'm here to ask a question of God. And probably also myself. Whether keeping secrets like I have is worth it simply to maintain the path I thought I was always meant to take, or whether I'm denying myself the chance to live as God is giving me the opportunity to.'

He nods at our intertwined hands. 'Love is the only thing that makes life worth it. I can tell you have something special. Keep it.'

The priest stands up and puts a bill on the table, then smiles at us one more time. *'Adio.'*

'Harika pu se ida,' Nikos replies.

We're left alone, except for a crowd of monks passing by. Nikos doesn't say anything for a few long minutes, and then he shakes his head, like he's clearing a daydream. 'Can I show you around? We can go see the church where I was baptised - it's gorgeous. Really... gold.'

'Sure.' I stand up as Nikos pulls money from his pocket to leave on the table. 'Show me your town. I want to see all your favourite spots. I bet this is where you snuck your first kiss.'

I elbow him in the ribs, and he laughs again, grabbing me around the waist and tucking me under his arm as we walk down a narrow side street. 'And my first beer. And my first cigarette. And my first joint. But none of them are as good as my *favourite* first.'

Looking up at him, I see that adoration again. That contentment. That emotion that I'm too afraid to name, written all over his face. My heart skips a beat. 'What's that?'

'My first time here with you,' he says as he holds me tight, like he's never going to let me go.

22

NIKOS

I'D EXCHANGE ALL the money in the world just for the chance to immortalise this day. Our last day in paradise. Our last day before we leave and return to our normal lives - not the little pocket of peace we've carved out with one another. The chaotic, awful life I'd been living before.

Oli hasn't realised it, but he's become the best distraction for me. Since the episode the other day when I walked in and saw him on the stairs, I'd not thought about my father and his threats. It was an issue I'd solve when I returned to London. But here, surrounded by old memories whilst making new ones, I exist only in the moment. The lack of phone signal has been cathartic, and we've chosen to leave our phones in the house for the majority of the time.

Last night me and Oli - bellies full of fried squid, chicken gyros, and enough ice cream to sink a ship - decided to sleep on the beach. We laid out on sheets I'd brought down with us, staring up at the star-speckled sky.

In the moment, drunk on wine and sugar, it sounded like a great idea. But waking up to a seagull on my chest, starring daggers into my eyes, wasn't the wake up call I imagined.

'Be gone, demon!' Oli shouts, flapping his arms like a mad man. 'Do thou not knowith of whomith you... something something... sittith uponith?'

The bird gives a squawk and launches into the air.

'What on earth was that?' I ask, dusting sand and a few stray feathers off my bare chest. I'm covered in mosquito bites, but I feel happy to have last night marked on my skin.

'I was acting,' Oli says, lounging back beside me.

I draw him in close to me, planting a kiss upon his head. 'How did I survive all this time without you?'

'Luck,' Oli says, planting his lips on the curve of my pec. 'And a healthy dose of pretty-privilege.'

'You think I'm pretty?'

Oli looks though his pale lashes at me. 'Oh shut up, Adonis.'

His hair is lighter than it was before we came, likely a result of the sun-and-lemon combination he boasted about. Turns out, when he was younger and his family took him to the beach in summer, his mom would soak his pale hair in lemon juice as an attempt to get 'natural highlights'. I mean, it works, I guess. It brightens the blue of his eyes, the colour so vibrant it gives the ocean a run for its money.

'Last day today - ' I start, but I'm silenced by the press of lips to my mouth.

'I said, shut up.' Oli hovers over me now, so much that

I have to plant my hands on his thighs. With the sun over him, he's haloed in light. I can barely think straight as the rays highlight every pore and mark across his beautiful face. I want to touch him, trace his body with my fingers like I'm moulding him from clay.

'What would you do if I said 'make me'?'

Oli lowers his mouth to mine, pressing his torso atop me until we're practically fused together. 'That.' His lips move to my neck. 'And this.' He trails his kiss down my chest, my stomach all the way to my navel. 'And also this.'

Before his fingers tug at the back of my shorts - stained with splatters of ice cream from last night - I stop him. 'Ah, ah, ah. Who said you've earned that?'

Oli pouts, his pink lips shiny with spit. He's ravenous for me, as I am for him. But today is important, enough that I wish to draw out the inevitable as much as I can.

'Do you want me to beg for it?'

To prove that no begging is required, Oli palms the hardened length beneath my shorts. I have to snatch his wrist to stop him from making me come too quickly. 'As much as I enjoy the idea of you on your knees, I have something planned for today. To make our last day special.'

'Stop calling it that!'

'But it is,' I reply, huffing a laugh at Oli's dramatic flop back onto the beach. 'Is the idea of going back to work that painful?'

My attempt to make light of our shared depression doesn't work. Even as I say those words, I regret them. But it's too late - they're out in the open. Now I find myself waiting to hear how Oli will reply.

'I'll manage,' Oli says, and I feel something jolt in my chest. A pain that I wish to evict, but can't. 'You? Will you cope when reality hits us in the face?'

'A pair of black eyes, some bruises and broken teeth - I'd take a lot in exchange for this time spent together. It's worth it,' I say, because what's the point in sugar-coating it? 'Thank you, Oli.'

'For what?'

Existing. Being you. Helping me understand myself. 'Just thank you.'

'I was expecting some grand declaration of your love,' he replies, his pout now unserious and mocking.

'Well,' I sit up, sand falling down my sun-kissed arms. 'We have an entire day left. Maybe, just maybe, that declaration will come later.'

'What do you have in mind?' Oli asks as I stare out across the calm body of water before us.

'It's a surprise,' I reply, enjoying the control for once.

'If it doesn't involve more donkeys, Nikos Adonis Ridge Drakos, I will punish you.'

I snap my attention towards him, letting the devious ideas fill my mind. 'Careful, Honey. With a promise like that, I might need to change what I already have planned for us.'

He pounces on me, all feverish kisses and grappling hands. We tumble off the sheets, rolling around the sand until we crash, side first, into the gentle lapping waves. Turns out we will be a little late to my plans, because we don't stop laughing for close to an hour.

THE MIDDAY SUN beats down on us, hot and unforgiving. Surrounded by nothing but the endless sea, islands speckled in the distance, not a cloud in the sky, we're forced to hide beneath the canopy on our little boat.

Oli sits on the bench, his legs drawn up beneath his chin, wet hands turning the pages of his book as his hair drips more water onto the crisping pages. I've been watching him for a while, devouring the peach in the cool-box I'd prepared. The juices run down my chin and chest, but I don't care. I'm so transfixed by Oli - how his expressive brow is always responding to whatever scene he's reading.

Right now, his lower lip is caught beneath his teeth. I can only imagine the filth he's reading. I bet good money, though, that it doesn't compare to the thoughts I'm holding for him in this moment.

'You need to drink some water,' I say only when I know he reaches the end of his chapter so as not to interrupt him. 'Dehydrating all these miles from any land wouldn't be good.'

Oli folds the page down, marks his place in the book, and puts it down. He hasn't stopped smiling since I brought him to the jetty earlier and revealed my surprise plans. An entire day out at sea, with no one but each other for company. Food, drink, books, swimming. Everything he loved, combined into one experience.

My perfect day, though, simply requires him.

'And you need to try and get some of that peach inside your mouth,' Oli replies as he takes the bottle of water from the cool-box and lifts it to his grinning lips. 'You're wearing it.'

I look down, and he isn't wrong. My dark navy swimming trunks are soaked with peach juice - even the dark hairs between my pecs are tangled with sticky the liquid. 'Do you want some?' I offer.

'I do,' Oli replies, and I swear my dick leaps in my shorts.

'Here,' I offer the half-eaten peach, but Oli doesn't take it. Instead, he puts down the bottle of water, gets on his knees as the boat sways, and shuffles over to me. He eases himself between my spread legs, hands running up my shins and inner thighs.

'I wasn't talking about the peach,' Oli says.

I watch, helplessly in his thrall, as he extends a tongue and traces up over my abs. He groans as he clears the peach juice from my skin, not stopping until his tongue is dancing circles around my nipple.

'I don't - remember there being - juice on my - nipple,' I groan.

Oli laughs. 'Oh, silly me.'

I grasp his jaw and hoist him up. The peach is now floating overboard, being feasted on by fish. All I care about is tasting Oli, devouring him as I guide his mouth to mine. The sweet taste sparks across my tongue. I groan into his mouth, as Oli grinds himself atop me. Suddenly, we're arranged down in the boats middle, Oli sitting atop me just as he had this morning when we woke.

'Now, I should thank you for the most memorable last day.'

I lift my hips, enjoying the press of his arse against my cock. 'I thought we weren't calling it that.'

'What shall we call it then?' Oli says, pinning my arms down above my head.

'The magical day,' I answer, because it was actually something I'd been thinking about.

'Magical?' Oli echoes. 'I like that. But snorkelling, reading, jumping into the water and swimming with fish is great and all. But what would really make today magical, is you being buried inside of me.'

'Is that so?'

Oli nods. 'Isn't it custom to buy a souvenir when on holiday? Something to mark the occasion, so we'll never forget? This memory will be better than any magnet for my fridge.'

I had plans to buy Oli something to commemorate this trip, but I do something better. I reach into the bag beside me, fingers grasping the cool metal of a phone. It's his, because mine is still back at the house. I haven't touched it since we arrived. But Oli has his today, snapping photos of the boat and the waves and the view of the shore. Except he hasn't taken a single one of us. I know why - he's respecting my privacy. And yet, right now, I couldn't care if the world found out. If this was the life I could have, I'd trade it all, every bit of fame and fortune.

I swipe up on the screen, open the camera app and hold it to our side.

'What are you doing?'

'Smile,' I reply, clicking the button three times to capture Oli's natural surprise melt to happiness. I hand him the phone. 'Now you have something to look back on and remember today.'

His happiness shifts to something else. It lasts only a moment, but there is no denying the sadness which flashes behind his eyes.

'Are you okay?' I ask, already knowing the answer.

Oli fakes a smile, but it doesn't quite reach his eyes. 'Yes, of course I am.'

He shakes his head as if dusting off the emotion, but it's clearly sunk its talons in deep. 'If you would prefer the magnet as a memento, I'll get you one.'

Oli sits back, still on my hips, although I fear the sexual tension has ebbed away. He presses the phone screen to his chests, takes a deep inhale and sighs. 'I just... it's silly but... as amazing as this trip has been, I don't ever want to think about it again.'

I swallow a lump in my throat, wishing to do anything in my power to go back to pretending. 'I'm sorry if I ruined the moment'

'No, it isn't you. It's...'

'Us,' I answer.

Oli looks at me, truly looks at me, and I see the ocean reflected in those brilliantly blue eyes. 'Life doesn't seem as exciting without you in it, Adonis.'

His words sink into my flesh, carving themselves onto my bones. I know what I need to say back to him, but I can't seem to gather the confidence to say it. Oli takes my silence as a way of me not feeling the same. He gets off me, takes his seat back on the bench and gathers his knees back up beneath his chin.

'Honey,' I say, numb to my core. 'I love - ' I almost say it, but I don't. 'I've loved the time we've spent together. Every moment. Not just here, but back in London. Those are memories I'll never forget.'

'You will,' he says, sniffling. 'And you should. You're Nikos Ridge, superstar, heartthrob. You'll go home, meet a lovely woman, make headlines, and have a beautiful family. And I'll be forced to go back to work and stare at your face whilst working on the campaigns you're plastered all over. You can run away from me, but I will never run away from you, not even if I want to.'

It's my turn to kneel before Oli. I clamber up in front of him, desperately laying my hands on his knees. 'I'll come back to you. No matter what happens in life, no matter where it goes, I will always visit you.'

'As your little secret?'

I nod. 'You'll always be my little secret.'

Oli draws back. 'Dirty secret.'

My eyes widen and I know I've worked myself into this trap. 'No, not like that. I didn't mean it like that.'

Oli fakes a smile as if this had been some joke and he didn't care, but there was no hiding the true pain in his eyes. 'I'm playing with you, Adonis. We both have our own lives. This has just been a little bit of fun to tide us over. Real life was always going to come knocking, we both knew that when we got into this. We've always had an expiry date.'

'Oli,' I say his name as though I'm begging.

'I think I'd like to go back to the house now, please.' Oli stares out at the ocean, blinking rapidly. 'I've got to pack before tomorrow's flight. And anymore sun exposure and I'll get sunstroke.'

'We haven't finished this conversation'

'Yes,' Oli says too firmly, 'I have. Now please, Nikos, take me home.'

Take me home.

I want to tell him that his request is impossible when *I'm* his home. Or he is mine? The concept of turning my back on him is impossible, but I know the risks - I know what I have to do.

'If I could promise you one thing, Oli, what would you ask of me?'

He takes in my question. I find myself holding my breath, unsure how he will answer. When the words finally come out of his mouth, I feel my world shatter.

'Never come back for me,' Oli says, his harsh words contradicted by the soft hand he runs over my face. I sense his regret, his pain, and yet he still wants to offer me comfort. Like the kiss of a mouth, while a knife is stabbed through my chest. 'It will be too painful to see each other again. For the both of us. I want you to move on. Be happy.'

'Is that what you want?'

Oli looks away when he replies. 'It's best for us both.'

'What's changed?' I ask.

'Nothing changed, Nikos. We both knew this was coming. And as much as I have loved every moment too, it is best we save the precious memories and move on from them... before...'

'Before they become impossible to ignore?'

Oli blinks and a single tear runs down his face. 'Yes. Exactly.'

'Okay, Honey.' I push myself to standing, feeling sick to my core but not from the swaying boat.

'Okay, Adonis.' Oli offers that smile again and I swear it shatters my fucking heart. He extends a hand to me in offering. I don't know what it's for until the final word comes out his mouth. 'Deal?'

'Deal.'

Oli picks up his book, opens the page again and hides himself in the pages. Although this time, I know he's not reading. His brows don't move and his eyes don't linger over the lines. They stay glued to one spot in the book as he attempts to conceal the tears rolling down his cheeks.

I'd experienced heartbreak before, but nothing like this. As I navigate the boat back towards land, I feel myself cracking little by little, until the pieces of me are scattered across the ocean for the creatures of the sea to feast on.

23

OLI

I DON'T WANT to go home, but it's inevitable.

The process of pulling away from Nikos is unbearable, and I want nothing more than to kidnap him and go back to the little house by the ocean that we've spent five magical days in. But Nikos is needed back in New York for more publicity, and I'm needed back at work to continue promotion of the next book in the series.

There was a time when thinking about my work made me happy, but now it just gives me a pit in my stomach. All I want to do is avoid it. I don't think I'm ever going to be able to think about *An Age of Dragons* again without visions of Nikos lying in the sand, feeling the heat of his skin and the way his fingers traced my body. And that's going to be more of a torture than Geoff leaving me ever was. When my ex left, I knew it was the end of a relationship, the death of a vision of my life that was expected and stable and boring and perfect.

Leaving Nikos feels like the end of *me*. The end of the carefree Oliver who'd thrown caution to the wind to run off with a movie star. The end of the Oliver who was worth enough to make Nikos Ridge - Nikos *Drakos* - bare his soul and sweep me off my feet.

I'm going back to my sad, pathetic life, and I know Nikos will have no trouble moving on without me.

'Oli?' Nikos is sitting next to me in the car, and he nudges my leg with his foot. 'What's on your mind?'

I swallow hard. It's difficult to speak, and has been since we'd pulled up to the shore in our boat the day prior. Every time I try to talk, there's a lump in my throat stopping the words from coming out.

A few deep breaths and I manage. 'I'm alright. Just thinking about everything that's awaiting me when I get back. I'm sure it's a lot.'

We haven't really connected our phones to the internet or cell service, an unspoken agreement to keep the fantasy going for a little longer. When we get to the airport in Thessaloniki, there's going to be no excuse, but we can cling to the isolation for another hour.

I'm sure that there's a pile of emails waiting for me, not to mention all of my notifications on social media, but at least that will be something to distract me from the total, abject heartbreak.

Nikos reaches out and puts a hand on my thigh, and I take the comfort. I feel like I'm stealing something from him, since there's no way that this can continue on once we step off the jet in London.

'I wish it could be different,' he says. 'I really do.'

'I know.' I do. I can see it in every line of his face. 'But these is are our lives, Nikos. We can't play pretend anymore.'

He sighs, and his hand tightens on my thigh. I watch

the landscape roll by out of the car's windows, and wonder what would happen if we just ran away together. If we returned to being anonymous, the way he'd been before he left Greece. The way I'd been before he noticed me.

'*Agape mou.*' He presses his lips to my head and breathes the words into my hair. 'I'm never going to forget this week. The one week of my life where I could truly be myself.'

'Neither am I.' I swipe at my cheeks with the back of my hand, wishing that I wasn't so quick to cry. I don't want to waste the few hours I have left with Nikos being sad. I want us to go back to being Adonis and Honey, the way we'd been able to have fun with each other and take pleasure in each other's bodies before we'd come to know each other. Before the reality of Nikos being unable to be open about being with a man came back to bite us.

Before -

Before I fell in love with Nikos Drakos. The real him, not the one carefully cultivated for the cameras to see.

It's hard to even admit it to myself, but I do. I've fallen fast and hard, and no matter what I do, he'll always have a piece of my heart.

The rest of the car ride is silent, since we've run out of things to say that aren't sad or goodbye. I just sit with my head pressed to Nikos' chest and listen to his heart beating, memorising the way that his skin is hot against mine. The solid, reassuring presence of his muscular body. I don't beg him to stay, to reconsider, and I'm proud of myself. I just imprint all of this on my mind so that when he's gone, I can at least dream about this week.

The airport is busy, but the car drops us off at a private

terminal. We're at passport control before I know it, and Nikos shifts his bag off his shoulder. 'Can you hold this for a second? I need to get the passports.'

He gives me his cup of coffee and his phone, which is currently vibrating like crazy. I can only imagine the sheer number of notifications on every single platform that Nikos must deal with, if he has access to his own social media. I can barely handle it when one of my posts gets a few hundred likes, and I can only imagine what it's like when we're talking about the tens of thousands of comments and likes and everything else that are generated every time Nikos posts a thirst trap. Not that I can blame the people, not when I've personally had my hands all over the man's incredible body.

The coffee is hot, and the cardboard sleeves aren't doing nearly enough to stop my hands from burning as Nikos talks to the customs agent in Greek. I need to put them down, so it's a good thing there's a counter nearby. But as I juggle the coffee cups, I jostle the phone and the screen lights up. It's a bunch of emails coming in - from the subject line, they look like offers for more movies - and texts from his manager Selina.

One, though, catches my eye. I touch the notification, causing the rest to slow. It's a text with a picture attached, one which turns my world upside down.

The thumbnail is small, but it's unmistakable. I know it because I've owned that jumper for years, and combined with my unruly curls I know it's me.

Someone has sent Nikos a picture of me walking somewhere. And based on the coffee cup in my hand, I know exactly where I was walking to.

The blood in my body runs ice cold as I take it in. I'm

not sure how to deal with this - how did Geoff get Nikos' number? Why is he texting Nikos? I wonder for a moment if Geoff has been blackmailing Nikos too, if I've already been used against him. So I do something that's so out of character for me that it turns my stomach - I click on the photo. The phone asks me for a passcode, and I put in the numbers that I'd watched Nikos type in a few times before whilst we were in London.

It's a single text from a unknown number, along with one line.

UNKNOWN NUMBER
Pay up, or I'll take him away from you

I act without thinking. My thumb and fingers race across the screen, typing a short and very clear message back to Geoff.

Fuck off, you're getting nothing.

Once I see the message is delivered, I swipe the conversation away and delete it.

Nikos turns to me after handing over our passports, and I quickly lock the phone.

'Oli?' He looks at me with concern, frowning. 'Are you alright?'

'Yeah.' My voice is strangled even to my ears. 'Fine.'

He's going to hate me. My crazy ex-boyfriend is threatening him? Demanding money, after I already *stole* for him? I wish I could call Geoff up right now and tell him off, maybe even go a step further and call his mum to embarrass him. Or file a police report that he's stalking me to scare him. But that would give me away - there's nothing I can do until we're back in London.

There's a terrifying chorus that echoes through my head as we board our jet. That Geoff is going to out Nikos, or that Nikos is going to have to support Geoff's newfound drugs habit to stop his sexuality from becoming the topic of every tabloid. The horror of that, of not being ready to tell the world who he is and yet being forced into a corner to stop it from happening? That makes me feel like I'm going to pass out.

I got him into this mess, so I have to get him out of it.

My legs are wobbly as I walk up the stairs of the jet, and Nikos puts a hand to the small of my back. Even now, he's warm and trusting, looking at me with concern in his eyes. All the while, I'm the one who's going to hurt him. I'm the one who's already ruining his world.

We settle into the leather seats of the jet and the air stewardesses serve us cocktails. I gulp mine down while Nikos thumbs through his phone. His mouth twists down momentarily, but then he shakes his head like he's dismissing something. I hope Geoff hasn't texted back.

'Are you alright?' I venture.

'Yeah.' He keeps scrolling. 'I'm fine. Just someone being an asshole. Par for the course. Nothing I can't handle.'

You know when you can tell that someone is lying, even though they say that they're alright? I know, in that moment, that Nikos isn't telling the truth. That he's actually really, really bothered by whatever Geoff must've sent in response to my reply.

I'm about to nudge him with a foot and insist that he be honest, but he looks up, his smile bright again. I can't tell if he's acting, but if he is, it's good. 'Do you want to play one of my favourite games with Selina? It's called *how bad is the movie pitch that Nikos got in his inbox.*'

He's clearly trying to make the most of the rest of our time together. We've not spoken about it, but I know we're going to go our separate ways once we land in London. So I decide to grow up and seize the normalcy he's offering me. I drain the rest of my cocktail. 'Lay them on me.'

We spend a few hours of the flight laughing over the stupid movie ideas and the even stupider amount of money being offered to Nikos and getting steadily more drunk. I'm glad I'm not the only one who needs an alternative way of dealing with this situation. It's only when the pilot gets on the intercom and tells us that we're descending that I see Nikos get serious again.

I want to stop him as he kneels before me and takes my hands in his, earnest sincerity in his eyes.

'I wish I was brave enough to keep you,' Nikos says. The image of him on his knees in front of me is something I'll never forget. 'I wish I was brave enough to say *fuck it* and claim you as mine. But I'm doing this for you as much as for me. You don't know everything about me, and the secrets I keep? They could rip you apart. It's so much safer for you this way, Oli. Honey. It's tearing my heart out, but there's nothing more important to me than you being happy. And I can promise you, even with the fantasy we've lived out this last week, you wouldn't be happy with me. Not when you know everything. Not when you learn who I really am.'

All the fake good humour is gone, now. I can't contain my emotion any longer. The tears are flowing freely down my face as I cup his jaw in my hands. 'I don't know what you're talking about, Nikos, but I *have* seen the real you. You're kind and caring and smart and funny. You're protective of those you care about. You make me laugh. You're one of the sweetest people I know.'

'It's not everything.' Nikos shakes his head as he reaches up to wipe away my tears with a thumb. 'It's not the darkest parts of me. I would never expose anyone I lo- anyone I cared about to them.'

My stomach drops, and it's not just the plane descending. He almost said it in English. In a way that wasn't a cute endearment. In a way that sounded like he meant it.

And somehow it's a million times worse knowing that we both love each other, and still we're going to let each other go.

24

NIKOS

WITHOUT OLI DISTRACTING ME, I would've spent the entire flight fixating on Selina's text message. At first I'd wondered if Oli had seen it on my phone when he held it, but he showed no sign that something terrible was about to happen.

Paradise came crashing down around me. I fight the urge to pull out my phone on the jet, knowing that staring at Selina's message would taunt me.

> SELINA
>
> The press have photos of you with Oli
>
> They'll be leaked by tomorrow
>
> Fuck Nikos
>
> We are trying to stop them
>
> Call me ASAP!!

I hoped this was all some big joke. How had my father taken things into his own hands? I'd not spoken with him since before Greece, and my answer to paying him was still up in the air. And yet something has provoked him. After we land back in London, I'm following Oli down the jet's stairs, trying to locate the messages I last had from him. But I can't find the thread. It's as if the entire string of threats have self-destructed - father hiding evidence like he did all those years ago.

'Nikos,' I hear Oli call beneath the roaring engines of planes and commercial carriers. I don't look up until he shouts it again, this time with panic lacing his words. 'Nikos!'

'What?' I bit back, unable to hold my tongue.

Shock passes over his face. Oli is hanging out the side of a private car, beckoning me to follow him. Our bags were being loaded into the back already, and here I was, left standing at the bottom of the plane's stairs, dumfounded.

What I'd give to get back on that plane and fly away forever.

'We need to go,' Oli says, gesturing towards the terminal. I see them, a wall of photographers and fans banging on the glass in the distance. 'You're giving the audience a show.'

As if my life couldn't crumble any more than it already was, my phone vibrates in my hand. It's an unknown number and I know instantly who is calling me. I answer it, locking eyes with Oli at a distance, using him as my confidence.

Heavy breathing sounds down the end of the line. I speak before my father gets a chance.

'Meet me at my hotel. I trust you already know where that is.'

More heavy breathing followed by a gruff voice. 'I do.'

The line goes dead, and just like that, I have a date with the man who's haunted my life.

I get into the car and fake a smile, pretending like everything is ok when the truth is the complete opposite. My body buzzes with unspent energy, my mind racing with the possibilities. Oli rests a hand on my knee, but I peel it off and lay it in the seat between us.

'Selina already on your case?' Oli asks, voice quivering with nerves.

I stare ahead as the car engine starts. 'Something like that.'

Oli is a smart man. He can tell that something's wrong. Just as I know I'm retreating behind walls of iron and steel, hiding myself. No matter how painful this is, I'm doing it to protect him. This is necessary to ensure his life isn't affected by my orbit any more than it already has been.

I lean into the plastic partition separating us from the driver. One knock and he has the window lowering.

'Everything suitable for you, Mr Ridge?'

It's hard to swallow the lump in my throat when it's as dry as the sand back in Greece. 'Can you make a detour for me? I need to drop my assistant off first at the following address.'

I list off Oli's address, all the while he sits next to me and stares out the window. Even after the driver agrees and the partition goes up, we both don't talk. Oli continues to gaze out the window, while I stare at my phone screen, fingers shaking.

I don't realise we get to Oli's apartment until the door slams closed. I've been so engulfed in the folder of images

Selina sent. In every one of them, me and Oli are traipsing around the town in Greece. It wouldn't take a genius to see that the two men were enjoying each other's company are more than friends.

But what is worse is the message that followed those images.

> **SELINA**
>
> The leaks came with a message. Whichever media firm that will pay the highest price, they're promising photos of a scandalous nature

> Define scandalous?

> **SELINA**
>
> I'm sorry, Nikos. I'm attempting to put forwards our own offer but I'm being blocked. It would seem the leaker has higher ambitions

I want to vomit. I feel it in the back of my throat, burning acid. I go to open the window but look up to find the seat beside me is empty. Panic overwhelms me as I look out the window and watch the back of Oli disappear into his front door, lugging his suitcase behind him.

Gone, just like that. And he'd think I ignored him purposefully.

I fumble with my buckle, throwing open the door just as Oli leaves my view. His name claws out of my throat, a garbled, panicked shout. But he doesn't turn around. I'm left to watch as his outline fades behind the warped glass of the door.

I don't even care for the driver who is looking at me like I'm a madman. He has no idea. Maybe, come tomorrow, he will work it all out when every newspaper, magazine and blog has mine and Oli's faces - and probably far more than that - plastered all over them.

Unless I can convince the leaker myself.

Panic melts to fury until I'm simmering in the back of the car. Sweat beads across my brow, even sticking to the skin at the back of my neck. I don't snap out of the trance until I hear a crack in my hand. Looking down, a jagged line has spread across my phone screen. It splits the photo of me and Oli, set as my background, down the middle.

I played with fire, and this was what I get in return. But it isn't my life that I care about anymore. It's Oli I worry about. How tomorrow, if I don't solve this issue with my father, his life will be turned upside down.

Hounded. Stalked. The comments on social media. The hate and aggression. I brought this all to his door.

This is my fault.

This is my fault.

This is my -

'Nikos, this is your fault. I warned you, and you didn't listen. In fact, you taunted me.'

I sit still on the chair, clutching my glass of vodka and ice as my father towers over me. Even in his old age, with the deterioration of his posture and the grey hairs, he still makes me feel like a little boy.

'Don't treat me like a child,' I snap, knuckles pale as I clutch the glass, contemplating how hard I need to throw it to break his skull. The liquid sloshes as I lift it to my mouth and take a sip. It's more like a desperate gulp, because the glass drains and my throat is left burning.

'Then stop acting like one, Nikos.'

I peer up at him, longing to wrap my hands around his throat. I haven't had a real conversation like this with him in years, and I'm remembering exactly why. 'Why? Why are you doing this? I've given you everything you've wanted for *years*.'

'You just had to take that little slut to our family home, didn't you? Surely you knew what you were doing - taunting me, playing with me as if I am just some fucking toy like those helpless people you plough through. No. I'm your *father*.'

I lean forwards, trying everything to still my breathing. 'Call back the leaks.'

Father shrugs and then smiles. 'Your secret is out there. Even if I withdraw, the press has access to images that will taint your image forever. But better this secret than the other one, right?'

My heart is pounding. 'Don't threaten me.'

Father pulls a chair, drags it across the room, and plants it directly in front of me. He takes a seat, smelling like alcohol and stale cigarettes. No different to me, I suppose. 'Now. About that money. You're going to need to exceed whatever is given to me by my highest bidder. Otherwise, the next leak will not one that taints your career, but ruins you completely.'

'You wouldn't dare,' I spit.

'Do you wish to test that theory, boy?'

I hate how he looks at me as if he has already won. Even though he has and I know it, deep down I'm helpless against him.

'Fuck off,' I seethe.

'Goodness, Nikos. Your language is terrible these days. Whatever would your mother think of you now?'

I jolt forwards, blinded by rage, and crack the glass into the side of his temple. Father rocks back, flopping off his chair like the pathetic prick he is. Blood seeps down his face as it pours out of my palm. Shards of glass have embedded into my hand and scattered in father's thinning hair.

'If you ever speak of her, I will -'

'Kill me?' My father laughs, pushing himself up, face a mask of blood and enjoyment. He's smiling wider than ever before. 'It wouldn't be the first time, would it? Mentally sick Nikos Drakos, who killed his mother, attempted to kill his father, and then took his own life.'

The scar on my hand aches, the place where the broken glass I'd used to cut him had opened my skin too. It's not the first time he's threatened to kill me, and I'm numb to it now. 'Lies.'

'Perhaps,' my father says, standing up on wobbly feet, the blood pouring down the side of his face. 'But imagine what would happen now, if I went and re-opened the case *I* closed. Do you think the police would second-guess the accusation when they see what you've done to me?' Father smudges the blood with fingers, making the wound look worse than it is.

'*You* killed her, not me.'

'And yet it is your fingerprints that were found all over her. Not to mention the bruises on my neck and the gash the broken glass from that stupid picture frame made across your arm and mine.'

'You killed her!' I scream, breathing hard, my fists clenched.

My father leans in close until all I can smell is copper and beer mixed together. 'Because she was weak. Weak enough to listen to you and try and run from me. You can never run from me. Never. You're *mine*. I *own* you.'

'You're a monster,' I say, shaking like a leaf caught in a storm. 'I hate you.'

'Hate is the best motivator. Don't you think?'

I spit at his feet. 'You've got what you want.'

'Not exactly. There is still the issue of money. Money makes the world go round'

'Money feeds your habits,' I retort.

A dark thought passes through my mind. It wouldn't take much to kill this man. To actually complete what I tried to do after he pushed my mother down the stairs. I'm stronger now, taller and broader. My hands, although numb from the alcohol I've consumed, are large. It would take little effort to wrap my fingers around his throat and squeeze the life from him.

If I was asked what I wanted most in the world in that moment, his demise would have been the answer.

'You're the one who wanted me to come here,' my father says, snapping me out of the murderous thoughts. 'Did you come just to assault me, or do you have an offer for me, one so good I cannot turn it down?'

I step in, so close that our faces are inches apart. I enjoy the fact he has to peer up at me just to hold my stare. 'Do whatever you want to me. Take everything from me. My money, success, my life. But touch Oli, hurt him, affect his world in any way, and I will kill you.'

Father's eyes narrow on me. 'I believe you.'

'That isn't an answer.'

'You didn't ask a question. All you do is threaten me - your poor, helpless father who simply wishes for a relationship with his son. A son who poisoned his mother's mind and wanted her to run from me. A son who tried to kill me. A son who - for all intents and purposes - is the greatest disappointment of my life whilst also being my pride and joy. Look at you. All that fury, the drinking, the obsessions. You really are no different to me.'

'I'm nothing like you.'

'Say it with your chest, Nikos. I might actually believe you.'

I don't care if I make the issue worse. I lash out, grasp his arms and hold him so tight that my fingerprints will likely etch themselves into his skin. 'Actually, you're right. I am just like you. I hurt people, I cause them pain, and more importantly, I have it in me to kill.'

'More threats?'

I'm so close, I know my breath assaults him. 'No threats. Promises.'

'So...' he says, enjoying every fucking minute of this. 'What now?'

'Call back the leaked photos.'

My father mocks a shocked expression, pulls back and breaks my hold on him. 'Do you know what. I completely forgot that I already accepted an offer on the way over here. Gosh, it must be my old age.'

My eyes widen. I'm frozen to the spot.

'But don't worry. There are a few more photos I have... in fact, let me show you so you know I'm a man of my word.' He fishes out his phone, clicks as few buttons and then holds up the screen to me.

I see the photo. Blink. And then empty my stomach across the floor. Vomit spills down my shirt, across my trousers and shoes. I can't breathe or see as tears stream down my eyes.

The photo is of me and Oli naked in bed in his house.

'Tomorrow you will be faced with the entire world asking questions about you. But it is nothing a little press tour and some damage control can't solve. You have a good team around you - people you can rely on to fix all your issues. But if these photos...' Father begins to swipe left, showing me just how many there are. 'If these photos ever saw the light of day, say goodbye to your films, your promotions, commercials, sponsorships. But imagine what it would do to Oli. You can hide away in your luxury apartment, close the door and live a life you've always wanted. But Oli... what do you think will happen to him?'

I *am* imagining it. It would ruin him, being the subject of so much speculation and stalking and ire from fans.

My knees crack on the ground. My father watches, eyes now glaring down at me, reverting us back into the position of weak, pleading son and controlling father. 'Please don't do this.'

'You know what is required of you.'

'I'll give you everything - just don't involve Oli.'

'He involved himself.' Disgust passes over my father's face, the very same I saw just before he pushed my mother down the stairs. 'But you have the chance to save him. I'm not the monster you think I am.'

Aren't you?

'Take this as a warning, son. The next time you taunt me, the next time you test my charity and kindness, I will tell the world who Nikos Ridge really is. No matter how good the team around you is, I don't imagine they can 'damage control' the news that Nikos Drakos was almost tried for murder. That is one fire you cannot put out.'

'Why do you hate me?' I'm crying now, a mess of blood and tears.

'You tried to take my wife from me.'

'I didn't do that,' I reply, numb to the core. '*You* did that when you hit her, beat her, treated her like shit.'

Father kneels before me, just shy of my puddle of vomit. 'She was mine.'

'That isn't good enough of an answer.'

He reaches a hand and lays it on my cheek. His blood-slick fingers smudge across my face, the gesture fatherly but unwanted. 'And you belong to me too. I think you've forgotten this over the years, but I am so glad we got to have this reminder. Ever since Oli came into your life, you've suddenly thought you had the power to refuse me. Let him be a lesson. Do as I say, give me what I need, and you can have the life you ran away from me for. Test me again, I will ruin everything. Do I make myself clear?'

My chest rises and falls with furious breaths. I lock eyes with him, wishing to grapple for control, but knowing the chance for that is long gone.

I drop my head and reply. 'Yes, father. You do.'

He pats my head like a dog. 'Good boy.'

Then he gets up, gathers himself, and leaves me more broken and alone than ever before.

25

OLI

Leaving Nikos behind in the car was the hardest thing I've ever done. He made it so much harder by calling after me in a broken voice. I shut the door behind me before he could plead with me to stay.

I know that I wouldn't have been able to say no to him if he did. I would have said *fuck it* and waited for him to come in with me. I would have let this continue, because Nikos makes me weak.

But there's no way that I can keep seeing him, not when I'm the whole reason that he might be outed, his career ruined, his life in shambles. I'm not worth any of that, not even close.

I know that Geoff is only doing this to hurt me, because he doesn't actually care about Nikos. He's doing it for the money, and for the chance to upset me. And good on him - he's gotten both. He got a watch worth more than my annual paycheque, and I'm sitting here crying over the whole situation in the bath.

I'm very, very upset.

Unlike my usual routine when it comes to returning from travel, I've left my suitcase in the entryway. Normally I'd unpack it straight away, but I can't bear to catch Nikos' scent on my clothes. I don't want any reminders of what I've lost. Even thinking about the selfies on my phone hurts so much I can't breathe.

I sink into the bubbles, trying to let the lavender scent relax me, but it's no use. I just end up rubbing my eyes and getting suds in them, which makes me cry even more. It feels good to be letting everything out, but I also hate being a sloppy mess.

Visions of what Nikos must be doing now flash before my mind. I wonder if he's going to be upset too, or whether the mask he can put on so well extends to the ability to wipe his mind clean. I almost hope for it - I don't *want* him to be heartbroken. And besides, he was probably less love-struck than me, more clear-eyed about what the limitations of our time together were, and what the risks were too. I've always been a dreamer, and I shouldn't have let the fantasy carry me away.

There was no world in which we would have had a life together.

I lived my fantasy, and now it's time to go back to the real world.

THE NEXT MORNING IS ROUGH. I feel wrung-out and rumpled, and it's not just my clothes. I cried myself to sleep after eating an entire pint of ice cream, and now my head is aching and my stomach is cramping enough that I'm worried I'll be sick on the tube.

I don't think that any number of affirmations on post-its is going to be able to pull me out of this one.

Why is this heartbreak so much worse than when Geoff left me? I'm not sure, but I think that it has something to do with the fact that when Geoff cheated on me, I at least was able to cut the sadness with well-deserved anger. Now, there's nothing for me to focus on except the ache of losing a man I know I could have spent the rest of my life with.

Nikos and I did nothing wrong, except be the wrong people at the wrong places in their lives at the wrong time.

Work, at least, should be a way for me to take my mind off things. Megan must be able to tell I'm sad, because she sends me a picture of a box of donuts alongside a text.

> MEGAN
>
> These have your name on them when you get to the office

It's a relief, in a way, that she knows what's going on. I need at least one person to talk with and cry on who isn't going to further endanger Nikos. And given that Megan knows - and totally hates - Geoff, she'll have all the facts for when I come clean to her.

I drag myself out of the tube and towards the office lobby. I've forgotten my umbrella and it's raining, so of course I get soaked. The grey weather is such a contrast to the sun of Greece, but in a way it's a relief. I don't want even the weather to be reminding me of what I've lost.

'Darling.' Megan meets me at the elevator bank, and I wonder if she's been spying on my shared location to tell when I've gotten to the office. 'I'm here.'

She enfolds me into a huge hug, and I let myself sink into the woman who's not just my boss, but also my closest friend and confidante. 'I fucked up,' I mumble into her shoulder.

'I know, love.' She squeezes me even tighter. 'Let's go stuff ourselves with sugar and talk about it, yeah?'

My co-workers are all staring at their computers and no one even looks up when we walk past. They're all buried in a mountain of work, I'm sure, especially given that I've just abandoned them for five days right after the premier of the movie. I feel guilty about that, but I'm not going to say anything as Megan pulls me along, her hand in mine. When we get to her office, I slump onto the couch, my head in my hands.

'Out with it.' She shoved a donut on a napkin onto my lap and then sits next to me. 'Tell your bestie what's gone on.'

I groan, then shove the donut into my mouth with an aggressive amount of force. 'I fell in love with him,' I confess through a mouthful of crumbs and sprinkles. 'That's part one of how I fucked up.'

'Oh *no*.' Megan puts her arm around my shoulders. 'I see why you're so upset. Falling for the out-of-reach movie star who sweeps you off your feet to a tropical getaway, and then leaves - it's practically straight out of a romance novel.'

I put my head on her shoulder, breathing in the smell of her coconut shampoo. I normally love it, but now it just reminds me of the beach, and Nikos. 'I thought it was just going to be fun. A way to forget Geoff. I thought I'd be able to forget about Nikos when he had to go.'

Megan hums, and then pauses, like she's trying to

decide whether to actually say something. She takes in a deep breath. 'Oli, babe, there was no way that you were going to be able to let him fuck you and then walk away unscathed. You have such a good heart, and you're so open to love. It's not a fault, far from it. But sometimes it means you get hurt. All you can do is wade through it. Eventually, it's going to fade.'

'I knew the two of us could never be together,' I whispered. 'I don't know why my stupid heart had to go and catch feelings for someone totally unobtainable.'

Megan grabs another donut out of the box and puts it in front of me. I'm about to grab it when my phone vibrates in my pocket. I pull it out, irrationally hoping that it's Nikos texting to tell me this has all been a big mistake and that he wants to run away together to live in blissful anonymity in Greece.

It's not. It's so much worse. My heart shrivels.

'I'll be right back,' I say to Megan, handing her the donut back. She looks at me, confused, but I just mumble about needing the bathroom and hightail it out of her office and into the hallway.

I almost get to the bathroom, where I can at least have a little privacy to deal with this situation, but I'm stopped by Megan dashing out of her office and grabbing me by the shoulder. She yanks me back so hard that I almost fall, but my windmilling arms prevent me from hitting the ground.

'Megan!' I snap. She's pulled me with surprising strength right back into her office, slamming the door.

'There's an email from corporate.' She sounds numb, like she's not believing what she's seeing. 'I just saw it. Oli...'

If it was possible for my blood to run any colder than it already was, it would have turned to ice. I stare at her, at the way that she looks completely and totally devastated.

'What is it, Megan?' It's got to be related to the text from Geoff, the one I haven't read yet, but I can't bring myself to look at my phone as she turns hers towards me so I can see what she's looking at.

'They sent this to us because it involves Nikos, so that we could be aware.' She gulps, and I study the screenshot in the email she's showing me. It's from the Daily Mail, and it's a grainy photo of Nikos in Greece with his arm around a person - very obviously a man - whose head has been blurred out. 'But they don't know.'

They don't know like Megan knows, because only Megan knows that I went to Greece. That *I'm* the one in the picture with Nikos.

That I'm the one who fucked this all up for him.

My mouth is as dry as the Sahara and there's nothing I can say.

'Oli,' she says carefully, like she thinks I'm going to break. 'I think maybe you should take some gardening leave, yeah? There's no way that corporate is going to be alright with you having…been with Nikos, and until we're sure that information isn't going to come out, you should probably lay low.'

It's smart, but my eyes sting. I'm hurt - Megan was comforting me, and here she is throwing me to the wolves.

'I'll come by your place after work, alright?' She's got her arm on my shoulder. I still have nothing to say. 'I'll bring takeaway and we'll figure this out. I know some good crisis communications people if it comes to that.'

I nod like my friend-slash-boss didn't basically boot me out of a job, then turn automatically and pull open her door.

This is all so fucked. Nikos is going to be so upset, and I'm not even there to comfort him.

It's only when I've slipped out of Megan's office and taken a shaky breath that I pull out my own phone.

There's another text from that unknown number, the one Geoff used to tell me I needed to give him the watch. Except now it's a longer, more detailed threat about going to the media with the nudes he'd emailed me if I don't convince Nikos to pay him even more.

How fucking *dare he*.

Before I can stop myself and think rationally, I give in to the white-hot rage currently consuming me, from the leaks and Megan and gardening leave and having to let go of Nikos. I mash my finger into the call button, fully intending to give Geoff a piece of my mind. The spineless shit is done playing games, and I know that when I get fully angry at him, he's going to cave and stop this. He's going to leave me alone once I show him that I'm not an easy target, the kind he always liked to toy with.

I get up and start to stalk out the door so that the rest of the office doesn't have to hear me laying into my ex about threatening me with more nude pictures, but I slam into the janitor. He's standing in the aisle of the office, and his phone is ringing too. I hit the end call button reflexively, starting to apologise to the poor man - he's got a bandage on his head too, and here I've just jostled him - but the minute I look into his face I freeze.

I've seen that face before. I thought it looked familiar

because it was Nikos, just aged. Now, I realise that there was a second reason it's been familiar.

He's been emptying my bin for weeks and weeks, now.

The janitor's eyes are narrowed, and before I can make more unfounded assumptions, I test my theory. I step away, apologising profusely, and surreptitiously hit the call button on my phone again.

The janitor's phone rings. He looks like a deer caught in the headlights.

It all clicks into place. My missing keys, which vanished from my desk at work and reappeared there. The detailed knowledge of when Nikos and I would be together, and where. This man *broke into my house*. He *stalked me*.

It was never Geoff. It was Nikos' *father*.

Oh, *fuck*.

26

NIKOS

I'M drunk - utterly fucked up.

Selina is so focused on the multitude of emails, wi-fi calls, and texts that she doesn't care that I'm draining the airplane's bar dry. I clutch the tumbler, hand shaking beneath the tautly wrapped bandage. I can only imagine what my father's face looks like right now. My hand caught little of the shattered glass, but the damage is there and a sour reminder.

But the more I drink, the more I'm pleased with the scars. In fact, by my sixth whisky I'm almost sad that I have no other reminders of last night.

By the time I make it back to my seat, I can barely walk straight. I tumble into the lap of an expensive looking man, splashing the remains of my drink on his suit and computer. My drunk brain tells me I've just broken his computer, the anger across his face certainly proves it, but all I can do is laugh.

How can he care about something so trivial when my life is in pieces behind me?

'I'm so sorry, sir!' Selina sweeps in from seemingly nowhere. She's laying square napkins over the spillage, attempting to mop up my mess.

'Fucking drunk,' he spits at me, standing up with his arms outstretched as if displaying the growing patch on his grey suit. 'Leash him, would you?'

'Yes, I will.' Selina snaps around to me, eyes ablaze. 'Get to your fucking seat, Nikos.'

I'm hit by the power in her tone and double back. I mumble another wasted apology and flop into my seat. Already an air stewardess is fussing over the man who is pointing at me, his face red with rage.

I can see it in him, the desire to punch me. I lock eyes and silently beg him to do it. Knock me out. Put me out of my fucking misery.

The scene of the chaos in first class is blocked out by a body. My lazy eyes trace upwards until they land on an equally pissed-off looking woman.

'Hello, Selina.' I slur her name as though it can't fit into my mouth.

'Drink this.' She hands me a glass of clear liquid. I take it, hoping for vodka but getting water. I wince at the crisp bite. Before I can give up, painted nails anchor at the bottom of the glass and tip it up, not relenting until the entire thing is down my throat.

I slump back on the seat, mind swimming, chin and chest wet with water and alcohol.

'You're a mess,' Selina says, towering over me.

'Can you - ' I actually hiccup, making her anger intensify ' - leave me to sleep.'

I check the screen in front of my seat and see that New York is only two hours away. We're so close to home - to reality - that I want to sleep the rest of the way.

At least in sleep I can't think.

'What's happened to you, Nikos?'

I close my eyes, hoping to ignore her but find the words tumbling out of me. 'I fell in love and was reminded I'm not worthy of it.'

I can't see Selina's reaction, but I hear it. She sighs. 'Oh, Nikos. When will you learn you're worthy of what you allow yourself to have? Start treating yourself with kindness, and maybe you'll understand that. Keep punishing yourself, and you're right. You can't love someone if you don't love yourself.'

In the dark of my closed eyes, my mind conjures faded images of Oli. I try and grasp onto them, but he slips through my mind like sand through fingers.

'How bad is it?' I ask next.

'Well,' Selina slips into the seat next to me, laying a hand on my knee so I know whatever she is going to say is bad. 'Every major and minor news site currently has your face plastered everywhere.'

'Fuck.' Hiccup.

'Luckily, our last counter-offer worked. Although the news is out that Nikos Ridge was seen in Greece on a romantic getaway with a man, they haven't linked it to Oli. Anonymity laws in England are strong enough that we were able to blur his face and protect him.'

I smile into the dark, not bothering to open my eyes. 'Good. This is good.'

Even though my father has won, I was still able to protect Oli. He may not know it, but I do. That eases some of the guilt, but not all of it.

'And damage control, what are... are they saying?' It's becoming hard to form words. With my eyes closed, my mind sloshing in alcohol and my stomach as empty as a church for sinners, I know sleep is close. Not sleep as I need, but a comatose state I can drink myself into.

'A couple of days of solitary confinement for you to gather yourself, then you're on a press tour to explain yourself.'

'Is loving a man such a terrible thing?'

'No,' Selina says, softly. 'Not at all, and please don't think I think that way. The issue is the fact that the second film going into production was riding on your proving your chemistry with your co-star. Everyone went wild over Armin and Gwen on screen, and it's your romance that is going to draw people back to seats in theatres. She is willing, for a price, to stand by your side during this time and keep up the flirtation we had going before the first movie.'

My stomach churns again with memories of how I'd had to act even off-screen to sell the 'romance' that was the heart of the movie. My co-star was fine enough, but right now I can barely even remember her name - let alone conjure a single shred of desire for her.

'She'll be meeting us at your first appearance with the host of *Mornin' America*,' Selina continued. 'You'll explain that the man you were seen with was a childhood friend, and that it is simply good-old-fashioned Greek touchy-feeliness between utterly platonic and definitely not gay mates that got you into this mess. Convince every straight woman in America it's nothing to worry about, just some very European...close hugging, and you'll convince the board at the production company to sign off on the second film - '

'I don't want to do it,' I say, peeking open my eyes enough to see her.

'I know, but you need to.'

'Because I'm broke.' Or near enough as of this morning, when I wired away the majority of my bank account to pay off my father. To keep him silent about my attack yesterday, to stop him sharing scandalous images that would ruin Oli's life - but most of all, to stop him from bringing to light the case of my mother's tragic demise.

'Because *we're* broke,' Selina corrects. 'If you don't work, it's the end of the line. Especially if Mr. Grey Suit over there presses charges that a drunk and careless Nikos Ridge assaulted him during a flight. We can sugarcoat some secrets, but not all of them.'

I roll my head over to face Selina, my neck aching at a strange angle. 'The more I work, the more money I get, the more my past will haunt me. Being broke makes me boring. I don't want the money, I don't want the fame - if it means I get... I get...'

Get what? Peace, quiet... the list is both short and endless.

'What do you want, Nikos? Tell me and I'll make it happen.'

I close my eyes again, giving into the quiet rush of alcohol induced silence. I have no control over my mouth in this state, which could lead me to more trouble than it's worth. But I hear my voice, broken and pained, reply through the roaring in my mind.

'I want Honey.' Tears roll down my cheeks. 'I want Oli.'

27

OLI

It must be the panic, because I do something I never would have done in my normal life. Instead of letting the janitor bolt like I clearly should, I grab the phone out of his hand and *run* towards the back of the office.

Good thing most of my colleagues are wearing noise-cancelling headphones, and even better that they're used to Megan and I screaming and getting up to God knows what on a daily basis. Otherwise, they might find it *very* suspicious that I ran into our janitor, started squealing, and then ran back through the office with him chasing me.

Megan is standing outside her office door, staring at me, and to her immense credit when I shriek 'get him!' she doesn't even hesitate to run after us, her heels clacking on the tile floor. I barrel into one of the spare recording booths at the back of the office - which, it isn't lost on me, is an honest-to-God converted janitor's closet - and Nikos' dad is right on my heels, grabbing for the phone that I've got clutched to my chest. I can feel his breath on the back of my neck and smell the alcohol. How did we never notice that our janitor was a blackmailing drunk asshole?

The door slams, and Megan screams 'got you!' I turn just as she tackles the guy to the ground, which is doubly impressive considering her six-inch heels and perfectly fitted trousers.

The janitor falls to the ground with a thud, his breath whooshing out of him, and I look around the small space. There's a chair in front of the recording setup, and a pile of cables sitting on top of it. Blessedly, there's also a pack of zip ties, like someone was in the middle of doing cable organisation and just gave up.

Actually, that was me, two weeks ago. I thank myself for my foresight and kneel down next to Megan, who has the guy in a very impressive headlock. Her lip is split and bleeding - he must have gotten in an elbow to her face, which makes me ill just thinking about.

If I have anything to say about it, this guy is done hurting the people I love.

'How do you know how to do this?' I pant as she wrenches his arms behind his back for me to zip tie. I do up his wrists as tight as I can without cutting off the circulation, then make the ties just a *little* bit more snug. The fucker deserves to suffer for everything he's done to us.

'Judo.' She grins, and for a minute I'm just a tiny bit terrified of my best friend. 'My ex did it, and she had thighs that could crush your head, and watching her throw people on the mat was *so hot* - '

'Now's not the time!' I squeak as she gets off Nikos' dad's chest and hauls the guy to his feet. Together we drag him to the chair, wrists bound, and shove him down. He's snarling at us, but Megan holds him in place while I zip tie his kicking feet.

Once he realises that he's good and stuck, the fight goes out of him - or his body, at least. He turns to me, grimacing.

'Who the fuck do you think you are?' he growls. His accent is a thicker version of Nikos'.

'Someone who cares a fuck-ton more about your son than you do,' I snap. I hold the phone up in front of him, dangling it before his face. This is the phone he must have all his blackmail on - and I'm sick thinking of how long this has been going on.

Megan straightens her hair, tucking a strand that's flown loose into her bun. 'What do we do with him now?

I eye the recording setup, and a plan starts to come to mind. I've read so many dark romances that I practically have a PhD in blackmail.

'We're going to fuck him up.' I say, pushing my hair out of my eyes and heading to the camera. 'So badly that he's never going to hurt anyone again.'

'Oh please.' The guy rolls his eyes. 'What on earth could the two of you *possibly* do to me? I have so much dirt on you, Oliver Cane, that I can ruin your life with the push of a button.'

'I know exactly what to do,' I say as I turn the camera on and hit record.

'Ah.' I can tell the moment Megan gets it because a smile spreads across her face. With the blood from her split lip, it's terrifying. 'Classic.'

'What are you talking about?' Nikos' dad has gone from dismissive to just a tiny bit intimidated. I don't blame him - Megan looks like she's ready to crack some skulls.

'Don't mess with bitches who read,' I snarl. 'We know *every trick in the book.*'

Megan laughs, and it's so evil that I laugh too. I've always been a side character, someone who doesn't take things into his own hands or take risks. But Nikos changed that.

For him, I want to be the hero of the story.

I hold up the phone again. 'I have this, and I'm very sure that it contains evidence of *numerous* crimes. So you're going to tell me *everything,* and I'm going to record it. And if you do, I won't go to the police right now with all of it.'

He gapes at me. 'How do I know you won't still go to the police?'

I shrug. 'You don't. But something tells me that you're really familiar with blackmailing people and then going back on your word, so I think this is actually just karma.'

He blanches, and for a moment I think he's just going to clam up. But then Megan steps out of her heels and picks one up, hefting it experimentally. 'How much damage do you think a stiletto to the eye would do?'

God, I fucking love my bestie.

'Ok.' He licks his lips, sweat breaking out on his brow. It's just like I thought - he's actually a coward. Once he isn't able to hide behind threats, once he's actually put in a position where he doesn't actually have the upper hand, he's crumbling. 'Here's what happened.'

It takes thirty minutes for me to wring the entire confession out of Nikos' dad. The worst part is when I start asking about his mother's death. That makes my stomach churn, because he's almost *proud* of the fact that he pushed a woman down the stairs and killed her in front of her own kid - and then held it over Nikos' head for his entire adult life, claiming that he would press charges and reopen a criminal case that would ruin Nikos' life, and maybe end with him in jail for a murder he didn't commit, of a woman who he still mourned.

All the while, Megan is tapping frantically on her phone. When I'm done and end the recording, she looks up at me. 'Selina sent me Nikos' itinerary and a plane ticket for you. You have three hours until your flight leaves - you better get going.'

My eyes sting with the tears that are threatening to spill at the way that she's supported me without question. I wrap her in a hug. 'Thank you.'

She squeezes me back. I pull away and look to Nikos' dad. 'Call the police. Tell them that the janitor pulled you in here and assaulted you. Your lip is proof that you fought back, and then you zip-tied him to the chair using your badass judo skills.'

'What?' Nikos' dad's eyes bulge out of his head. 'You said you wouldn't if I confessed!'

I shrug. 'I said *I* wouldn't. Megan is her own woman.'

She laughs, and I do too. I'm going to make this right. 'I'll let you know when I land,' I say, pressing a kiss to her cheek. 'Thank you for everything, really.'

'Go get your man,' she says, and so that's what I do.

28

NIKOS

My co-star, Michelle, sits beside me, so close I can smell the overwhelming kiss of her perfume. It chokes me. Even the slightly cracked-open window cannot alleviate the stench. Then again, I know why she's done it - it overwhelms the smell of alcohol that clings to my skin, my hair. Hell, the suit I'd rocked up to the TV studio in still smells of last night's mistakes.

Once H&M - hair and makeup - fix me up, smudging concealer over the shadows beneath my eyes, trimming my unruly hair and spritzing my neck with some matching obnoxious aftershave, I will get changed, follow our chaperone and begin to weave yet another lie around my life.

There are so many that even Charlotte would be jealous of the web I've woven.

I clutch the script in my hands, unable to focus on the swirling mass of ink on the paper. Selina had given it to me, reluctantly, on behalf of our management. Michelle has one too. And from the way she is memorising her lines out loud, I want to scream or punch the mirror before me.

'...Nikos was so kind to take my dearest brother to Greece with him. I would've been in the photos, but my kind-hearted *fiancé* had booked me in to a five-star spa in the hillside.'

I could vomit. Which, as it turns out, is something I'd already spent my night doing. I'd reached the point of alcohol consumption where my body rejected it. And no matter how much more I drank, I just couldn't keep it down.

I can't control my life, what makes me think controlling my body is any different?

I press my fingers into my eyes until I see shapes in the dark. 'Michelle, please. Shut up.'

'Oh, he speaks!' she scoffs, the script crinkling in her fist. 'Do I need to remind you that I'm here to help?'

'I didn't ask for your help.'

'Grow up, Nikos. Stop playing the victim.'

You have no idea. 'How - how much are they paying you?'

They being the big-wigs behind *An Age of Dragon*'s sequel film.

'To save your arse from the embarrassment? Hmm. Not enough, clearly.'

I watch her reflection shift from disdain to pride. Michelle flicks her hair over her shoulder, forcing that ungodly scent to stuff up my nose. She's looking back at the script again, smiling to herself.

'You know, Nikos. A lot is riding on us being able to work on a second film. I hardly think the fans are going to want someone of your...ilk leading the role. I told them

THE ACTOR AND HIS SECRET

just to re-hire, write it into the script that the original Armin Wolfe died in some horrible accident, and you had to be replaced with another dragon rider. But alas, they want you or nothing at all. So here I am, like your knight...ess in glittering armour. Come to save you from your *dirty little secret* ruining your life.'

I blink and see red. I tell myself I'm not an aggressive man, but that would be a lie. I am my father's son, and he is a killer.

My fist strikes the mirror, shattering glass. Michelle erupts in a scream so brilliant, it's like she's trying to prove her skills as an actress for award season. Shame those skills were lacking during filming for *An Age of Dragons*.

She's sobbing now, fumbling away from me like I'm some kind of ogre. Blood seeps across my shattered knuckles, splashing on my suit and the floor beneath me. 'Don't you ever - say that - again.'

Dirty little secret. Oli is nothing of the sort. He's not someone or something to be ashamed of. *I'm* the problem. *I'm* the one with secrets so dirty they'll taint my life forever.

'Fuck your film,' I spit, seething as the door flies open and Selina rushes in, followed by security guards and show runners. Michelle flops into Selina's arms, but Selina promptly pushes her off into the arms of a security guard.

'Nikos,' Selina spits, arms raised as though she is wrangling a dinosaur in Jurassic Park. 'Calm down.'

I can hardly think, let alone breathe.

'Fuck your sequel. Fuck your job. Fuck everything.'

Selina snaps around to the hysterical Michelle. Miracu-

257

lously, there are no tears on her beet-red face. And yet she wails like she's just been told someone died. The only thing dead is the chance of her helping me.

'What did you say to him?'

It takes me a moment to actually register what Selina just asked Michelle. When the actress doesn't formulate a reply, Selina shouts at the security team. 'Get her fucking out of here. Now.'

They listen, as though she's the one paying the bills.

'Fuck you, Nikos Ridge.' Michelle finally finds her voice apparently, just as the door begins to close. 'Fuck you, and your dirty little secret. May it ruin you forever.'

'We go live in three minutes,' one of the show-runners says, her eyes wide with panic and shock.

'I need two,' Selina barks back.

As the door clicks closed, I feel the adrenaline fade away from me like a tide drawing out from shore. I sag forwards, breathless, hands on my knees, trying to stem the ache in my skull.

Selina is beside me, arm wrapped around my side, guiding me back to the chair. Glass is scattered all across the seat and make-up desk, shards speckled alongside glitter. Just like the shards of broken glass that signified the death of my mother, and the attempt I'd made on my father's life.

Scattered shards just like me. Broken into so many pieces there's no hope that I can ever be put back together again.

'I can't do it,' I mumble, voice broken.

'Can't, or don't want to?' Selina asks.

'Both.' My ribs ache as though someone has taken a hammer and slammed it into them, over and over.

'Nikos, listen to me. I need you to hold on for only a few more hours, okay?' There's a hope in her voice that is almost infectious. But I have to care about my life to allow that hope entry into my soul.

'I have nothing left to do this for. I go out and lie, and I'm not only disrespecting myself, but Oli. I can't do it to him - I won't. Both.' I know I'm not making sense, but the words come pouring out of me. 'But I have to protect him. I brought demons into his life. How do I protect him from them when I can't even protect myself?'

Selina clasps her hands on either side of my face, thumbs gently stroking my skin. Her eyes bore so far into my mine that I'm sure she sees the truth of my soul. Then she replies, words so cold and honest I believe them.

'I know,' Selina says, tears slipping down her cheeks. She looks sad and furious, blended into one.

'You know?'

Her jaw grits, muscles feathering. 'I know. Everything. Which is why I'm asking you to just hold on, a few more hours, and I promise it will all work out.'

'How can you promise me that, when this is rock bottom? When there is no further depth I can possibly sink to?'

'Because - ' Selina takes a deep, rattling inhale as a calculating shift passes behind her eyes. 'Because there is somewhere you can go. Welcome to rock bottom, Nikos Drakos. You feel that floor beneath you? Push up. That is where you go. Use all that anger and grief, and fucking push up. Kick. Fight. But don't you dare give up now the floor is beneath you and you *finally* have something solid to launch off of.'

Her words settle over me like the cool kiss of snow. I

long to close my eyes and lift my face to the sky, soaking them in.

Selina uses my name. Not the one she'd only ever known me by, but the one I was born to - the true secret I left behind. My eyes snap open, and I see her nodding, as if reading my mind. But before I can question her, there is a hesitant tap at the door before the show-runner pops their head around.

'One minute to go,' they say, biting nails.

Everything is happening so quickly. I look to Selina for support, knowing I will always find it, no matter what.

'If you can't find the strength to push up yourself, do it for someone else. Do it for Oli.'

For Oli.

'Forty-five seconds. And please, do something about his bleeding hand. It's morning television.'

'Then get out,' Selina snaps on my behalf. The door closes. The timer is counting down.

'Ready for a quick change, Mr. Drakos?'

I swallow hard, unable to shake her previous words. *For Oli. Do it for him.*

'Into whom?' I ask, 'Nikos Ridge? The fake persona?'

Selina shrugs. 'To be honest, I don't care. You decide who steps out onto the studio floor. This is your story, Nikos. Write it. Beginning, middle, and end. Just make it fucking epic. Can you do that?'

Can I do that? It's a question I've never even contemplated. But I know the answer. I know now what my lies will ensure. Oli's safety. Oli's protection. I will do this for him, because he reminded me of who I truly was, outside of Nikos Ridge, the actor.

'Michelle?' I ask.

'I get the feeling you're on your own on stage,' Selina says, 'but you know that is never the case in life. Not when I'm around. I'll be there, stage left. You need me and I will come out on that stage and save you.'

'What would I do without you?'

'Figure that out later.' Selina winks. 'Time to show the world the person you want to be.'

29

OLI

THE PLANE CIRCLES around JFK airport for fucking *ever* before it lands.

I'm bleary-eyed through the descent, the flight one of those weird red eyes where it lands still practically in the middle of the night. It's going to be 5am in New York, but my body is all messed up with the combination of adrenaline and exhaustion.

It doesn't matter. I'm going to see Nikos.

The moment the plane touches down on the tarmac, I'm up and out of my seat, clutching my backpack and ready to pull my carry-on out of the overhead bin. But then an air stewardess glares at me, and I sit back down sheepishly. When the pilot comes on the intercom to announce that we need to wait for a gate, I start to get anxious.

I check my watch - it's nearly 5:15am now. I'm going to have to sprint through the airport and pray that I get a cab quickly and that there's no traffic. The morning show tapes live at 7am. I have to catch Nikos before he goes on the air.

I need to tell him that he's safe. That we caught his dad and cornered him. That I have the evidence on my phone, and it's also been sent to Megan's computer and loaded onto her hard drive and a USB, as well as uploaded to the cloud. We're taking no chances with this one. Nikos' insurance is as safe as can be.

The first thing I check on my phone is the mornings news. Pain cramps in my gut as I see that Nikos is set to reveal a big secret live on air today, and all signs are pointing towards an engagement. Half of me wants to die, knowing this is what my presence has pushed him towards. But I know it is the price to pay. If only I can tell him that he is free from his fuckstick of a dad, then maybe he can see that his life is his own to do with as he pleases, with me or not. If this engagement to his co-star is actually what he wants, at least he can make that decision with a clear mind.

There's a heavy weight in my pocket, and I can't wait to get rid of it - the watch I stole from Nikos. His dad was wearing it when we caught him, hidden under the cuff of his janitor's uniform. I bet that he just hadn't had time to pawn it yet. I'm relieved that I'm going to be able to give it back to Nikos and make things right - I didn't end up hurting him after all.

I'm going to fix this whole fucked-up situation.

The way the plane inches to the gate is excruciating. I'm bouncing my leg up and down as if that could make the plane go faster.

'You look like you're excited for your trip.'

I almost jump as I turn to the old lady sitting next to

me. In typical grandma style, she's spent the entire flight knitting an enormous scarf. It's heathered grey and looks incredibly soft.

She eyes me through her thick glasses, her hair pulled back into a fashionable bun. 'Or, on second examination, are you visiting someone in hospital? Because you look like you're about to vomit all over this plane.'

'I think I have to go confess my love for a man I met two weeks ago on national telly,' I say without thinking. 'Before he makes the biggest mistake of his life.'

'Oh!' The woman puts down her now-finished scarf and pulls out a little notebook and pen. 'What channel?'

'Uh, I think it's *Mornin' America?*' The plane inches forward a little more, and I almost get out of my seat again when I feel it jolt, the plane connecting with the walkway. I bite my lip, looking at my watch again, counting the minutes.

'Ah, young love,' the grandma sighs. 'How exciting!'

So exciting that I feel like the vomit emoji personified. Which is really more like abjectly terrified. 'Yeah,' I manage weakly. 'Exciting.'

The boarding door opens and people start to get up. Just before I get out of my seat, something warm and heavy lands around my neck like it's trapping me.

'Everyone about to make a public declaration of love needs a scarf,' the grandma says. 'It's the law here in the United States, and you know they take their laws seriously.'

She winks at me, and my throat tightens as I touch the scarf. 'Thank you.'

'Now go!' she says, making a shooing motion. She

stands up, barely reaching the top of the seats. 'Let the boy through! He has to go confess his love on the telly!'

She screams it loud enough that everyone turns and stares at her. My face is flaming, but I take the chance. I grab my carry-on, sling my backpack over my shoulder, and bolt off the plane.

———

GETTING through the airport was a total nightmare. I get lost twice in the crush of people as my watch edges closer to 6am. I don't even have time to stop in the bathroom to make sure I don't look like a corpse - I dash right through the crowds and to the taxi stand. The line is a mile long, and I practically dance in place with nerves as I wait my turn.

I pull out my phone, which has now loaded the text messages from Megan that were sent during the flight. She must have been up all night. I'm now on a group chain with Selina, the two of them pinging updates back and forth.

I eye the last one from Selina. *Bit of a situation. Nikos freaking out. We're off to the studio but it's not going well.*

Don't worry, Megan had said back. *Oli's on the way.*

I am. I get to the front of the line and fling myself into the back of a cab, suitcase and all.

'Broadway and 44th street, please,' I gasp out. 'Times Square.'

The cabbie doesn't respond, just pulls out from the curb so quickly that I'm pressed back against my seat. I nervously check how long it's going to take to get to the studio. 45 minutes, *fuck*. It means I'll get there right as they start taping.

We inch through traffic, which appears to be caused entirely by a truck sitting in the middle of the road, surrounded by cones, with workers holding signs saying *slow* for literally no discernible reason. By the time we reach the city, morning traffic has started up in earnest, and the number of stoplights we hit and the number of pedestrians we have to wait for makes me want to shake apart.

I've never been to New York City, but I couldn't care less about the view or the sights or whatever. The enormous LED screens of Times Square make me feel like I'm going to have a seizure, or maybe that's just the lack of air from the crippling anxiety strangling me.

I need to get to Nikos. I need to make sure he's alright, because right now, he's very clearly *not*.

We reach the TV studio and I just about die when the credit card reader takes forever to process my contactless payment. As soon as it clears, I'm shooting out of the cab like a bullet, my suitcase wheels not even touching the street. The security guard looks alarmed and holds out an arm to stop me, but there's a production assistant standing there with a clipboard and a set of headphones on. 'Are you Oliver Cane?'

'Yes,' I pant out. 'I am.'

'We're rolling,' they say. 'Come with me, quickly now.'

The security guard relents and the production assistant grabs my suitcase handle, speeding us through the lobby's security barriers with the flash of a badge. We get into the elevator, and head to the top floor of the building. There's a little television inset into the elevator wall, and I see

Nikos on it. He's sitting on a couch, looking more terrible than I've ever seen him. Tortured, like everything that's happened has taken him to the bottom of the ocean.

It's ok, I tell myself. *I'll pull him up to the surface.*

'This way.' The production assistant grabs me by the scarf and tugs me along, and we're at the side of the stage and Selina is there.

'Oh thank fuck,' she whispers, hugging me. She shoves some blank cue cards into my hands, along with a marker. 'They're taping, but for the love of God, tell him how you feel, Oli. Help him find a reason to be his real self. The self he is with you.'

Her eyes are shining with unshed tears, the only crack in her otherwise perfect facade. It's clear that she cares about Nikos far more than just as a client, and I realise that she's good for him. She'll be good for Megan, too.

'Ok,' I whisper, as I pull the cap off the marker. I put my tongue between my lips, trying to figure out what I say, and then I start to write. And when I'm done laying my heart out, I nod.

'Go,' the production assistant says, pushing me forwards. And with a deep breath and an arm full of cue cards, I step out behind the cameras to go save the love of my life.

30

NIKOS

Harsh studio lights blind me. It's like I'm sitting in a room, engulfed in unnaturally white light, the silence of the crew watching on almost deafening. The interviewer is a striking woman with red-painted lips, wide green eyes, and pin-straight brown hair that looks as manicured as the pre-written questions she has on the interview cards waiting on her lap.

I take it all in, the raised plush chairs we sit on, the empty one at my side, the fake flowers, flashing screens with pictures of my face followed by images taken of me and the 'mystery man' in Greece.

Maybe I should've paid more attention to the script I was given. All my excuses were in there, written down for me by someone else trying to navigate the story of my life. Not that it would matter anymore.

Big issue, though - Michelle is nowhere to be seen. Not that I can blame her. Now my head is clear, I'm already plotting all the ways I can make it up to her. I don't feel like a bunch of flowers is enough for someone like her, but I would give it a go.

I'm going this alone. And instead of running away, this time I'm forced to face it.

'Live from New York in ten seconds,' the red-faced show runner calls from stage left.

The interviewer leans forwards, tapping her nails on my knee. 'Are you ready to break the internet, Nikos?'

I swallow hard, forcing down the sickness to the pit of my stomach. 'I am.'

'Five seconds!'

I close my eyes and take the deepest breath I can in through my nose. I'm aware of some commotion just off the set, but I don't care enough to look. I think of Oli - my Honey - his warm smile, kind eyes, and gentle, encouraging touch. I imagine he's here with me, his presence guiding me through the next ten minutes.

Ten minutes - that's all I have. Ten minutes to re-write my story. To forge a web of lies so strong, it's ironclad and unbreakable.

When I open my eyes just as the 'live on air' button flashes red, I adorn the mask of the actor and leave everything else behind.

The show's jingle plays around us, silencing in time for the interviewer to unleash the same welcome she's given every morning for as long as she's been doing this job. I look at her and smile, unable to gather the strength to find my camera and face all of America who are watching.

I'm hot beneath my suit. I see the glass of water on the coffee table before me, plastered with the logo of the TV show, and find myself dying for a drink. I take it, just as the interview turns her attention to me and introduces me.

I lift the glass to my lips with shaking hands, and I almost choke when she goes silent, leaving the floor to me.

'Thank you for having me,' I say, catching a drip of water from sliding down my chin, with my thumb.

'You must be exhausted, what with all the movie's release, press, and your secretive trips to Greece. It's an honour you've fit us into your busy schedule.'

I lift the glass in salute. 'It's my pleasure. Although I admit, I'd rather be sunbathing on a beach than being back here at home. There's just something less aggressive about the birds in Greece - the pigeons in the city are deadly.'

The interview barks out a laugh. 'Coming from the dragon riding warrior we've all come to swoon over! Do you hear that America? Nikos Ridge is scared of some little birds.'

'Little? Have you seen those pigeons? They're the size of small dogs.' I give her my winningest smile.

She narrows her eyes at me, flaying me open with a single look. 'Now, are you trying to distract us, Nikos?'

'Whatever from?' I retort, my heart beating in my throat.

I can't move before she strikes out and lifts up my hand. There is no time to stop her, before she focuses on my finger - to the place an engagement band would've been if I were Michelle.

Shame I left it - and her - back in the dressing room.

'Looking for something?' I asked.

'Well, I *was*. actually.' She drops my hand, leaning back

in her chair in a mock stature of comfort. 'The streets are talking, Nikos. Those little birdies you are so frightened of are chirping about a potential engagement. Anything you want to share?'

'I told you those birds are a nightmare.' I go for a wink, but it falls flat. It takes everything I have not to focus on the empty chair beside me.

She laughs again, this time sicklier than before. It's fake, as is everything here. And I can tell that she's just worked out that I didn't read through my script.

'Nikos. We're friends here, aren't we? Between me and you, have you got anything you'd like to share?'

I lean forwards, wondering if those watching from the comfort of their own homes can see the sweat beading on my temple. My breathing is uneven, my chest constricting as though a python has tangled itself around me.

'Actually, yes. I've been keeping a secret from you all, but clearly not very well.'

The interviewer claps her hands together. 'What a way to start a boring Thursday morning off. How thrilling. Now, I have my speculations, as does all of social media apparently…' She gestures to the large screens behind me, where the photos of me and Oli have been circulating. Of course, they don't show his face. I admit, the excuse of him being Michelle's relative works - no matter how the lie makes me ill. To my relief, the photos fade into something new. Screenshots of social media comments flash up, each one as irritating as the next. I see Michelle's name next to mine, the mention of marriage, the talk of on-screen chemistry spilling over to real life.

I stare at it, dumfounded and frozen.

'So…' She drawls out, tapping those nails on the side

of her chair, the sound grating through me. 'What have you got to share with us, Nikos?'

I turn away from everything, unable to focus. This is the moment I secure my future, but at the cost of taking the power away from my past. From Oli. I search the dark shadows of the set for Selina, hoping her encouraging nod or smile will help me through this next lie.

But what I find has my body and mind shutting down.

Oli stands to the side, concealed by shadows, but even in the dark I would be able to find him. I blink - not once, but four times, wondering if the ghost would disappear. But he is real, *very* real, all sun-blond wavy hair, wide eyes, and a heart-shaped face that my fingers and mouth have memorised.

He is holding large cards in both hands, so big they cover his torso. And on it, written in black ink and rushed handwriting, is a few words.

He can never hurt you again. You're free.

Time seems to stretch on, but perhaps only milliseconds have passed. I don't know. I'm not aware of anything but the words he's holding up. Selina shadows him, nodding as if offering the confirmation of what my thoughts are piecing together.

Oli reaches into his pocket, making the card hit the ground with a thump. I watch him, his every movement, and see him withdraw a watch. My watch. The one my father had taken from me.

He can never hurt you again.

He - my father.

You're free.

'I'm sorry to the folks watching, but it would seem that Nikos is teasing us with his big announcement,' the interview says from next to me. She jabs me in the side playfully with a fake nail, but I can tell she's getting irritated.

Before I take my eyes off Oli, I'm certain he mouths three more words to me.

I love you.

'Nikos? Earth to Nikos?' When the interview taps my knee again, it's with a harsh bite. Clearly, I'm embarrassing her. But I don't care. I care about nothing but the fact that Oli is here.

My ears are ringing, my head an empty space of disbelief. I can hardly think straight, but somehow that pressure on my shoulders has eased.

'I'm sorry,' I say, unsure who my apology is for.

'Are you ready?' she encourages, waving her hands impatiently at me. 'We are all bursting to know what Nikos Ridge's secret is.'

A small laugh bursts out of me. One little bark, followed by another.

'Where do I even begin?' I reply.

My secrets. I've had so many. When I was seventeen years old, I tried to escape my abusive home with my mother. Because of my attempt, my father killed her. I tried to kill him in return. I ran away from home, leaving behind the promise of being blamed and convicted for my mother's death - although I wasn't the one to push her, my actions are what drove my father to do it, so I suppose it was my fault. Since then I have been running from demons - my father - who chased my success, holding my past over my head like a guillotine, unless I paid him. But all that running forced me into the hands of a man who opened my mind in ways I never believed possible. My life changed in a split second when my mother fell down those stairs, so it is not impossible to believe that it would take two weeks with Oliver Cane for it to change again.

I take a deep breath, find my camera and stare deep into the lens. I have a sense of the millions of people watching, those ready to post my admission across social media. I have an image of the big-wigs at the film studios, sat around a TV in a board room, leaning in with anticipation, waiting for me to make my career or break it.

But what is success without a person to enjoy it with? A waste. Like my life has been until Oli.

'My name is Nikos Ridge, and I am head over heels, unequivocally, unapologetically and viciously in love with a man. His name is Oliver Cane, and you all saw him in those pictures. He is not my friend, my publicist, or the brother of a woman who you all believe me to be engaged to. He is Oli. He is simply my Honey, and I am his. And I love him because he loves me, past, present, and future - I hope. And he's here right now.'

The studio is silent. Hell, the entire world goes quiet. But I don't. Now I've started, the words just flow out of me. And I tell the watching world our story, from beginning and through the middle. I would've told them the end, but there isn't one yet.

I don't ever want there to be an end.

I can feel the cool kiss of eyes on the side of my face, and I know Oli is watching. But I can't have a distraction. Not until the last words fall out of my lips. Only then do I turn off stage, extend a hand for him and offer him four words.

'I love you, too.'

31

OLI

I CANNOT OVERSTATE the utter fucking relief of hearing Nikos say that he loves me.

I don't care that I'm dishevelled, jet-lagged, and wearing yesterday's clothes. I take one look at Nikos' outstretched hand and the pleading look on his face and know there's no way I could leave my man alone up on stage, not with what he's just done. Not with the way he's just told the world that I'm his.

Shrugging off the enormous scarf I'm wearing and pulling off my coat leaves me in just a jumper and jeans - not the best showing for the lover of Nikos Ridge, international heartthrob. But the way he's grinning at me, like I'm his entire world, shows me that he couldn't care less.

Nikos never cared about anything other than who I was inside. It's the best gift he could have given me - showing me that who I am is enough. That I'm worthy of being the centre of a love story, just as I am.

He stands up as I walk onto the stage, a production

assistant literally shoving a mic into the collar of my jumper as I walk. When I wobble across the set, delirious with relief and excitement and exhaustion, Nikos is there to catch me. He grabs my hand and then pulls me to him, wrapping his hand around the back of my neck and kissing me like it's the last time our lips will ever touch.

It's not the last, I think as I relax into him, breathing in his familiar scent, letting him hold me close. *It's just the first*.

I pull back and he chases me, pressing a kiss to my forehead. His eyes are shining, and I put a hand to his chest to steady him. His heart is thumping against his ribs so hard that I'm impressed he's still standing and not in a dead faint.

'Thank you, Honey,' he whispers.

I'm choked up now, so all I do is nod. And then I remember that right now, I'm live on nationally telly, and I freeze. But Nikos squeezes my hand and sits, tugging me down into the chair next to him.

'Oh my God,' is what the interviewer says. She looks like she's about to have a heart attack, or vomit, or both. I can see the producers off to the side, looking somewhere between gleeful and terrified, likely calculating just how much this one interview is going to net them in streaming revenue or something of the sort.

If I was their publicist, I'd be having a field day. Nikos Ridge coming out as some variant of not straight and in love with a man on my morning show which normally only breaks the news of different types of muffin recipes? I'd have died and gone to marketing heaven.

But right now, I turn my attention to Nikos. Because for once, I'm not telling the story - I'm a part of it.

'Well,' the interviewer continues, pulling herself together. 'This is *quite* the revelation. Oliver, it's lovely to have you on. How did you meet Nikos?'

I'm impressed with the way she's pivoted. I can see the notecards shaking in her hands, though, and for a moment I feel bad that we totally hijacked her morning. The poor woman is going to need a strong drink after this debacle. 'In the toilets, actually.'

The interviewer is in the middle of taking a drink of water, and I can see her choke on it and try valiantly not to cough as the water goes into her lungs from the shock. 'I'm sorry, did you say *the toilets?*'

'In America, we'd call it the bathroom.' Nikos' laugh is warm, his eyes sparkling. His hand tightens in mine, like he's never going to let me go. 'I was panicking before the premier of *An Age of Dragons*. A lot has happened in my life that I've never been open about, and anxiety is one of those things. I was having a panic attack, because publicity makes me nervous. I'm scared of crowds, and sometimes my social anxiety is awful. Oli was kind enough to help me. It was the first moment in my adult life I felt seen by another person as a man first, and not an actor.'

Nikos looks to me, and I lick my lips and continue, hoping that my voice doesn't wobble. 'I actually had no idea who he was.'

The interviewer's eyes bulge. 'You what?'

'I didn't recognise him one bit.' I smile at the expression on her face. 'I know, I know - it seems ridiculous to not recognise one of the planet's biggest heartthrobs, especially when you've spent months working on the book tie-in to his movie. But his hair was different, and he wasn't dressed in dirty leather.'

Nikos snorts. 'Not usually my outfit of choice, at least in public.'

'Ooo,' the interviewer titters. She's clearly relaxing into this, the shock wearing off. I start to relax too. 'In private?'

Nikos winks, and he lets go of my hand to put it on the back of my neck, like he's claiming me. My cheeks heat of their own accord. 'Now *that's* something that's going to stay a secret. But yes, Oli clearly had no idea who I was.'

'And you didn't tell me!' I yelp indignantly, elbowing him in the ribs. He bites his lip as he smiles and then ducks down to kiss me on the cheek. 'You let me call you Adonis!'

'Well,' the interviewer says, laughing for real now. 'He *is* a Greek god.'

'Oh no.' I groan and roll my eyes theatrically. 'Don't stroke his ego. He's bad enough as is.'

The interviewer, and the studio, erupt in honest laughter.

'I promised him one night,' Nikos says. 'And when I left - yes, *yes*, the next morning, if you're wondering - I couldn't stop thinking about him. I was in Paris for the next part of the press tour, and it was literally the only thing on my mind. How sweet and kind and caring he was. Not to mention delicious enough to eat - just like his namesake.'

'You remembered me because you stole my affirmation post-it,' I grumble, giving him the stink-eye.

Nikos laughs, and the sound is so happy and free that my heart soars. 'I did.' He shifts in his seat to pull the wallet out of his suit pocket, and withdraws the now-crumpled post-it. He flashes it to the camera - *you are enough*. 'I needed something to remember you by. But I left something in return, didn't I, darling?'

How did he know? Nikos is looking at me expectantly, and I flush deeper. Because when I pull out my own wallet, the post-it he left in return is right there.

As sweet as Honey, you are certainly enough.
- Adonis.

'I needed this,' I explain to the interviewer, holding it up. 'He didn't know how much confidence he'd given me, just by showing that he cared. That *I* was enough. I'd gone through a horrible breakup a few months prior and my self-confidence was low enough that clearly I was leaving myself little messages on my fridge. Nikos saw me, too. Maybe I saved him from that panic attack, but he saved me from a whole lot more.'

'We saved each other.' Nikos turns his warm brown eyes on me. 'We saved each other, Oli.'

'Yeah,' I reply, my voice rough. 'I guess we did.'

'Well,' the interviewer interjects as we get lost in each other's gaze. 'The actor and his secret, everyone. A modern-day love story if ever there was one. And now for a commercial break…'

———

AFTER WE WERE HUSTLED off the stage and traded for some pop star or another, Selina mercifully gets us a few minutes alone in the green room. I immediately fall into Nikos' arms and start to cry.

He holds me close and pets my hair, and when I sniffle and pull away, I choke out, 'I'm so sorry for leaving.'

'It's not just you.' His voice is rough. 'I'm sorry for leaving too. For not fighting more for you.'

'I think I understand,' I admit, because I do now. 'Your dad? He was the janitor at Sky High Publishing. That's who stole my keys. I - I got an email the morning after you'd stayed over with photos of us from the security cameras in the house, and we'd just seen Geoff so I'd thought it was him. The email told me that if I didn't steal your watch and leave it in my spot by the Thames that the photos would be leaked. So I did, and I'm so sorry, but I thought I was protecting you. And then there were more threats, and I just, I didn't know what to do. But then the number texted me again while I was at work and I was just so mad because of the gardening leave that I called and the janitor's phone rang and Megan tackled him with her judo skills for the blackmail tape that we made - '

I'm totally out of breath by the time Nikos puts his finger to my lips, stopping me. 'Breathe, Honey.'

I do, gulping in air. My stomach is twisting in knots that Nikos will be mad at me.

'First off, I'm so sorry that my father did that.' Nikos steps back and exhales, running a hand through his gelled-up hair, messing with the style. 'He's been blackmailing me for years. It's why I did *An Age of Dragons* - I needed more money to pay him. But I realised that he was never going to stop, no matter what I did. He threatened to blame my mother's death on me and have the police in Greece reopen the case unless I complied. I was stuck, but then he started to threaten *you*, and I lost it. The only thing I could think to do was leave you to protect you. But you didn't need protecting from me, did you?'

'No.' I shake my head. 'I don't, I guess.'

He smiles brilliantly. 'What did you say about Megan and judo?'

'We pulled your dad into the supply closet, held him down, tied him up, and then threatened him with the police until he recorded a video with his confession on it.' I hold up my cell phone. 'We have it in a million places so he can never hack in and delete it. And besides, I think he's in jail right now? Megan called the police when I left because he elbowed her in the face. She was going to tell him that the janitor assaulted her in the podcast studio so that he's at least off the streets for a bit while you figure out what you want to do.'

Nikos looks dumbfounded. 'You did all that for *me*?'

'Of course,' I answered simply. 'I love you.'

Because that's all there is to it. I would do anything in the world for this man.

I hadn't noticed the door crack open, but a throat clears and I turn to see Selina standing there, holding up her phone. It's displaying a banking app with a balance so large that I think it must be a mistake. 'My badass newly minted girlfriend did more than just call the cops. She must have threatened your dad in some other fucking amazing way, because the money that you've sent him over the years? A *very* substantial chunk of it was returned right as Oli got on the plane.'

Nikos looks completely and utterly overwhelmed, tears falling freely down his cheeks now.

'I'm free,' he says, like he still can't believe it. 'I'm free?'

'Yeah,' I say, putting my hands on his face to pull him in for a kiss. 'You are.'

'You two go collect yourselves,' Selina says. 'I'll tackle things here for a bit.'

'Thank you…I just can't believe I'm free. I'm my own man, for the first time,' Nikos says simply, and there's the promise of a lifetime in those words. 'Thank you both so much. I need to thank this Megan, too.'

'I'll do that for you,' Selina says. She's tapping away at her phone with her crimson-painted nails, and I have no doubt she's texting Megan, letting her know exactly what happened. 'It will be my pleasure.'

'Oh, and her judo skills are incredible,' she says, looking straight at me without a trace of irony. 'I fell in love with her the moment she crushed my head in between her thighs when we were - '

'Oh my God,' I gag theatrically. 'Please, pity me. Not a single word more. She's like a sister to me, I do *not* need to hear about her sex life.'

Selina smiles wolfishly, and I have a feeling she and I are going to get along great. 'Now you two go home. You have a few hours before we're going to need to start tackling what all this means, and I think you can find something worthwhile to fill the time with.'

'She's right,' Nikos says. He hugs me close. 'Come on, Oli. Let's go home.'

32

NIKOS

I OPEN the door to my apartment, and for the first time, don't dread the silence waiting for me inside. Because Oli is by my side - actually, he's in my arms, because I've just literally swept him off his feet.

'What are you doing!' Oli manages through a fit of hysterical laughter. His hands grasp at my jacket, anchoring himself to me. Although I'd never let him fall. I've got him now, tomorrow, and for all the blissfully endless days to come.

'Mind your head,' I reply as I duck into the apartment, careful not to bump his head on the door frame.

'Fuck me,' Oli gasps as he takes in my apartment. 'Is this your home?'

I watch the awe in his eyes as he sweeps them over the open-planned living room, the high-tech kitchen and the tall walls covered in expensive art pieces. 'Truthfully, it's never felt much like home. But I suppose it does now.'

I put him down on the ground carefully, admiring the

glow in his eyes, the way his reaction isn't born from admiring my apartment, but likely thinking what a waste of money it is. That's something else I love about Oli, his ability to not be blinded by fame.

'It's... impressive.'

'It's over the top,' I say, scrutinising the rooms before me. 'In fact, I think I'm going to sell up, get myself a small little apartment with a nice view.'

'But this is your home,' Oli retorts. 'You just said that.'

'No.' I take him into my arms, embracing him tight. 'You're my home, Honey. Home isn't a construct of brick and mortar, but a feeling. For fear of sounding like a sappy fool, *you* are that feeling for me. New York, London, Greece - fuck, it could be in the desert surrounded by nothing at all, and still I would feel totally at home if you were beside me.'

Oli is silent as he looks up at me. His mouth parts, his bright eyes wide. I watch his reply turn to ash on his tongue, and I suddenly regret saying so much.

'Now, that wasn't the reaction I was expecting,' I say, forcing out the sarcasm to protect me from what must be coming. The inevitable reminder that I'm moving much too fast.

'Well.' Oli withdraws. 'It's just we both have our lives. Mine is back in London. And yours... yours is here, or wherever the work takes you. You're free now. I don't expect you to nail yourself down to the first twink you set your eyes on.'

I take his face in my hands, loving how small he is in comparison to me. 'Ask me a million times, and I will always choose you.'

'Bloody hell,' Oli squirms with his cute little English accent. 'What are we like?'

I dip my face to his, holding my lips inches from his mouth. 'Star-crossed lovers, fated mates, forbidden romance.... I admit I don't understand the bookish terms you use, but surely we're something like that.'

'You've been doing your research,' Oli says, narrowing his eyes.

'I have.' I kiss him, laying my emotion and desires out on the line. It's soft and careful. My lips guide his, parting his mouth to allow for my tongue to enter. I sweep it around his mouth, entangling myself with him, tasting mint and coffee and loving every moment of the contrasting flavours.

When the kiss ends, I lay my forehead on his and exhale a breath full of all the tension I've ever held. 'I love you, Oliver Honey Cane.'

His reply comes so quickly, he practically interrupts me. 'And I love you, Nikos Adonis Ridge Drakos.'

'That's a mouthful,' I reply.

'You certainly are.'

I open my eyes a millisecond after Oli's hands begin fumbling with the buttons of my trousers. His gaze is aglow with desire and want, matching my own. He doesn't need to tell me with words what he wants from me. I see it as clear as day. But Oli, ever the best at words compared to me, parts his pink-tinged lips and says, 'take me to bed, Adonis.'

I swallow hard. 'With pleasure.'

I deserve happiness, as does Oli. It's a feeling so overwhelming in this single moment that I can't help but wish it for everyone in the world, my father included. Whatever happened to him to poison his heart and ruin his soul - what cruel circumstance broke him enough to allow for him to become a monster - I pity him for it.

He had love in his hands in the form of a woman who was the best I'd ever known. My mother. And he crushed it. But as I guide Oli to my bedroom, his eyes fixed on me, his hand in mine, I know that I would never jeopardise what he and I have.

Regardless of how the world reacts to my 'little secret,' it was worth it. I'd give it all up to simply exist in the same space as him.

Oli is not only my secret - he is my love and my honour. And for him, I'll face the world with a confidence as bright as the sun. Because nothing has the power to eclipse this.

My new world. My new life.

We stand at the end of my bed with its pristine sheets and plush pillows. Oli's mouth is on mine, my tongue twisting alongside his. With eyes closed, and our hands touching, we undress one another - one piece of clothing at a time, until a puddle of material waits at our feet. I break away long enough to lift the t-shirt over his head, but it gets stuck. We fall to the ground, laughing.

I'm completely overcome with joy.

Once we're bare, I draw him up onto my lap, working his legs over my thighs until our chests are pressing together, my back into the rug. Oli arches into me, my hand tracing down his spine, conjuring shivers across his skin. I nip at his neck, kissing his throat tenderly. Oli is so frantic that his hands barely stay in one place. Nails score at my back, leaving marks in my skin just as my kiss does with his neck and shoulders.

By the time we're done here, our stories will be written onto one another's bodies.

At some point, we move from the floor to the bed. In a cloud of duvet and pillows, we lose ourselves. Oli's mouth is on my cock, sucking me, proving his early statement of me being a mouthful. I offer him the same pleasure, taking him onto my tongue, palming his balls as we fit ourselves together like a puzzle.

His groans of pleasure encourage me. I've never wanted to make someone lose themselves before, not like this. With him, I want to hear every beautiful sound come out of his mouth - regardless of if his moan of pleasure are muffled by my cock in his mouth.

I spit on my fingers and reach behind him. I could find his centre without sight. As I press the tip of my finger against him, Oli shivers.

'Do you like that, Honey?' I ask, circling his entrance, knowing that a single move would make him buckle from ecstasy.

Oli doesn't answer with words - instead, he takes my entire length in, burying my cock down his throat until there isn't an inch left dry. He heaves around it, the sound sparkling a feral reaction in me. Blinded by the pleasure of his throat rubbing over my bell-end, I take my wetted finger and plunge it inside of him.

I almost come in that moment. I have to practice the control of a monk just to stop myself from finishing.

Oli is so tight against my finger. He's clenching purposefully, telling me with his body just how incredible he will feel once I put my cock inside of him. So, partly rushed and partly desperate, I snatch his hair and withdraw him from my cock.

'Sit on me,' I command, lying down on the bed, head propped up by two pillows.

Oli does as he is told, clambering over my hips, knees bending. 'Are you going to fuck me dry, Adonis?'

'Yes, but not today. Your hole needs training for that kind of feat. If you want, though, we can practise. We have all the time in the world.'

Oli's brow peaks, his eyes mischievous as his grin. 'I would take you up on it, but I need you in me *now*, Adonis.' He offers his hand and gives me a one worded command. 'Lube.'

Not one to disappoint, I reach into the side drawer and retrieve an - almost full - bottle of lube. The milky liquid is thick, the kind with a slight tingle to it. Oli notices that some has been used.

'I believe the Brits call it a 'posh-wank',' I tell him.

Oli laughs, the sound rumbling across the room. 'That involves a condom, you fool. But I do like the idea of you touching yourself.'

'I prefer when you do it,' I reply, watching as he pumps four measures of lube into his palm. He discards the bottle amongst the mounds of bedding and reaches behind himself. Pleasure overcomes me as he begins working the liquid across my length. 'However, one day, I'd very much like you to make me kneel, wank over my face, and cover me in your come. If that sounds like something you'd be interested in.'

'Is this - your - kink?' I pant. In Oli's hand, I am a mess of uncontrolled breathes and stumbled words.

'One of many,' he replies, rolling a condom onto me and guiding the end of my cock to his hole.

'Many? What have I gotten myself into?'

'The best thing in your life,' Oli replies, then thrusts himself down on my cock with such vigour, I find myself arching into him.

'Fuck me,' I cry, feeling like I've died and gone to heaven.

'Okay,' Oli says calmly. 'I will.'

And he does.

With thighs of steel, Oli bounces on my cock. First he's slow, then the speed and pace picks up. His forehead creases in concentration, his mouth parted in a perpetual o-shape. I grip onto his thigh, burying my fingers into his skin. My spare hand wraps around his cock and I begin jerking him.

We play this game of pleasure for as long as I can handle. I move him around, shifting Oli until he is on his hands and knees, and I'm behind him, pounding his arse from behind. But in truth, no matter how incredible he feels in this position, I want to see his face. There's an enjoyment in watching his expressions. It's so fucking sexy. So, we end up in the position we started in, Oli atop me, sliding down on my length over and over.

I stare him deep in his eyes, as he does with me. 'You're the best part of me.'

Oli gasps, his eyes rolling into his head. 'You're only saying that because you're about to come.'

'Yes,' I say, pressing into him, wanting to feel every possible inch of his arse upon me. I give Oli credit, he is a champion. He takes my cock like a pro. 'But it's also true. You are the best part of me. And I love you. I love you. I love you. I *love* you.'

Oli leans down and presses his mouth to mine. Before the kiss intensifies, he replies into my mouth, the words vibrating over my swollen lips. 'And I love you. Now come for me, baby.'

Not wanting to disappoint, I do just that. And from the wet splash of liquid over my stomach, I know Oli has finished too. Both of us, in tandem, joined in more ways than one. We finish together, because we *finish* each other. Completely, in all manners of the sense.

He completes me. And I, for the first time in a long time, recognise that I have the potential to complete another person, too.

———

MORNING LIGHT SPEARS in through my large windows, casting the bed in a golden glow. Central Park looks magical from this view, with verdant trees and vivid colours as summer truly encompasses the world.

Oli is nestled to my side, his head on my chest. After a night of lots of passion and very little sleep, we find ourselves brave enough to check social media - as per Selina's request. She just called and woke us up.

'Incredible,' Oli exhales.

'It is,' I say, staring at the screen as I continuously scroll through the trending tab.

I'm overwhelmed with positivity. Comments, tags, pictures, posts, videos - every form of media I can imagine is outpouring with love for me and Oli. For our story. And they only know the half of it.

Selina has just emailed over a list of TV-shows that would like to host an interview with us. The film studio is offering more money for a sequel, and the author of *An Age of Dragons* has even proposed to write in a new romance for Armin Wolfe in book three. In her words *'a topless man in leather, riding a dragon - what's gayer than that?'* She isn't wrong.

Oli closes his eyes and exhales against my skin. I peer down my nose at him and see him smiling. I can't help but mirror the emotion. 'Not such a dirty little secret after all,' Oli's says.

'You never were, not to me.' I love the feel of his skin against mine. We're both sticky from a night of sex, but I can't bring myself to get out of bed just yet. I lock my phone screen, lay it on the bed and give my entire focus to the man at my side.

'So,' Oli draws out with a yawn. 'What next?'

What next? 'Us?'

'Well, I'd hope so. But I have a job to get back to, and you have a film to prepare for.'

I laugh, almost the idea of being separated is nauseating. '*If* I accept, I'll be filming in the UK.'

'If? What do you mean if?'

'Maybe I don't want to do it.'

Oli leans up on his elbows, his stomach rolling up into cute bundles. 'And deprive me of the gay, dragon-riding, leather-wearing, muscled hero of my dreams? You *better* not decline it. I'm like the number one biggest fan of that book. I've *annotated* it.'

'I thought I was free and could make my own decisions,' I retort with a chuckle, planting my lips on his cheek whilst drawing him back down atop me.

'I mean, you *are*,' Oli says. 'But you are literally the man of my literature dreams. An honest-to-God book boyfriend, come to life.'

'You just want me to do it so you can tell all your friends you're fucking Armin.'

Oli's tired eyes flick to my turned-down phone. 'Oh, they already know. But that doesn't stop me from wanting you to fuck me *in costume*.'

'The world knows.' I grin. 'And if you want me to fuck you in costume? I will. Every damn day, if you'd like.'

'So, the world is ours,' Oli says. 'But the world doesn't stop just because this has all happened. I have bills to pay, a job that I love - and now, a man who can come and stay with me during his long filming sessions.'

I close my eyes, my smile growing wider. 'I like the idea of coming home to you every night.'

'Home,' Oli repeats.

'Us,' I answer. 'But first, I need breakfast, 'and then we can discuss all our grand plans.'

'Built up an appetite, have you,' Oli says, finger tracing patterns over my chest.

'I have.'

'And what do you fancy to eat?'

In one swift motion, I draw him up and lay him flat over me. My mouth nuzzles in his neck, my hands grasping his bare arse, massaging the smooth skin that I love so much. 'Something sweet enough to rot my teeth. I fancy eating you, Honey.'

'Mmhm,' Oli groans, leaning down over me. 'I like the sound of that.'

With a swift motion, the man of my dreams spins around and offers his arse to me. Mouth dripping wet, cock already hard, I drag his arse to my outstretched tongue and devour him.

I pause long enough to whisper two words. '*Agape mou.*'

Oli mumbles something back, but his face is buried into the bedding so I can barely make it out. But I know, as I return my tongue to his arse, his answer was the same.

'*Agape mou.*'
My love.

PART 3

THE HAPPILY EVER AFTER

33

OLI

-One Year Later-

I'M MORE exhausted than I've ever been, and happier than I ever thought possible.

'You really need to stop looking at those, or you're going to strain your eyes.'

Nikos prods me in the back with a finger. I'm hunched over the desk in our office, sitting on a pile of Nikos' scripts because I couldn't be bothered to move them off the chair where he'd left them. He has so many offers coming in these days for movies he actually *cares* about that I keep finding scripts everywhere - including once, memorably, in the shower, propped up on the shelf with the soap.

'I'm not done yet,' I mumble, my tongue between my teeth. 'I want to look at them *all*.'

Twice. Maybe three times. I'm type-A, what can I say. And this day? It's got to be utter perfection. I'm not going to settle for anything less.

When Nikos proposed six months ago, lying on our little private beach behind his childhood home in Greece, I spent an hour crying my eyes out from happiness until I got so thoroughly dehydrated and dizzy that he had to carry me back up the path and force me to lie down. We'd gone out to dinner in town that night with Selina and Megan - who'd very conveniently managed to buy a small, abandoned vacation home down the road from us and were currently renovating it - and they'd both screamed loud enough when I waved my hand with a ring in their faces that half the population came running.

We'd managed to keep the engagement a secret for a few blissful days. When we're in Greece, now that Nikos doesn't have to sneak around anymore, we're welcomed with open arms. And while each of the Yiayia's in the village could win a contest in prying into our lives, they've turned out to be fiercely protective of Nikos and his privacy when it comes to the outside world.

A herd of donkeys very memorably chased a reporter down the street and nearly off a cliff when she'd dared to sneak too close to our house. We laughed about it until we couldn't breathe.

When we'd arrived back in London, we'd announced it on Nikos' Instagram page, a simple black and white shot of us holding hands. The response had been an outpouring of love and support which overwhelmed the both of us. All the comments from fans and friends alike kept me going as Nikos had left for a month-long filming stint in Scotland to complete the second *Age of Dragons* movie.

Yes, he did fuck me whilst in his Armin Wolfe

costume. And yes, it did fulfil every single one of my bookish fantasies - and then some.

The only way to keep our wedding from being a media circus is to keep it incredibly small and covert. I knew from the moment Nikos proposed that the longer planning went on, the more likely it was that the media would catch wind of what was happening and intrude on something that I want to be just for us.

'Oli, love. They're *napkins*.'

'Yes,' I snap waspishly. 'And they come in *so many colours*.'

I yelp as Nikos literally picks me up off the chair and cradles me to his chest. Now that he's still all bulked up from playing Armin - and staying that way, for the already-announced third movie - he can toss me around easier than ever. It's so unfair.

It's also incredibly hot, though, so I guess it's alright.

'Honey, darling.' He presses a kiss to my forehead. 'All napkins have to do is wipe food off your mouth. No one will even remember what colour they are a week later.'

'They'll be in all the pictures,' I moan. 'I'll remember them *forever*.'

'The only thing you'll remember is that you're marrying the love of your life.' His warm brown eyes gaze into mine, and my heart flips the way it does each and every time that I remember this man is mine. For the rest of forever.

I sigh, putting a hand to my forehead like I'm a fainting maiden. 'Oh Armin, thank you for rescuing me from the terror of our decorator's hundred-page PDF of napkin colours. However can I thank you?'

'Oh,' he says, steering us out of the office and into the

kitchen, where he sits me on the counter. 'I can think of a few things.'

He's clearly been cooking dinner, because I can smell the delicious Greek spices in the air, coming from the direction of the oven. We decided to keep my house in London, because even though it's where I was heartbroken over Geoff, it was also where I fell in love with Nikos.

And as he looks into my eyes and sinks down to his knees, I'm so, so glad it's the choice I made.

My life has turned out better than I ever could have dreamed, a true fairytale romance. I'm the luckiest man in the world. And I can't wait to write the rest of our story - together.

34

NIKOS

I NEVER IMAGINED GETTING MARRIED. For me, growing up, it was never in the cards. But as I stood at the end of aisle, facing a room full of adoring friends and family, I felt as though I was the happiest man on earth.

Of course, it was mainly friends that came for me. My family were either buried six feet under, or behind bars for blackmail and intention to spread revenge porn. But, as I saw Oli walking up to greet me, I knew that wasn't the case.

He was my family - my home.

The wedding, despite Oli's begging me to not go overboard, cost a fortune. But I would pay it ten times over just to experience those moments with him again, and I wanted him to have the wedding of his dreams. And now, as our driver sweeps us away from the over-the-top manor house venue, we wave at our guests, old tins and bottles clattering on the end of string, attached to the bumper of our car.

Oli's hand finds mine, and I catch the glint of silver.

Plain and simple, just as he liked it, glittering next to the diamond eternity band I'd proposed with. 'Are you sure you want to do this?'

I offer him a smile, feeling the answer come swiftly. 'I do.'

'We should turn this into a drinking game. How many times can we say 'I do' in one day?'

I lean into him, resting my head on his shoulder, my suit pulling at the recent muscle gain after filming *An Age of Dragons: Ruin*. 'I would drink the ocean dry just to get to say those words to you, over and over.'

'Until I'm sick of them?'

I smile. 'You'll never be sick of them.'

'You're right,' Oli replies. 'Never ever.'

Unbeknownst to our guests, we have no plans of attending our reception. Instead, while they are enjoying the food and drinks, the music and games, me and my Honey are jetting off to the warm Caribbean. But first, we have someone to visit.

―――

THE METAL CHAIR is nailed to the floor, inches from the table. Everything in here is metal - even the baton the guard is holding. I sit in the - almost - empty room, staring at the man who spent his life trying to ruin mine. I smile at him, still dressed in my wedding suit, the blush of joy and my happily ever after painted across my face.

'Did you come for my blessing?' My father spits, his tired old hands worn and beaten as he lays them on the table.

'No,' I reply.

THE ACTOR AND HIS SECRET

The last time I saw him, it was from a bench in the courthouse as the judge read out his charges. Now, all I see is a pathetic man whose actions finally caught up to him. Although he was only sentenced to ten years, which would likely be halved due to good behaviour and limited prison space, at least he knows that it would take just one replay of the voice recording of him admitting to killing my mother, and he'd be locked up for a *very* long time.

'Then to what do I owe this displeasure?' he asks, accent thick.

'I wanted to see you,' I reply. 'One last time.'

His eyes widen. It's brief, but I enjoy seeing him squirm. All my life he has held my mother's death over my head - it's only fitting that it's my turn to do it.

A truly full circle moment.

Father leans in close, his rotten breath washing over me. 'You made a promise.'

'And as our bloodline seems cursed when it comes to promises, I may just break this one. Depends on if you hold up your end of our deal.'

The deal being 'stay away from me and mine, and you can be free. Never come near, think of, contact or hell - even speak the name of me or my husband' or ten years will look like playtime compared to what he'll get if his true secrets came out.

'You came to see me,' my father says, as though reminding me of the obvious.

'I did.' I lean in, mirroring his stance, expect the smile on my face has not yet wavered. 'I want you to see me, the real me, the one you never gave me the chance to be. And I want you to recognise that I'm the happiest I've ever been.'

'Good for you,' my father spits.

'It is. Oh, and I married him. Oli. I know you remember him.'

'Your dirty little - .'

'Ah, ah, ah, father.' I shake my head like a displeased adult speaking down to a child. This is a power play, and I'm high on it. 'Words are very hurtful. I wouldn't want you to say something you may come to regret.'

The guards catch my eye and I nod, letting them know all is well. I see him fiddle with his pocket, to the stack of money I'd handed to him as I came inside. Bad, I know. But what is a little bribery, if it means I get to do what I've come here for?

'I hope you rot, father. Here, alone. Never experiencing love. Even when you had the most precious woman in the world in the palm of your hand, you carelessly broke her, all because you were small and pathetic. But I didn't just come to gloat, although truthly, it feels fucking amazing to do so. I came here to look you in your eye and say how sorry I am.'

His furrowed brow softens, the lines around his glaring eyes easing a touch. 'What do you mean?'

'I'm sorry for whatever happened to you to make you into such a hateful person.'

The look of shock lasts but a moment before he spears forwards, spittle flying beyond thin lips. 'How dare you - '

My fist connects with his jaw, the crack a beautiful symphony. My father's head lolls back, his body slumping over the chair where he topples to the ground. Steadily, I stand, my own chair squeaking against the floor.

'Yes,' I say to myself. 'That really was worth the money.'

My father doesn't hear me because he's howling like an animal in a trap. I've said my piece, so I prepare to leave, thanking the guard with a wink and a smile. As I make my way to the exit, I find myself wanting to say one more thing.

'Oh dad,' I call out, turning back to face him. 'Orange really suits you. Brings out the devil in your eyes.'

'Fuck you - ' he shouts, slamming fists on the table. In moments the guards grab him, but I don't stick around to watch. I hear him thump to the ground, groaning and bellowing. He is a man who finally understands that he's lost. His screams are full of torment, and I admit, the sound is blissful. Beautiful.

'Goodbye father,' I say, mostly to myself. In my mind I picture Oli, sitting in the back of the car, nervously biting his nails, likely thinking we would miss our flight. The sun is shining down on me as I leave the prison, but no ray is as bright as the smiling, golden-haired man who waits for me. And when he opens his mouth and speaks, I know I've made the best decision of my life.

'Nikos Adonis Ridge Drakos, we're going to be late!'

I climb in, then clamber atop him until I'm laid atop him on the back seat. My hand brushes his hair from his face, and I can't help but feel overcome with love.

'Oliver Honey Drakos, my husband, I think you are completely wrong on that one.'

'What?' He barks, giggling as I bury my mouth into his neck, my hand already unbuttoning his white shirt.

'Shh, my love. There's something more pressing I need to do.'

'But the flight - '

I lean up, mischief glittering across my gaze. 'The

private jet can wait. That's what you pay the big dollars for.'

'I said no private jets!'

'And I said I bloody love you.' I mock his English accent, just before diving back into feasting on his neck. 'So are we consummating our marriage now, or will you make me wait until we reach our destination?'

Oli ponders my question, or at least he pretends to. Because I know his answer the second a hand reaches between us and cups my hardening cock.

'Five minutes.'

'With an arse like yours, I'll only need three.'

Oli laughs and the sound of it completely muffles the echo of my fist connecting to my father's face. 'That's a generous estimate. You normally last two - '

We laugh, and I kiss him, and right now the only thing I can think about is how a secret meant to ruin me turned out to be the single best thing in my life.

ALSO BY BEN ALDERSON

LAURA'S BOOKS:

The Sins on Their Bones

The Way it Haunted Him

BEN'S BOOKS:

If you want more retelling romances, check out the:

Darkmourn Universe

Lord of Eternal Night

King of Immortal Tithe

Alpha of Mortal Flesh

Prince of Endless Tides

How about Gay Fae princes sleeping with their male guard and a Fae hunter:

A Realm of Fey Series

A Betrayal of Storms

A Kingdom of Lies

A Deception of Courts

A Games of Monsters

Dragons, mages and spice? Read my:

Court of Broken Bonds Series

Heir to Thorn and Flame

Heir to Frost and Storm

Heir to Dreams and Darkness

If YA Fantasy Romance is more your cup of tea, check out the:

The *Dragori* Trilogy

Cloaked in Shadow

Found in Night

Poisoned in Light

LAURA'S BOOKS:

The Sins on Their Bones

The Way it Haunted Him

Printed in Great Britain
by Amazon